SON

EL

DAUGHTER

SOMEONE ELSE'S DAUGHTER

JENNIFER HARVEY

Bookouture

Published by Bookouture in 2020

An imprint of Storyfire Ltd.
Carmelite House
50 Victoria Embankment
London EC4Y 0DZ

www.bookouture.com

ISBN: 978-1-83888-725-4
eBook ISBN: 978-1-83888-724-7

For my parents, Vincent and Maureen, with much love.

CHAPTER ONE

Katie

I suppose, in our hearts, we all knew she was dead. But hope kept us looking for her. Hope kept us calling out her name. All afternoon we searched for her, scouring the beach as the sun blazed over the dunes.

"Isa! Isa!"

Never a reply. Just the wash of waves on the shore and the screech of gulls as they swooped overhead watching us, while the sun traced its arc across the sky. Over and over we called her name, telling ourselves she was just asleep someplace. Sheltered and safe in the dunes, curled up on the sand and hidden from view by the high marram grass. Eventually, through the fog of sleep, she would hear her name, rub her eyes and call back to us.

"I'm here. I'm over here."

But she never did. We found her, at dusk, caught in a hollow where the tide had ebbed. Face down in the water and buffeted by the waves, her hair tangled and matted by salt and sand, her skin violet and mottled as a bruise.

And I can't stop thinking how strange it is that we were sitting around the bonfire, drinking and singing and joking, and oblivious to it all, while she floated alone in the darkness. Perhaps she even heard us singing, as she spluttered and choked and drowned.

Isa, poor Isa.

I still can't believe she's gone. She was the girl we all wanted a piece of, the girl we all wanted to be. So funny and sassy and cool. So clever and beautiful and kind. A girl like Isa wasn't meant to die.

And okay, so she was also vain and careless and irresponsible. And she could be secretive, and arrogant and cruel. And yes, it's true she thought the world revolved around her. But that was just how she was, that was just Isa.

She was my best friend, and my worst enemy. My confidante and my rival. She was the most exhilarating person I have ever known and the most irritating. But whatever I thought of her, good or bad, she didn't deserve to die like that.

Not really.

CHAPTER TWO

Louise

Nothing was the same after that summer, yet the vacation began the way it always did. The SUV piled high with too much stuff, the four of us squeezed in between the bags and the suitcases. Not so much a vacation, as an enforced retreat. A mad dash to Long Island, to escape the summer chaos of Manhattan. It was a city that had always been too much for me, and from the very beginning, I'd insisted on a house by the sea.

That annual escape to Montauk had become something vital over the years. Just knowing there was a wide-open space I could run to made the rest of the year feel less claustrophobic.

But that summer, things were different. That summer, there were five of us. An odd number. A break with the usual routine. Everything out of balance. I had hesitated when Sarah asked if Isa could join us, not because I didn't want to help her, but because it felt like an encroachment. As if my hideaway had been discovered and the summer spoiled somehow, before it had even started. But Sarah had left me with little choice. At least, that was how it felt.

"Willem and I need to get away," Sarah had practically begged me. "Just the two of us, so we can sort things out and see if we can salvage anything from this mess."

She told me she wanted to treat it as some sort of second honeymoon which meant it was better if Isa wasn't with them.

"It would just feel awkward," she had explained.

Which was true, I suppose. It was awkward. But, my God, *second honeymoon*. I had cringed when Sarah called it that, because it sounded so hopeless for some reason. The idea that it was necessary—a second chance. The failure contained there, in that insipid little phrase. You failed the first time so now you need to try again. Poor Sarah.

But I found myself blindsided by the request and agreed that Isa could join us at the house in Montauk. What else could I do, faced with Sarah's desperation?

It's terrible to think that everything was set in motion by such a poorly considered decision. I caved in, despite my better judgment. I allowed my emotion to get the better of my intuition.

Perhaps, if I'd paid more attention to Katie, I would have come to a different decision. I had expected her to be excited when I told her that Sarah wanted Isa to spend the vacation with us. I thought the prospect of having her best friend around for a whole month would have had her rushing to call Isa and start making frenzied plans. But she was strangely subdued when I mentioned it.

"The whole summer? With us? At the beach house?"

"Yes. That's okay, isn't it?"

"Sure. I guess so."

I guess so. That was a warning in a way, when I look back. But I chose to ignore it.

"You don't sound too keen."

"No, I am. I'm just tired is all. But it's cool if Isa comes with us. And anyway, they're not going to want Isa tagging along with them on their second honeymoon, are they? That'd be weird."

"You know about that?"

"Mom, Isa's my best friend. Do you really think she wouldn't talk to me about something like that?"

"That's true. It must be strange for her too, I suppose. All this fuss and bother?"

"What do you think? She almost died of embarrassment when they told her about it."

And I can spend the rest of my life going back over that moment. I can torment myself with the idea that this was the moment I should have stepped back and really thought about what Sarah was asking us to do. I should have recognized Katie's reticence for what it was—she had her doubts, she wasn't sure. I could have waited a few days and then asked her again, asked her why she wasn't so keen on the idea. But I didn't. And I'm going to have to live with that.

I tried to explain my misgivings to Peter, hoping, perhaps, at some subconscious level, that he would dissuade me.

"Four weeks is a long time, don't you think?" I asked him. "A lot can happen in four weeks, and I'm not sure I have the energy for all that worry."

"Worry? What's there to worry about?"

"I don't know. When it's someone else's child, you worry about them more than your own, don't you?"

"Maybe, but Isa's seventeen now, she can take care of herself. And let's face it, Sarah does have a point, they can hardly take her with them on their honeymoon."

"Second honeymoon," I'd reminded him.

"Okay, second honeymoon," he laughed. "But you know what I mean. They need time to sort things out, and if we can help them out, then I think we should."

But that was the problem, in a way. Seventeen. It was a dangerous age. I remembered how I felt myself, at that age. More adult, more capable, than I really was. Never able to ask for help, or admit I needed it. Floundering because of it. You needed guidance at that age, perhaps more than ever.

I thought all this but never mentioned it, because... well, how old-fashioned it sounded. How provincial of me. Like I wanted to interfere or spoil the fun. Kids had more freedom these days, especially in a city like New York, that's just how it was.

And Katie and Isa were on the cusp of adulthood, so you had to give them room to make mistakes, it was part of the deal. But there was a wildness to Isa, I had always felt. An adventurousness and boldness that unsettled me. That smile of hers, that glint in her eye, that feline stretch of arms and legs that always suggested something indolent and untamable. There would be trouble, there would be mess. I could feel it.

"Listen," Peter had said. "If Willem and Sarah think Isa can handle it, then it's fine with me. They know their own daughter. So, I guess it's going to be up to you. If you don't want Isa with us, then that's fair enough, it's our vacation too, so…"

Which meant nothing, in the end. How could I be the spoilsport? Say no, when everyone else seemed to think it was fine?

So, I kept my thoughts to myself, ignored my instincts and, instead, found myself driving along West 80th Street on my way to collect Isa.

I can still see her outside their beautiful brownstone, waiting for us. She was standing at the top of the steps leading up to the house and jumped up and down, waving when she caught sight of the car. When Katie spotted her, she opened the window and leaned out, waving back and whooping, "Hey! Isa! You ready?"

It was a quick pickup. New York is an impatient city, and a line of cars formed immediately behind us, honking their annoyance as soon as we stopped and forcing us to zip back and forth quickly with Isa's bags.

I remember Isa jumping into the back of the car too quickly, forgetting Willem and Sarah were there and that she had yet to say goodbye to them. Not caring, it seemed, that it would be a month until she saw her parents again.

They had needed to lean into the car to say their goodbyes, just a brush of a kiss on a cheek, all of it very informal and rushed.

"You guys have a great time too, okay?" Isa had called out to them. And they had nodded and laughed.

"Okay, we'll try."

I remember I looked in the rearview mirror as we pulled away and watched Willem and Sarah as they stood on the sidewalk, arm in arm, waving until the car pulled out of sight.

Not once did Isa turn to look back at them and wave a last goodbye. She was already gone, off on her summer adventure, her parents forgotten, leaning on Katie as they both stared at something on the screen of Isa's phone and laughed.

And I still wonder if my memory of this moment is more vivid than Sarah's or Willem's. I imagine it is, but I can't explain why I remember it so clearly. The banality of it all didn't lend itself to being remembered. And yet, there it is, fixed in my mind. Sarah and Willem on the street waving as the car turns the corner, neither of them knowing this was the last time they would see their daughter alive, blissfully unaware that Isa had apparently forgotten them already.

We'd driven to Long Island filled with the same easy forgetfulness, and I'd been relieved to feel the looseness in my shoulders as we sped down the interstate. Katie and Isa chatting in the back, James leaning against the window and snoozing, the radio on low, and Peter humming along with it.

Just like every summer.

Yes, I thought. *Maybe I've been wrong to worry too much about Isa coming with us. Everything will be okay.*

Three hours later, we pulled up at the beach house and tumbled out of the car. The salty smell of the sea was like a welcome home and the cool Atlantic breeze blew away any last traces of doubt.

Summer could begin at last.

CHAPTER THREE

Katie

Summer, I thought it would never come. For weeks it was the only thing I thought about. I kept waiting for the moment when Mom would turn around and say she'd changed her mind and that Isa couldn't come with us after all. I planned and imagined every detail because I wanted it to be perfect. A fun summer, an exciting summer, an unforgettable summer. It had to be. Just me and Isa together for a whole month. We could start anew and learn to be friends again. The anticipation was almost unbearable.

That first morning in the beach house, I woke up, roused by the gentle shush of the sea and the flicker of sun on my eyelids and forgot, for an instant, that Isa was there. When I turned and saw her sitting in the window seat staring out at the ocean, it made my heart jump.

I lay in bed, heavy with sleep, and watched her for a while, admiring the looseness of her, the way her head rested against the glass, like she didn't have a care in the world. She was simply sitting there staring out the window and watching the day begin.

Being tucked away by the sea, away from New York, seemed to have worked its magic already; she seemed happy, and it was nice to see her looking so relaxed again. And watching her, I thought we'd be able to put all that trouble behind us. Just forget all the arguments and disagreements and get back to being friends again. Good friends. Close friends, just as we had always been.

Isa could forget all that crap with her parents, she could forget all about Alex, and all the stupid shit she'd done the last few months, all the lies, all the trouble she'd caused. She could learn to be herself again.

Looking at her sitting in the window, the pale light of the morning shimmering around her like a halo, it was possible to forget the secrets behind her fake bright smile. It was possible to ignore the truth and pretend everything could be forgotten, and I lay in bed and looked at her and felt sure of it: the summer was going to be the best ever.

"You look like an angel sitting there like that," I said.

And she turned towards me and smiled, then leapt from the window seat and onto the bed beside me.

"Damn it, Katie," she laughed. "I thought you were never going to wake up."

The house was quiet, everyone asleep still and enjoying the fact that there was no need to get up early. When I turned the clock towards me it read 6 a.m.

"Shit, Isa, you're not going to wake up this early every day, are you?"

"Dunno, depends what we get up to I guess."

"Swimming, sunbathing and sleeping," I told her.

And Isa laughed. "Well, that's a start, I suppose."

"Why? What else were you planning on doing?"

Isa simply smiled and shrugged, the sort of shrug that suggested "you'll see." The sort of shrug that suggested she had plans, lots of them, and they were going to be messy. And if that made my stomach lurch a little, then I decided to ignore it. It was summer after all, and the whole point of summer was to loosen up and let go. And besides, I had plans of my own.

We spent an hour or so sifting through our suitcases, pulling out summer dresses, sandals, bikinis and agreeing which ones we would swap during the vacation. Isa pulled off her nightshirt and slipped on a yellow sundress she'd lifted from my pile of stuff. It was a perfect fit, tight in all the right places and looked good against her skin, which was golden brown already from all the running she'd been doing. An attempt to get healthy after her recent bout of partying.

I watched as she stood by the mirror, smoothing down the creases, messing up her long blond hair, and checking herself from every angle to be sure she looked good. When she was satisfied with the pose, she grabbed her phone and took a photo over her shoulder before swiping the screen and uploading it to Instagram.

I knew what was coming, though I'd hoped things would be different here, that the sun, the sea, the change of scenery, would prove a bigger lure than the glitter and instant gratification of Instagram. That Isa would realize there were plenty of other ways to feel good about yourself and would stop needing that sort of attention, even if it was just for a few weeks. Stupid really. Isa was still Isa and a change of location was never going to alter that, no matter how much I hoped for it.

I watched her posing in front of the mirror and knew the rest of the day would be punctuated with pings and notifications, and Isa checking her phone every few minutes to read the comments and keep count of the likes. Isa always got plenty of likes.

Likes that would keep on coming even after she died, the tally of little red hearts maintaining a ghoulish upward tick. Even in death, Isa would lose none of her allure.

"Hey, okay if I wear this today?" she asked me.

And I wanted to say, "Actually, no." I wanted to tell her that the dress was a gift, something my mom had picked out especially for the vacation, but I said nothing. I think I understood it was a test, of sorts. Isa's way of asking me, "Are we really still friends?" So, I let her have the dress.

"Sure, but take a shower first, yeah? I don't want you stinking up my new clothes."

"Hey!" Isa laughed, and she picked up a T-shirt from the floor, and threw it at me. "I don't know about you, Katie Lindeman, but I plan on getting sweaty and sandy and dirty this vacation. It's summer, time to live a little."

"Isa, if you want the dress, you get in the shower."

And she laughed again, "Yeah, yeah," and made a show of sniffing her armpits and scrunching up her nose, before peeling off the dress and sauntering to the bathroom, comfortable in her nakedness, a confidence I wished I also possessed.

There were other girls at school who had the same ease, a self-assurance that came from sport and toned muscles and long limbs, and something else, something indefinable, though none of them had the easy grace Isa possessed.

I knew I would never be one of those girls, an Isa sort of girl, and it was a thought which made me scratch at my arm and try to think of something else.

From the shower, I could hear Isa singing, some song I didn't recognize. Probably something she was making up as she went along. She was like that, spontaneous and in the moment. One day, I would figure out how she managed it.

Sweaty and sandy and dirty.

I thought about what my mom would think if she'd heard Isa announce this. It was the kind of thing that made her nervous and super vigilant.

But Isa's right though, I thought. It was summer, it was time to loosen up. It was what seventeen was all about. Messing things up, creating chaos, getting into trouble, and having fun. Mom had just forgotten what it was like to be seventeen, her memory fogged over by middle-age and the horrors she imagined might befall her daughter. Sex, in other words.

And as if Isa had picked up on my thoughts, there came a yell from the shower.

"Hey, Katie, any boys in this town worth getting to know?"

And I almost said it. I almost told her: "Yeah, there's this one boy, Luka."

But I wasn't ready to share Luka with Isa yet. Not after all that had happened between us. So, I said nothing. Just listened to the shower run, and Isa sing, and tried to swallow down the unease I already felt rising in my throat and burning my tongue.

We had always shared our secrets. Not so much lately, perhaps, but we were confidantes still. We leaned on one another as friends always do. But when it came to Luka, I held back. Kept it to myself without really knowing why. A secret like that was the sort of thing friends were supposed to share with each another. But something had held me back. Instinct, I suppose.

Luka, no, I couldn't tell Isa about him. Tell her about the feelings I had for him. Feelings which had crept up on me unexpectedly. I still wasn't sure just what it was I felt, or where it had come from, this… well, what was it exactly? Infatuation? A crush? I had no way to articulate it, not without sounding gushing and pathetic. It made me cringe just thinking about it.

Every time I thought about him though, that was how I felt. A tingle somewhere—everywhere, in fact, from scalp to toe. Just saying his name could bring it on. "Luka," and there it was, that shiver across my skin and down my spine.

He had always been there, a regular part of the Montauk summer. But the feelings—they were new. They overcame me last summer. The two of us were headed to the beach, Luka hanging on the porch, waiting for me just as he always did, smiling when I came running outside, my hair still wet from the shower, T-shirt half on, my beach bag half open so everything fell out and had me cursing and blushing and feeling clumsy and geeky as I tried to pick it up and stuff it back in.

He kneeled to help me. That was all he did, he just kneeled, and I looked up from my crouched position, felt the wet of my hair as it started to soak through the back of my T-shirt, caught a whiff of shampoo—the awful medicinal smell of the brand James used, a bottle I'd seized by mistake in the morning rush—and it was as if I could see myself, so awkward and flailing and hopeless. And I'd wanted to run inside and never come back out. I'd thought he would laugh at me and shake his head, smell the crappy shampoo and back away in embarrassment, but all he did was crouch down beside me, pick up the sunscreen and put it in my bag saying, "Hey, what's the rush? It's summer, remember?"

And he could never have known, of course, what this did to me. He was just being Luka. Just being how he always was with me. A friend, a pal, someone to walk to the beach with. Until that morning, that was all he'd ever been to me, as well.

Or maybe that wasn't true. Maybe I had noticed the blue of his eyes before. A color I found so hard to describe. Darker than a sapphire, bluer than a jay, indigo almost, it had caught me unawares a long time ago, just like the flop of his dark hair. Boys weren't meant to look like him, was what I'd thought. Beautiful, like this. They were meant to be rough around the edges and not worth my attention.

But there he was, looking this way, looking beautiful, and I'd had to stare at the ground, just to stop myself from blushing, just to catch my breath. Some days I'd even gone out of my way to avoid him, just to be sure he wouldn't figure it out.

Because if he did, that would be the end of that loose connection we had. That ease we had around each other would be gone. And I would have spoiled it for nothing. I knew we could never be anything more than friends. I would never be brave enough to tell him what I felt and then stand there watching him squirm as he told me he didn't feel the same way. I wasn't stupid. I knew he was the sort of boy I could never have.

And, if I'd trusted her completely, I would have asked Isa what to do. There were even a few times, over the last year when I'd come close to it.

Hey, there's this guy…

But I never dared, I always held back. And a piece of me knew why. Some instinct I preferred to ignore, a little voice that said, *She'll hurt you, if you tell her. She'll hurt you in the worst way you can imagine.*

It wasn't the sort of thing you were supposed to think about a friend, and I was ashamed of thinking it, at the time. Even now, when I know how true it was, when my instincts were proven correct, I still prefer not to think about it. Prefer instead to remember all the good things that happened that summer, before it all went wrong.

I've thought about that every day since Isa died. How it was possible that a vacation could turn into something so disastrous. Because the start of it had been so much fun. That first day, when I think back to it, it seems impossible that it was actually the moment we started moving closer to Isa's death. There was a shadow hanging over us all that time, but we just weren't aware of it.

*

By the time we had showered, we could already hear the sounds coming from the kitchen, the clatter of pots and pans and the radio playing. Dad was already up and about making breakfast. It was his little vacation thing, a full-blown affair of pancakes and fruits and freshly squeezed juices. Warm bread rolls and eggs and expensive artisan jams (no one ever knew where he found them). Coffee on the stove from a percolator he brought with him from home. Strong, black, powerful stuff that caused goose bumps with the first sip.

This breakfast extravaganza was something he never did back home. He didn't have the time. Back home we rarely saw him on weekday mornings, he was always up and gone long before we even opened our eyes. Breakfast in Manhattan was a quick toasted bagel and a gulp of juice, if that. No one talking much, save to say if they were going somewhere after school.

It was my favorite thing about staying at the summer house, those breakfasts, the fact that we all sat together and talked, as if we were a normal family. So as soon as the smell of coffee filtered through the house and up towards us, I shouted out to Isa to get a move on, so we would be downstairs before James scoffed the lot.

He was already there though, by the time we made it into the kitchen, sat at the table with his plate piled high. On his fork, a pancake, halfway to his mouth when we walked in. Isa in the yellow dress, her wet hair piled up on her head, the water dripping onto her shoulders and seeping into the thin pale cotton, the wet fabric clinging to her so that, in the morning light, against that tanned skin, you could almost think she was naked.

James simply stared.

"Morning, James," I said. And I winked at him because it was so easy to tease him, which made him drop his fork and caused his cheeks to blaze a furious embarrassed red, and Dad to shout out to him that he was, "such a klutz still."

And Isa? She noticed none of it, or pretended to, I couldn't be sure. She just slipped into the chair facing James and smiled at him and asked if there was any coffee left.

Poor James, I thought. So damn awkward. So shy.

Still young enough not to realize that girls had started to notice him and that they liked what they saw. Not just because he was basically an okay kinda guy, the sensitive kind, but because he was pretty good-looking, and the fact he didn't realize it made him all the more attractive.

"You know who he reminds me of sometimes?" Isa had said to me once. "Johnny Depp when he was really young, but just nowhere near as cocky."

And I had laughed at that, not because I couldn't see it, but because I could never imagine Isa looking at my brother that way.

"You should get yourself some glasses," I told her. And Isa had shaken her head and shrugged again. That same shrug she always did when she knew she was right about something. "You'll see, Katie. You'll see."

Until that summer, girls had never veered into James' line of vision. He was always busy with other things. But now there he was, sat at the breakfast table facing Isa and trying desperately not to look up from his plate.

I gave Isa a dig in the ribs and mouthed a whispered "stop" when I caught her smiling at James, all coy and girlish. If they hadn't known each for so long, it could have been funny, but something about the way Isa smiled at him felt weird. A joke too far. She should know that there were some boundaries even she shouldn't cross, and the fact that she didn't seem to consider this made me nervous.

Dad finally finished up in the kitchen and came to the table with a flourish and a "Ta-da," as he laid down a massive pile of fresh pancakes. He was already relaxed into his summer self. Sloppy and casual in a faded old T-shirt, the one with the album cover of *London Calling* on it.

Mom always joked he wore it as an ironic statement. But I never saw it like that. He was just relaxing was all. The rest of the year, he lived in expensive tailored suits, and wore a watch that cost as much as a small car. And okay, so maybe he'd never come close to being punk, and maybe Joe Strummer wouldn't have liked him all that much, at least, not when he was in high finance mode, but on mornings like this, with a pile of fresh pancakes on a plate and the sun pouring through the windows, maybe they'd get on okay.

Because he knows enough about the small things that matter. And when he gets the chance, he cares. Which makes his absence the rest of the time acceptable, sort of.

"Tuck in," Dad told us, and James wasted no time forking three more pancakes onto his plate, glad of the distraction. Happy he could do something to take his mind off Isa and her relentless gaze.

"Hey, come on, James," Dad laughed, "leave some for the rest of us."

And he pulled the plate away from James and offered it to Isa.

When she hesitated, he smiled at her and said, "Hey, you're too young to be worrying about a little pancake. All the swimming and goofing about on the beach will burn off any excess calories."

I could tell Isa was embarrassed. Annoyed with herself that he had caught her hesitation and understood what was behind it.

"Thanks, Mr. L," Isa murmured as she lifted a pancake onto her plate. Just the one. No syrup, only fruit salad on the side and a cup of black coffee.

I did the same but made sure to eat only half the pancake, piling a mass of fruit around it so Dad wasn't aware. I'd worked hard to hit my target weight of 114lbs before the vacation, and I wanted Isa to notice it, I wanted her to say something.

But if Isa noticed it, then she never said a word. She simply lost herself in her phone checking it every time it pinged, the Instagram likes coming in thick and fast.

Dad couldn't help but notice.

"You're popular," he said.

And while Isa smiled at him, I butted in.

"It's the dress," I explained. "All the guys online are going wild for it."

And he seemed to notice Isa then. Notice that she was no longer the little kid he had once known. That she was closer to a woman than he realized.

"Oh yes," he blurted out. "I can imagine. You look great, Isa. That dress fits you perfectly."

And as he admired her, in walked Mom, her face ashen.

It was like one of those snapshot moments when everything freezes. There was James, his eyes fixed on the plate in front of him. There was Dad, staring at Mom, the first traces of a worried frown creeping across his brow. There was Isa, head back about to laugh, her arms stretched across the table towards James. And there was Mom, standing in the doorway, taking it all in.

"Good morning," Mom said. "You're all up bright and early." Though she only looked at Dad. It was as if there was no one else in the room with them then. It was just the two of them, eye to eye, in a way that had become so familiar the last few years. I thought they could argue without a word ever passing between them, only cold stares. My father finally breaking the silence, "Breakfast?" as Mom pulled a chair up and sat down beside me.

"Just coffee for me, thanks."

And all the while, James stared at Isa, and Isa stared back, and I could see what James was thinking: *What would it be like to touch her?*

*

We headed to the beach at noon, sauntering through the dunes laden with beach bags and with James in tow.

He didn't want to join us, and I would have been happy to leave him at the beach house, but I'd heard Mom coax him out the door.

"Give me and your dad a few minutes together, will you, James?" she said. And it didn't take much to guess why.

Day one and Mom was already nervous. It was going to take some effort to get her to relax about having Isa along with us. And Isa had noticed it too but had mistaken Mom's anxiety for something else. For the start of some sort of argument.

I could almost hear Isa thinking, *So, all parents are pretty much the same*, and I had wanted to tell her that this wasn't true, that my parents were good together. Mom was just a worrier, and sometimes it could get on Dad's nerves. He'd be telling her to calm down. Which would only make things worse, of course.

I'd have to explain it to Isa later. Let her know that she hadn't fled the tension and chaos of her own home only to land smack in the middle of someone else's problems.

As we walked through the dunes the sounds of the beach grew louder and more enticing. I could hear laughter and voices, a radio blazing, shouts and squeals, and when we rose over the top of the dune, the sight of the beach was a relief, so colorful and alive and buzzing. The perfect antidote to parents and all their stressed-out marital bullshit.

Even James brightened at the sight of it, forgetting everything for a moment and sliding headlong down the sandy slopes, a great big stupid, "woohoo!" bursting out of him.

Isa watched him careen down the dune then followed, charging down the sandy banks and yelling her heart out. James watched her from the bottom, and the sight of her, flying and goofing about, and following his lead seemed to release something within him. Even from up here, looking down at him, I could see it, a sort of broadening of the shoulders that came over him, like he'd given himself permission to become someone else. Just like that. With one childish whoop. And the sight of him, so bold and full of energy, so keen to follow Isa's lead, put me on guard.

Keep an eye on him, I thought.

From high on the dune I could see Isa strolling along the sand, scouring the beach for a place where we could pitch up for the day. I could tell from the way she sauntered along that she was looking at the guys on the beach. Checking them out to see if there were any good-looking ones she fancied getting to know.

She looked up at me and yelled, "Hey! Are you coming?"

And I shrugged back a reply, then slowly eased myself down the dune and onto the beach.

"This is as good a place as any then," Isa said, and she thumped her bag down on to the sand and began to lay out her things. Everything was color coordinated. A navy blue and white striped beach towel, which matched her sun hat and her bikini. A book—hefty and serious-looking and definitely for show. A chic little thermos water bottle, also in navy blue, and some expensive brand of spray-on sunscreen. Last of all, she pulled out a little transparent plastic box with a click-on lid. It was for her phone, and when she dropped it in, after checking it for messages, I laughed.

"What?" Isa shot back. "It's to stop the sand getting in it."

I just nodded.

"Here," she said, and she popped open the lid, "put yours in too. Seriously, sand's a phone killer."

"Gee." I smiled at her and dropped in my phone. "You're too damn organized. Did you honestly color coordinate all this stuff?"

And Isa beamed, happy that I had noticed.

"You like it?" she asked me. "I went and got some nice stuff a few days before we left; I wanted this vacation to feel special, you know?"

I did. Though I hadn't realized until then that Isa wanted it to be special too.

James laid out his towel and flopped down on it, pulling off his T-shirt and jeans and unaware of Isa's gaze.

"Is it special?" he asked her. "This place? I mean, it's just Montauk."

And Isa glanced at him, appraising his physique, which had changed so much the past year, the muscles taking on a definition that could only be described as masculine, seriously masculine. If he wasn't my brother, I would be the first to admit he was a boy worth looking at.

And Isa was certainly looking. I gave her a gentle dig in the ribs and chided her.

"Hey, Isa, that's my baby brother."

"So it is," she smiled. "So it is."

And James was suddenly conscious of Isa's gaze again.

"I meant this place," he murmured. "What's so special about this place? We're here every year. It's not a vacation, is it? It's just a change of location."

But he didn't wait for an answer, just stood up and headed to the sea.

"I'm going for a swim."

Isa watched him go, then turned towards me and smiled.

"Okay, I promise I'll let up on him. He's too immature still." And I nodded.

"Still, you've got to admit it, Katie, he's going to be gorgeous in a couple of years."

"He's my brother, Isa," I reminded her. "My stupid kid brother."

"Spoilsport," Isa laughed. "Still, someone's going to nab him one day, Katie, and you're just going to have to get used to it."

"Yeah, and that's fine, but, you know, it would just be fucking weird if it was you, so lay off him okay?"

And Isa had pouted a jokey, "Aww," then lay back on her towel and laughed. "Whatever," she said. "Hopefully someone else will come along to amuse me while I'm here."

I decided to ignore that. I'd had enough of Isa amusing herself, the last few months.

For the next few hours we lazed around on the beach, drowsy from the early rise and the heat of the sun.

At some point James came back and snapped up his towel and clothes, telling us he'd found a bunch of friends along the beach and was going to hang out with them instead.

I didn't blame him, but Isa sighed and said, "What a shame." Then the relentless pings on her phone distracted her from her woes once again, and James was forgotten.

I spent the day listening to her laughing and providing me with running commentary on the messages she was getting about her beach photos. Every now and then she pulled out her phone and took a snapshot of herself. Photos of pieces of her—painted toenails, a teasing shot of her tan lines, a sneaky shot of 'Katie's well-toned butt,' as she captioned it, taken as I lounged half asleep in the sun. The inevitable cleavage shot.

The ping, ping, ping, of her phone, the click, click, click as she snapped open the little protective box, punctuating the day like the tick of a clock.

"Dammit, Isa," I eventually snapped. "Can you turn the notifications off? It's getting annoying."

"Geez, what the hell is up with you?"

"I just want to chill without all that racket."

"Oh, come on, Katie. It's just a few Instagram likes. Chill out for a bit, will you?"

And I wanted to ask her who it was exactly she was posting those shots for. Those flirty, heavily filtered photos, they weren't only for showing off to school pals and followers, they were meant as a tease for someone very specific, I was sure of it. A way to make him jealous. Let him see Isa could have a good time without him. It made me want to scream, knowing that he was still there in the background, like a bad dream you can't shake off.

I was close to just coming out and asking her, but Isa didn't give me the chance.

"Is everything okay? Is it your folks?" Isa asked me. "They seemed a bit tense back there. Is everything good between them?"

It wasn't the moment to get into all of that. I just wanted to have a day when we didn't have to talk about any of that messy sort of stuff.

"Maybe," I said. Then, "No, not especially. Listen, forget it, I just want to have a day on the beach, you know?"

"A day away from stupid parents, you mean?"

"Yeah, something like that."

And with that, Isa got up.

"You're right," she said. "Fuck 'em. Let's go for a swim, get away from all this *racket* for a bit."

"You go, I just want to lie here and get some sun."

"Oh, right, okay then."

I'd disappointed her, I knew I had. But these things worked both ways, and I felt like being petty for a bit.

I watched her head off down the sand to the sea, breaking into a light trot as she reached the harder, wetter sand. Athletic, and healthy, and strong. Nothing moved on her body, and the taut tension of muscle in her legs was almost too perfect.

And for a moment I envied her. Her perfection, her easy nature, her happiness. Her complete lack of self-awareness at times.

Not once, in all the hours we'd lain beside one another, had Isa looked at me or noticed a thing. She didn't notice the deep purple of my nail polish, a color I picked because I knew it was Isa's favorite. I had even done a full Isa and picked out a lilac swimsuit to match it. She didn't comment on the weight loss, the way my hip bones jutted out so beautifully when I lay back on the sand, the little dip in my belly as it hollowed out, something I'd worked so hard for.

How can she not have noticed? I brooded. Why has she said nothing? Just sat there all day admiring herself on Instagram and posing on the beach? Why did she always have to be so fucking self-absorbed?

I sat up and tried to find her among the crowd of swimmers in the water and thought about joining her for a swim. Maybe it would help to float in the sea for a while instead of lying there seething. It didn't take me long to spot her. Her striped bikini remarkably easy to spot in the waves.

She was splashing around and laughing, talking to someone, her arm draped over his shoulder. It took me a moment before I realized it was James.

Shit! I thought. You promised you'd lay off him. What the hell is wrong with you, Isa?

CHAPTER FOUR

Louise

A dress is just a dress, you could say. Teenage girls swap clothes all the time and play around with their appearance so much, it's hardly worth noticing. So why let a dress bother you?

But it did bother me. I'd bought that dress at Saks Fifth Avenue, as a surprise for Katie especially for the summer, because yellow was her color; with her dark hair and the deep suntan she always got in summer, it was a color she could pull off. But she never wore it. Not one single day. It was as if Isa had decided to live in that dress for the duration of the vacation.

I had come down to breakfast on the first morning and there she was, sitting at the table wearing it, and I knew straight away what had happened, because I knew my daughter, those little moments of self-doubt that crept up on her, the self-criticism. Katie would have taken one look at Isa in that dress, blue-eyed and blonde, her skin like honey, and decided she was never going to look as good in it herself. And that would have been all it took for her never to wear it. It sapped my energy to see Isa wearing it and drained the color from my cheeks.

Because something about the way she wore it, not just that morning, but for the rest of the summer, her casualness, it was as if she hadn't given it any thought; she'd simply claimed that dress as her own, as if she had a right to Katie's things. Even now, I flinch a little still when I think about it. Because, again, I missed a signal. That's what I think. As soon as I saw Isa in that dress, that was the moment I should have paid attention, made the decision to watch them closely. I should have done something more than just take my seat at the breakfast table and make breezy conversation while I pushed away the niggling doubt which had returned again: I should never have agreed to let Isa join us. Why didn't I just stand my ground and say it wasn't possible?

"Hey, just relax," Peter had said, when I shooed the kids out the door and sent them to the beach. "Let's take it easy and let them all settle down first. They're just excited to be spending the summer together."

I'd wanted to take it further, to tell him there was something else worrying me, but how to explain it? How to tell him that the sight of Isa in Katie's summer dress made me nervous? That there was something about the way Isa had taken control which tipped me off balance. That the blush on James' cheeks when he stared at Isa also worried me, not because James was staring at a good-looking girl, he was at that age when girls were bound to start coming into his field of vision. No, it was more the way Isa had stared back at him, there was something flirtatious about it, teasing. And it felt wrong. James should be out of bounds, and Isa should know that. Our long family friendship should mean Isa would never throw even a glance in James' direction. I had every right to feel awkward about it, surely?

But all I did was mention to Peter that it might be an idea to establish some ground rules.

"I can see them running wild if we're not careful."

And he had laughed and suggested that perhaps that was what the summer was all about for teenagers and that maybe we should be glad that the kids could blow around here on the beach rather than be at a loose end in the city. "It's a bit safer here, don't you think? I mean, think of all the trouble they could get into in Manhattan."

"I guess," I agreed. "But I still think we should set some limits or something. Don't you?"

"Listen," Peter said. "If anything happens, if they get a little too rowdy, then we can always call Willem and Sarah and ask them what to do."

"On their honeymoon?"

"Hey, second honeymoon, remember?"

And I'd smiled at that.

"Yeah, okay…"

"Listen, all this mess Willem's caused, it's bound to have left Isa a bit upset. I'd figured on her letting off steam while she was here. I just assumed you had too. And anyway, don't you think Isa has a right to be angry with him? I know I'd be pretty pissed off if I was her. If it was my dad who had screwed around like that."

It wasn't something I'd considered, if I'm honest, and the judgmental tone in Peter's voice made me anxious. *Screwed around.* That he had an opinion about Willem's behavior was something I'd never have imagined. I'd always considered Peter to be relaxed about such things. Other people's marriages were their own business, that was what he thought, and he always said he preferred to "avoid all that gossipy crap." But Isa being dragged into all the mess was something different apparently.

"I'm not sure that fills me with confidence," I told him. "The thought of a teenager letting off steam."

"Yeah, well, she's been through a lot, so let's just give her some space."

"I suppose she has—"

"You suppose?"

"I just mean I've been focusing so much on Sarah, on what it had done to her, that I never really thought about Isa, that she's been caught up in all of this too."

"Really? Wow…"

"Hey, Peter, please… don't…"

"Sorry."

"I just thought she had Katie for that, was all. I figured she had someone to talk to, you know?"

"Yes, well, as long as Willem starts thinking about what he's done then that's all that matters. He created this mess, so it's about time he started cleaning it up and making amends, don't you reckon? Take some responsibility."

"You think he can? Make amends, I mean? With Sarah?"

"Who knows. She has every right to be angry with him."

"True, but she could have handled it better. Not made such a drama out of it."

Peter had looked at me then, surprised that I would criticize my friend so easily. I guess he thought I'd defend Sarah out of some sort of female solidarity or something, and I found myself needing to explain.

"I just mean that it's not the end of the world, is it? After all those years together. What is it now, twenty years? I just think she could have forgiven him a lot quicker is all, instead of making such a fuss. And all this honeymoon business, all the melodrama. It's cringeworthy. And if you ask me, I think Isa's mortified about it all."

"She's a teenager, Louise. She's supposed to be mortified by her parents. And besides, everyone reacts in their own way to things like that. For what it's worth, I think Sarah's holding up pretty well under the circumstances. I mean, can you imagine if it was the other way around? If it had been Sarah who'd been caught with another man? Willem would have filed for divorce without even blinking."

"Oh, come on, Peter. I don't think so."

"No? I do. Guys like that are all the same. He'd never be able to withstand the humiliation."

"You say that like it would be justified."

"I just think that's how he would see things, is all. The fragile male ego and all that."

"Yeah, well this is all hypothetical. Sarah did nothing wrong, remember?"

I'd left it there, unable to say any more. The fact that he'd been so quick to judge had left me too flustered to speak.

It was only later, when I thought about it again, that it hit me. Maybe this was how Peter would react too. Though it seemed the crime was not so much the infidelity, as the humiliation it would cause. The fragile male ego. He was right about that. It was a dangerous thing.

But I knew as well as anyone that discretion was one of the foundations of a solid marriage. That was something we both understood about each other. That was the unspoken understanding we had. Only now, I wasn't so sure. If Peter thought an indiscretion, a meaningless fling, was a good enough reason to call time on a marriage as long as Sarah and Willem's... God, it made me feel sick to think of it. Sick and afraid.

I sent Sarah a message anyway, just to be sure.

> *I think the girls are a bit too excited about all this. We'll keep an eye on them make sure they don't run wild.*

I'd expected a quick reply. Sarah was usually so good that way. Within five minutes a response always came. But not this time.

A day later, I tried again.

> *Hey! How's Sardinia? Good, I hope. We're all settling in here. The girls spend all day at the beach. Believe it or not, we have sun! Okay, call me when you get the chance.*

But again, no reply. Though as the days passed and there was still no word from Sarah, I started to relax. No reply could only mean one thing. Sarah and Willem were having too much of a good time to be bothering with text messages. When she resurfaced, no doubt she would get around to calling me.

In the meantime, I figured I might as well take my lead from Sarah and enjoy the weeks ahead. The heatwave was forecast to continue, and the prospect of a long stretch of uninterrupted sunshine and a lazy summer was too good to spoil by worrying about friends.

Though the more I thought about Sarah and Willem enjoying their romantic getaway, the more I wanted the same thing, to turn the vacation into something more than just the usual retreat to the coast. It would do our relationship good, I thought, if we paid a bit more attention to one another. Not that we needed it. Extravagant gestures, second honeymoons and all that, were not our style. *But you could indulge him a little, Louise*, I thought. *Have some fun together.*

Fun. It had been missing the last few years. Both of us would admit to that. Close to twenty years of marriage took the edge off things. The predictability of it all. No one could escape it. And if I knew the phone calls telling me he needed to "pull an all-nighter" at work were not always true, well, I could live with that. And besides, I had ways of coping, it wasn't just husbands who got bored. I knew how to amuse myself.

I suppose some people would no doubt call it what it was: infidelity. But I had never looked at it that way. When both parties understood the need to be discreet, to turn a blind eye, to quietly acknowledge they were both adults who were free to choose, there was a mutual respect to it all which neutered any need to blame the other. Do no harm. That was all it was about.

And that was how it was. We did each other no harm. I thought Peter understood this. And if that looks like I'm trying to justify my behavior then fair enough, but one thing I do know is that it's the secrets you don't share, it's the things you don't reveal, that make a marriage strong.

When Sarah had first told me about Willem's affair, I had thought of explaining some of this to her. But Sarah had been so black and white about it all. Willem's affair was a betrayal, nothing less. I don't think she would have listened to anything I had to say. She was furious with him and humiliated by the whole thing.

And that slight primness she had, her very proper way of doing things sometimes, she was less cosmopolitan than she imagined. It was why I never fully confided in her. Right from the start of our friendship I understood it was better to keep some things to myself. Telling her about my own liaisons, about the dalliances and the short-lived affairs, would have been a futile and dangerous thing to do. I could imagine Sarah rushing to tell Willem all about it, or worse, Peter. And she would do it out of a sense of obligation. She would justify it to herself somehow.

"I just thought that you should know, Peter," I could imagine her saying, her voice sweet with sympathy and trembling with righteousness.

So, I simply offered a sympathetic ear and sat around listening while Sarah tried to grapple with what Willem had done. I never told her I thought her tears were indulgent and self-absorbed, though maybe I should have. Maybe if I had told her to get a grip, we could have saved ourselves from everything that was to come.

But I figured my role was to hold Sarah's hand and be the dutiful friend. To drink bottle after bottle of wine over countless afternoons and listen to her woes while I wiped away tears and tried to convince her that it was not the end of the world. These things could be sorted out. Reconciliation was not unthinkable.

I can't remember when she came around to that idea. What it was that finally caused her to listen. All I remember is Sarah asking me, "Do you really think we can get through this?"

And I'd been pretty blunt about it; there was no point, by then, in holding back or softening the blow.

"It's going to mean you need to forgive him, Sarah. So, I guess that's what you need to ask yourself. Can you? Really, I mean? Can you forget about it? Stop tormenting yourself about it and forgive him."

"You make it sound easy," Sarah had said.

"It's not. I just think that, if it was me, if I'd had an affair, say, and Peter had found out, I'd hope he'd forgive me. That almost twenty years of marriage would come to mean something in the end."

I noticed her reaction to that, of course. The small intake of breath, the little crease between the brows, as if the very idea of that, of the tables being turned, and the woman being the transgressor, seemed absurd. I'd needed to control the urge to laugh and so I'd pushed it a little.

"And, you know, I don't think Willem would want a separation. I don't think he'd want to leave you to fend for yourself, especially in such an emotional state. I mean, it would be so difficult for you."

She'd blinked when I mentioned that and looked at me and tried to say something but found herself incapable of speech. I took that as my cue to leave and left her sitting there pondering the dilemma and coming to a rational and mercenary conclusion: I was right, forgiveness was possible after all.

*

When the reply to my texts finally arrived, it seemed that forgiveness and reconciliation was also a lot of fun.

Hey! Sorry for not getting back to you earlier. You know how it is, been a bit, preoccupied, shall we say? How's things in Montauk? Are the kids behaving themselves?

I had sent back a quick reply, just a short, *Glad to hear you're having fun. Enjoy yourself! All okay here*, and left it at that, annoyed that it had taken her so long to reply. It was as if we were an after-thought or some pesky interruption to her precious honeymoon.

Enjoy yourself. I couldn't stop thinking about that. I had weeks ahead of me, and as relaxing as it always was, fun and enjoyment were not really on the cards. At least not the sort of enjoyment I longed for. And I felt a pang of jealousy then. That feverish immersion in someone else, there was no beating it. And when I thought of that, I thought of him. The two things were inseparable.

And I allowed my thoughts to drift, my skin prickling and alert just thinking about him. It was ridiculous really to feel like this at my age. To let myself be carried away with that youthful abandonment, with the sheer pleasure that came from losing yourself in something sensual and to hell with everything else.

But that was how he made me feel. Young. Myself. Carefree again. The woman I was before marriage and kids and responsibility enveloped me. Oh, and I wasn't stupid, I knew his compliments were simple flattery, that his attention was simply a way for him to get what he wanted. He was clever that way—good at spotting a weakness and exploiting it. But I didn't care. I accepted it, because he made me feel young again, he energized me, and I needed that more than I cared to admit. That was the deal. We both got what we wanted. Pleasure, pure and simple.

And I wondered what he would think, if he saw me now, wearing only a bikini and a chiffon sarong, lounging in a hammock and gleaming a little from the heat of the midday sun. Would he feel the same longing? Would he recognize it as desire?

He had always admired my body, the muscle tone maintained from years of Pilates and running. My skin, supple and hydrated and always protected from the sun. Not a blemish or stretchmark to be found, I'd made damn sure of it.

"You're like a twenty-five-year-old," he told me the first time we slept together. And I had laughed and jokingly called him a liar as he ran his finger down my stomach and over my hip bones, tracing the firmness, appraising me. Then he squeezed my thigh and smiled at me, and said, "You should be proud of your body. It's perfect."

"Well, you certainly seem to like it," I said. And he nodded and laughed.

"Oh, I do. I really do." Then he rolled me over and said, "Anyway, enough talking."

And I knew then that I would have to be careful, because I could feel the power he had over me. He could do as he pleased with me and I would let him. More than that, I would enjoy it.

Oh God, and what the hell was I to do now, with all these days ahead of me and that tingle of unsatisfied energy shivering through me?

And I thought of Peter, and a forgotten spark of longing resurfaced somewhere in my stomach and took me by surprise. I could almost hear his voice mocking me, "Well, well, well, Louise." But what else was I to do? Peter was here, and the summer was long, so…

I had acted on it immediately. Waited for him to come to bed that night and made my move before he could turn over. Sitting astride him and smiling. Whispering, "I don't see why it should just be Sarah and Willem who get to have all the fun, do you?" Ignoring the surprised look on his face. Closing my eyes and letting myself go with it.

Surprised, when it was over, to discover that during the whole thing I had not thought of *him* once. And I was happy to let my amnesia last the whole summer.

He'd be waiting for me when I returned home. In the meantime, I had found a way to channel my excess energy. And suddenly, the summer didn't seem such a daunting prospect after all.

CHAPTER FIVE

Katie

Isa and James. They had always been easy together, always relaxed and laughing and just really loose in one another's company. Oh, and loud, so damn loud, their laughter always two steps ahead of them, you always heard them before you saw them. Sometimes I wondered if Isa considered James more of a friend than she did me. That's what it could feel like sometimes, that I was the one tagging along with them, rather than the other way around. They had a way of always finding one another when they needed to and then shutting everyone else out. It wasn't a conscious thing, it was just the way they were together sometimes. They'd get chatting and laughing and then forget everyone else. It was cute when they were small, but now, for some reason, it seemed too intimate. As if their closeness now was a step towards something else, something forbidden.

Watching them goofing about in the sea that day, I wondered what they would be like around one another if the childhood friendship wasn't there. If our mothers weren't friends. Closer than they allowed themselves to be now, was what I figured. Much closer. And I realized I wasn't entirely confident I could trust Isa not to cross that line.

From my vantage point on the beach I could hear their shouts as they batted a ball about, playing beach tennis. I watched James jump in the air as he leapt to return a shot Isa had aimed deliberately high. He stumbled as he ran backwards through the water, then fell into a wave and came up grinning and yelling at Isa that she wasn't playing fair.

Isa just laughed. "But it's so much fun to see you crash in the sea like that!"

They kept it up for about half an hour, and eventually I grew tired of watching them, and fell back in the sand and pulled the parasol round so I was in the shade, then closed my eyes and tried to doze for a while in the heat and the lazy atmosphere. But it was impossible. Too many thoughts crowded my head.

I would have to say something to Isa about the dress, otherwise I would spend the rest of the break thinking about it, holding it in, and feeling crap about the whole thing. But it seemed so petty to start moaning about something so stupid. A dress. God, was I really prepared to put something so insignificant between us again when we had just made up after all that Alex business? And in any case, it was just Isa being Isa. Never noticing anything, just taking what she wanted, without really thinking. I knew what she could be like, and if I couldn't handle it, then that was my own fault. But Mom would be upset about it. God knows how much she'd paid for that dress. Too much, probably. And it definitely wasn't money she'd wanted to spend on Isa.

I watched them splashing about in the waves and thought about joining them. Just going along with it all, but the sun was so hot, and my head was so woozy with too much thinking. *Fuck it*, I figured. We've got a whole summer to sort this shit out.

And I pulled out my book and read for a while before falling asleep.

*

When I woke it was gone four o'clock and James and Isa were nowhere to be seen. Their stuff, gone.

I headed back to the beach house sunburned and annoyed and found Isa lounging on the porch happy and lazy from a day of sun and sea.

"Hey, sleepy head," Isa said.

"Damn it, Isa. Why didn't you wake me up? I almost fried alive out there."

"Oh, sorry. You just looked so relaxed, so we left you to it."

And she looked at my red shoulders and winced, "Oh, that does look nasty."

"Thanks a lot. Where is James anyway?"

"Dunno. In his room? I think he might be bored of me already."

"Not funny, Isa. I told you already, leave him alone."

Isa just waved a limp wrist in my direction and picked up her phone to check what the latest ping was.

"Is that your folks?" I asked her.

"They're on their honeymoon, Katie. You think they have time to check in with me?"

"Right, too busy with each other, huh?"

"Eww, gross me out why don't you?"

It was just an aside to break the silence and clear the air. A way of getting some of the tension out of the room.

"Seriously, though," I told her. "I thought one of them might have sent a message or a photo or something, you know?"

"Oh, they did," Isa replied. "Mom sent me a text to check we'd arrived, and ask if I'd settled in."

"Isa, that was almost a week ago."

"Yeah, I know, but it's my parents we're talking about here, so why are you surprised? You know how attentive they are."

She had a point. It wasn't a surprise. But still, to hear her say it out loud like that, that it was nothing unusual, just her folks ignoring her, it seemed sad.

"Give them a call then, ask them what's up," I suggested.

"Yeah, maybe." Then a quick change of subject. When it came to her parents, Isa was never in the mood to dwell on things too long and I can't really say I blamed her. "Listen, enough about my stupid folks, I'd much rather know what the hell is up with your mom. I swear, it feels like she's watching me all the time. Just waiting for me to do something wrong."

"Nah, you're imagining it. She's good."

"Honestly? She's not mad at me or anything?"

"She just gets like that sometimes is all. She's a worrier. Hell, you know that, Isa. She's always on my case. More likely my dad or James have done something to annoy her. Dad can be a bit of an asshole sometimes, if you haven't noticed."

"What? Your dad? Come on, Katie, that's bullshit and you know it. Your dad's cool. Seriously. I mean, do you see my dad flipping pancakes for us, huh?"

"I guess. But don't go thinking he's like this all year. This is just his summer vibe."

"Summer *vibe*?" Isa laughed.

"Yeah, that's a direct quote."

"Very retro. Does your mom ever get into the spirit of it too?"

"Huh?"

"The *summer vibe*, has your Mom got one too?" Isa laughed. "Coz seriously, I don't fancy spending all summer knowing she's watching me all the time."

"Isa, my Mom will *never* have a summer vibe, she's far too neurotic. Trust me. So, just ignore her, that's what I do."

"Yeah?"

"Yeah."

"Maybe I should do the same? Just let my folks get it out of their system, ignore them too for a bit?"

"You want to do that?"

"I dunno, maybe. What do you reckon?"

"Just give them a call, Isa. Let them know you miss them."

"Miss them? That might be taking it a bit too far, Katie. I guess I should check they haven't forgotten me though."

"Hey, come on, they haven't forgotten you."

"No?" she laughed. "I'm not so sure about that. I think they're so caught up in this honeymoon thing, they've forgotten everyone."

"Well, they're doing it for a reason, remember? I mean, they want to stick together, that's not so bad, is it? Or would you prefer that they go back to screaming at one another?"

And Isa shrugged her shoulders and laughed a little, as if she thought her parents were bound to fail, so there was no point in even talking about it. "They really think this honeymoon thing is going to set them straight. Like they can start again or something. It's pathetic."

"Why? Seriously, what's wrong with that? Isn't that what you want? For things to be okay between them again?"

"Yeah, maybe. It's just, you know, the idea they can 'start again.' Where does that leave me?"

"Huh?"

"I mean, it's like I'm erased or something. Like their whole marriage was such a mess, and they need to start from scratch, correct their mistakes."

"Oh, quit with the melodrama, you know they don't mean it like that, they wouldn't want to hurt you."

"No? Then why didn't they just take me with them? I mean, if they deserve a swanky trip to Sardinia then why don't I?"

And she had a point there, but I didn't have an answer. Though selfish, is what I thought. They were selfish. Having Isa along with them wouldn't have been so bad. Whether Isa deserved pampering was a different thing. If Willem and Sarah knew half of what Isa had been up to the last few months, they'd have been more likely to ground her forever than take her on a fancy vacation.

"Listen, no one's perfect," I told Isa. "Parents are allowed to fuck things up too, you know?"

"That's very mature of you, Katie. What's the word? Magnanimous. Yeah, that's it."

"Ha! Whatever," I laughed. "I just mean, they can make mistakes the same as everybody, so cut them a bit of slack while they're away. And anyway, you're not exactly miss goody two-shoes, are you? So, you know, maybe you should let other people fuck things up too sometimes?"

"*Goody two-shoes*? Katie, what century were you born in? Goody two-shoes, for fuck's sake."

And she picked up a cushion from behind her head and threw it at me, then laughed.

"I'm not kidding though, you know, when I say your dad is cool. I wish he was my dad."

"Aw, poor Isa."

"Poor you, more like, for not appreciating him. You should be glad you have a dad like him. Someone who gives a shit."

"Listen," I said. "Do me a favor, will you? If my dad wants to act cool, and pretend he's everyone's best friend, then just let him get on with it, let him bake pancakes the whole summer if that's what he wants. He's just making up for all the mornings he's never around. It's kind of a family tradition, you know? Pretending everything is hunky-dory. It's what we come here for. And anyway, one phone call from the office, and you'll see. He'll be driving down that interstate as fast as he can in his rush to get back to Manhattan. It's why he agreed to get a place here. It's close enough to work for him to be able to relax."

Isa lay back in the swing and sighed, then closed her eyes.

"Sorry, Katie," she said, and she meant it too. "I thought it was just my folks that were screwed up. I thought it was all okay for you. That your parents, at least, were basically alright, you know?"

"And they are. Honestly, they are. They're just not perfect. But who ever said they had to be?"

"Yeah, whatever. Anyway," Isa said, jumping up from the porch swing and grabbing her phone from her beach bag, "I guess you're right. I'm going to text my folks. Just coz they're on their honeymoon doesn't mean I can't let them see what a great time I'm having."

And she swiped through some photos she'd taken that morning on the beach, turning the phone towards me now and then and asking me, "What about this one, you think they'd like this one?" and laughing.

The photos were definitely not something Sarah would want to see, Isa posing in her bikini, looking like some tacky celebrity on the cover of a gossip magazine.

"Shit, Isa," I warned her. "Don't send them that stuff, they'll freak out."

"Too late," she laughed. "It's gone."

And the weird thing was, she got no reply. No freak-out, no comment. Nothing. For another five days, the line stayed dead. Five days in which Isa sent them about ten photos a day. Bombarding them with every boring, minute detail of her day.

When her phone finally rang, and she saw her mom's icon appear on the screen, she almost didn't pick up. I saw her expression—*fuck you*—and had to tell her to take the call.

I'd expected more anger, Isa yelling down the line or complaining, at least.

"Hey, where have you been? I've been messaging you for days!"

But all there was, was a quietness, as if Isa couldn't turn her anger towards Sarah, even though Sarah probably deserved it.

I wanted to tell her to do it. *Scream at her if you want, Isa. You've got every right.* But I knew she never would. Sarah was too delicate, and it held everyone back in the end, kept everyone on edge, watching their words when they were around her. As if we were frightened of breaking her. And we were, of course. Everyone was. Willem had hurt her more than he realized, everyone could see that.

But that didn't make it right, her parents' silence the last days. It wasn't an excuse.

And even now I wonder, I'll always wonder, if I should have explained that to Isa. Told her it was okay to come down on your parents if they were being assholes. She didn't need to feel responsible for the mess they had made of things.

Just tell her you think she's a piece of shit for ignoring you. Or words to that effect.

Yeah, I should have said that, I should have let Isa know she had every right to be pissed off.

But Willem and Sarah were angry too. Angry with Isa for what she had done, the way she had brought them so close to the brink. Their own daughter.

So their silence was understandable, in a way. They needed time away from Isa. Until then, I hadn't thought about it like that. The excitement of having Isa around for the summer meant I preferred to forget everything that had happened over the last few months. Let's just have a great summer, that was all that mattered.

But Sarah's silence made me wonder if it was possible to forget. To act as if Willem and Sarah's honeymoon was a spontaneous thing, and not the result of an emergency precipitated by Isa.

A couple of times I even thought about telling Mom all about it. Letting her know that her instinct was right, she should be wary of Isa. But if Mom ever found out about the trouble Isa had caused after all that business with Alex, it would only make her worry even more and it would spoil the summer. Perhaps it was better if some things remained secret. That was what I figured. If there was any trouble, I could sort it out.

And if I had told her everything, would it have made a difference? Probably not. I could no more keep Isa out of trouble than I could fend off a charging bull. And it was stupid of me to have ever believed I could.

CHAPTER SIX

Louise

About a week after we'd settled into the beach routine, I found Isa out on the deck one afternoon and asked her how her parents were doing and if they were enjoying Sardinia. "It's such a beautiful place, the sand on some of the beaches is so unbelievably white and it's as soft as silk. They must be having an amazing time."

"No idea," Isa had replied.

And I misunderstood, I thought she meant that Sarah hadn't said much about what they were doing. A honeymoon was a private sort of affair after all, even if it was the second time around.

"No? They haven't sent any photos?"

"Nope," Isa replied. "I guess I'll just have to wait for them to remember I'm here."

I remember I paused because I wasn't sure I had understood correctly.

"Sorry, have you not heard from them at all?"

"No. Nothing. Why? Have you?"

"No. But, I mean…"

"You assumed they'd at least drop me a line just to ask how it was going?"

"Well, yes. Of course."

"Yeah, well, then there's a lot you don't know about my folks, I suppose."

And there was a touch of venom in her voice, I thought. More than just hurt at being left behind, at being ignored. There was an anger there which hinted at some deeper sort of pain. Though why shouldn't she feel angry? I thought. The more I thought about how easily Sarah had been prepared to leave Isa with us for the summer, the stranger I found it, and the more I wondered if there were things Sarah hadn't told me.

"They must have a reason," I suggested. "I can call Sarah if you like, check everything is okay?"

"Don't bother," Isa had replied. "She won't pick up."

"Oh, come on, I'm sure—"

And Isa had exploded then, fierce and full of rage.

"Louise, they don't care, okay? Don't you get it? This is all about them. All about their stupid marriage and 'sorting things out' and 'getting back to where they started,' and all that kind of crap. Nothing else matters. No one else matters. It's just this. This is the make or break honeymoon. Honestly, my mom? She thinks this is her last chance or something. That if she doesn't get it right, then it's all over. Her and my dad. Her whole life. All those creature comforts. That's how far she's gotten herself worked up about it all. If she fucks this up, then she's lost everything. And while they're in Sardinia, I don't exist. I'm a problem she would rather forget. A problem she would prefer to ignore."

"Isa," I interrupted. "They don't think you're a problem. That's silly. Why would they think a thing like that?"

"I dunno. You'd have to ask them."

"Listen, I know for sure that they wouldn't ignore you."

"Oh no?" Isa replied. "Why not? It's what they've been doing these last couple of months. I mean, Katie must have told you, I guess. That I've been 'going off the rails' as Mom likes to put it. Staying out partying too late, in town with people my parents don't even know. Flunking pretty much everything at school. All the usual teenage mess."

I tried to interrupt her and tell her that Katie hadn't told me anything and was surprised that Isa didn't realize that Katie would never break her trust like that. A secret meant something to Katie. Loyalty meant something. But Isa didn't give me the chance. She just carried on, spurred on by teenage indignation and the need to get it all out of her system at last.

"Not that my parents seemed to mind," she said. "I mean, do you know how many times they've pulled me up for any of this? How many times they've asked me where I was or who I was with? Do you know how many times Dad has stayed up at night waiting for me to roll through the door, so he can give me a piece of his mind? Huh? Let me tell you. None. Big fat zero. Not once. Seriously, they have *no* idea. All they care about is sorting out their own mess, and that's God's honest truth. And it's the reason they haven't called. I mean it's not just me, is it? They haven't called you either, have they? To ask how everything was going? Don't you think that's weird? Don't you think that's out of order? If nothing else, don't you think it's just rude? To dump me here with you guys and then waltz off into the sunset?"

I couldn't answer. But "yes," was what I thought. It *was* rude, it *was* weird, it *was* out of order. But it was also out of character too. Sarah always worried about what other people thought of her. That was the Sarah I knew. And that Sarah would never act like this. That Sarah had never acted like this before. So there had to be a reason. Something they were keeping from me. Because none of it made sense when I thought about it. Leaving Isa behind was more than just convenience, it had to be.

But Isa was in no mood to explain further.

"Sorry, Mrs. Lindeman," she said. "You shouldn't be worrying about any of this. Honestly, it's fine really. I just get a bit pissed off with them sometimes is all."

"To be honest, at the moment, I feel a bit pissed off with them myself," I admitted.

And Isa had laughed at that and told me that I shouldn't let it ruin my summer.

"I mean, if Mom and Dad can kick back and enjoy themselves and not worry about anything, then we should do the same, right?"

And there she was again, that carefree, don't give a shit, flippant Isa I knew so well. And she was right. What else could we do?

So, I agreed. "I guess so," I replied. "But, Isa, if you want to talk to me about any of this, you know you can, right?"

And I'd been met with a smile and a flick of the wrist. A light-hearted dismissal.

"Don't you worry, everything's fine. Really, everything's fine. Maybe the three of us need a few weeks apart. It'll do us good."

Now, when I look back at the summer, I wonder how I missed it. All those stupid photos Isa posted to her Instagram. Photos designed to provoke. The late-night parties, the bikini pictures, the flirtatious poses each time with a different group of boys. You put the two things together, that wildness, that anger, and what did you get? Not a picture of a stable, happy child, that's for sure.

No, you put those things together and what you got was a girl begging to be noticed, begging for attention, begging for her parents to look beyond their own problems and see their own daughter.

You got a picture of who Isa really was. And the picture wasn't pretty. Poor Isa.

CHAPTER SEVEN

Katie

Luka came up later than usual that summer. I thought I was going to burst with anxiety, waiting for him to arrive. Then, after two weeks of waiting, there he was at last. We hit the beach in the morning, and he was already there, stretched out in the sand with the rest of the gang. And the way my stomach lurched when I saw him, oh man, it felt like the tumbles I got in in my belly as a kid, when Dad drove too fast over small dips in the road. Or when I got too excited in the run-up to my birthday.

When he turned to see me scrambling down the dunes and called out to me, my head spun, and something fluttered in my throat.

"Hey, Katie!"

He was happy to see me, and I stumbled down the dune excitedly, desperate to say hello to him again. But Isa got there first. She ran ahead and sat down beside him in the sand, spread out her towel and said, "Hey, are you a friend of Katie's?"

And Luka had turned to face her, leaned on his elbow and smiled at her, a smile I'd never seen from him.

"Yeah," he said. "I'm Luka."

And Isa had laughed and tilted her head in that infuriating coquettish way that seemed to charm everyone but me.

"Isa," she replied. "I'm staying with Katie for the summer."

I had to remind herself that it wasn't Isa's fault. She had no way of controlling how people responded to her. No way of changing the way she looked. And at that moment she glowed. There was no other word for it. There was something shimmering about her hair, her skin, she had this aura around her. It almost made me laugh out loud.

How can I ever compete with that? I thought. It was impossible. And I knew, right then, that I was invisible now, that Luka would barely notice me. That "Hey, Katie," was as far as his attention would stretch.

Yet something about it was so expected, as if I'd been preparing for the inevitability of this moment for the last two weeks. Luka and Isa—I'd given in to it days ago, I realized. She would flirt with him, mesmerize him, and that would be it. I'd disappear in the nuclear haze that was Isa Egberts.

Though that didn't make the truth of it any easier, the actual reality of it, there, in front of me, glowing and giggling in the sun. And I tried not to acknowledge the small hope that still existed. *Isa wouldn't do that to me, would she?* But, deep down, I knew the answer: she would, if she felt like it. Of course she would.

I'd lain down beside them and pulled my sun hat over my eyes and pretended to sleep. Listening to them talk and laugh, blocking out the chitchat by trying to listen to the sounds of the waves and the background noise of the beach. Tomorrow, I'd remember to bring music. I'd plug myself in and pretend I was someplace else.

But the attention of boys on a beach soon wanders. Even Isa could only distract them for so long.

She came and sat beside me, touched my skin and said, "Hey, you need some more sunscreen." And I could feel the energy in her, the burn and tingle of her frustration.

I'd lifted my hat and nodded to her, drowsy and only half-aware, and watched Isa pop the lid on the tube of cream and squeeze a blob of it onto the palm of her hand.

"Here, let me do your back." Something about the way she did it seemed agitated and a little annoyed. I soon realized why.

"Oh my God. A ten! Definitely a ten!"

Luka. He was watching the girls walking by on the beach and grading them along with his friends. I had been vaguely aware of their game but had chosen to ignore it.

Let them be dicks, if that's what they want, I'd thought.

But this was the first ten, so even I had looked up and tried to catch a glimpse of the perfect creature that must have just walked by.

But there were so many people on the beach and everyone looked the same. I couldn't see anyone perfect, girl or boy. It was all just a hot shimmering mass of garish swimwear and reddening skin.

"Did you get it?" Luka asked, and one of the guys, an older boy I didn't know too well, leaned across to him and showed him his phone.

"Just posted it," he told Luka, and everyone laughed.

The photo was of some girl with bobbed black hair. She was long limbed and thin but in a worked-out sort of way, and she oozed good health. You could see the muscle tone in her stomach, and she was showing it off in a red bikini, the halter neck sweeping down her shoulders and presenting her cleavage like some sort of 1950s pin-up. She was now an object of lust on Facebook, though she didn't know it. Or perhaps she did. The way she walked down the beach suggested she was aware everyone was staring at her.

"So that's a ten, eh?" I said to Isa, and Isa looked at me for the first time that day and pouted her lips in a sad little show of dejection.

"Betty Boop of the beach, who'd have thought?" I said, and Isa laughed.

"Ha! That's a good one."

"Hey, want to go for a swim, leave this heaving pile of hormones to their own devices for a bit?" I asked her.

I just assumed she wanted to get a break from all the laddish bravado as much as I did and couldn't believe it when she looked over at Luka and with her best smile, said, "Sure! Hey, you fancy coming too, Luka?"

And I wanted to run into the sea then. Just crash right into the water and sink below the waves and see if I could hit the bottom.

But Luka just looked up from his phone and said, "Nah, I'm okay," then went back to goofing around with his friends.

I could tell Isa was disappointed, so I touched her elbow and repeated my offer, and asked her again, with a smug little smile, because how could I resist? Luka had snubbed her, and I wasn't going to lie, it felt good.

"Come on, let's go," I said.

And Isa relented and got up from her towel with a shrug. "Might as well, I guess."

It was nice in the water. After weeks warming in the sun, it felt balmy and calm, and for a while we just lay back and bobbed on the waves, the sun on our faces, the sounds of the beach drowned out by the sea as we floated, half submerged, ears filling with salty water. It felt good to be away from the bustle of the beach and the constant chatter, and when I sensed Isa floating beside me, I reached out my hand to her and she took hold of it.

We floated like that together, so peacefully, until Isa flipped over and started to swim out to sea, away from the shore. I turned over in the water and watched her go, waiting for her to check that I was following. I wanted her to turn around and look for me, wait for me. I didn't want her to just assume I would be there swimming behind her, following her like some mindless, obedient puppy.

It took about twenty meters before she noticed I wasn't there, and she stopped swimming and treaded water until I caught up. I took my time swimming over, a slow breast stroke, barely using my legs.

Let her wait, I thought.

When I finally drew close, she smiled at me, oblivious to my mood.

"We should have come out here earlier," Isa said, "run away from that lot and their stupid commentary."

"Yeah, they've been pretty annoying," I agreed. "I swear, if they keep it up then I'm leaving them to it. The Betty Boop beach babes can have them."

Isa flopped back in the water and stared at the sky.

"It's kinda innocent though, I suppose. Just a bunch of scores and a few laughs."

I didn't even try to contradict her. I knew Isa cared that Luka had been scoring the girls. I knew she was desperate to know what her own score would be.

But I knew she would defend him if I said I thought he was an asshole for going along with the stupid banter. When Isa was interested in someone, when she liked them, there was never any chance to criticize the object of her desire. And I'd been watching her all day and she desired Luka alright. The way she tried to grab his attention, and the stupid way he tried so hard to ignore her, making like he didn't see her, like he was not interested, like he hadn't swiped a glance at her while she lay sleeping on the sand. They were both playing stupid, coy games.

Poor Luka. He thought he had it all under control. Playing hard to get. Teasing her then turning away. But just what was it he thought Isa was doing then? Every time she rolled onto her belly and asked me to rub some sunscreen on her back. Didn't he realize it was all a show? He probably didn't. And it was kind of sweet in a way, a very Luka thing to do, to be so clueless like that. It was always one of the things I liked most about him. That behind the bravado and laddish behavior, he was pretty naïve. He was certainly no match for someone like Isa.

And what if I'd just been upfront about it all right then? Told Isa exactly how I felt and how much it hurt me to see Luka looking at her like that? What if I'd told her to stay away from him? Would it have changed things? Who knows?

But Isa must have noticed it. How could she not have seen the way I glanced at him? If they were handing out scores, then Luka was my perfect ten and Isa knew it.

And I thought about Luka; if he had to give me a number, what would it be? A seven? A six? I didn't want to think about it.

But Isa was a ten, I knew that much. Though right at that moment she thought she wasn't. Right at that moment she was as disappointed and forlorn as I was. She was floating on her back in the sea thinking about that Betty Boop girl, and wondering, *Just what it is she's got that I don't have?*

And I could have told her the answer. *Nothing.* She's got nothing on you, Isa. But just thinking that left an acid taste in my mouth and made me want to dive deep into the ocean and never come back up. Because soon Isa would gather herself together and her confidence would return. Soon, she'd look in the mirror and see it. She was a ten and everyone knew it. Her dip in self-confidence was just a temporary setback.

"Hey." Isa's voice bobbing on the waves towards me. "You okay?"

"Yeah, fine. Just floating here and thinking is all."

"About what?"

"Oh, nothing. Just stuff."

"Boys, huh?"

"Some of them."

"Any one in particular?"

And again, I thought of telling her, just coming out with it and letting Isa know how I felt about Luka. Setting down a red line and letting her know that she shouldn't cross it. Testing her, the way she had tested me. But Isa didn't give me the chance.

"Fuck me but Luka's pretty hot though, eh?"

"Luka?"

"Oh, come on, Katie. Don't tell me you haven't noticed him. He's *so* fucking sexy."

"I suppose. He's just a friend."

"Yeah? You mean you don't want it to be more than that?"

You know I do, is what I thought. I couldn't count the times I'd imagined being with Luka. I thought about him all the time. But then a sort of panic would set in. A realization that it would never happen, that he would squirm and shy away from me if I was even to suggest it. And that would be the end of our friendship. And I didn't know if that was something I wanted—the risk that Luka would disappear altogether because of some hopeless fantasy I held.

So, I floated in the ocean and turned the question around.

"Why, do you want more than that then? With Luka I mean?" I asked her.

And the quickness of Isa's answer surprised me. It was as if she had been waiting for me to suggest it. Waiting to tell me, and now the moment had arrived, and she reeled me in.

"Well, if I'm not allowed to have Alex, then I might as well have someone, don't you think? At least no one would complain this time, eh? I mean, he's the same age as me after all."

And then she laughed a little. A small vicious little laugh that was swallowed up by the sound of the sea.

But I understood where that laugh came from, what it contained. *Alex.*

That was all Isa wanted. And if she couldn't have him? Well, then she figured she was free to do as she pleased. And she would. She would do exactly as she damn well pleased, and no one was going to stop her.

"Hey," Isa called out to me. "Come on, I'll race you back."

And she took off through the water and made for the shore. But I left her to it. *Let her have the boys, let her have the beach.*

All I wanted to do was lie back in the water and close my eyes and feel the sun glow like amber through my lids. I wanted to float and imagine that Isa wasn't there, that I wasn't there. None of us were. But Isa's words kept slapping against me, like a wave.

I might as well have someone.

It was a provocation, I wasn't stupid. And it was an accusation too. You were never happy about me and Alex, so now I won't let you have Luka. Isa's petty revenge. She couldn't help herself.

But I knew how to handle it. I knew what I would need to do. All I had to figure out, as I lay there in the sea, with the sun warming my face, was whether I wanted to play her stupid games. Because we'd come here to stop all that nonsense, hadn't we?

CHAPTER EIGHT

Louise

The boredom was a killer though. More so than usual, because this year I had choices, this year I had alternatives. And though I could amuse myself for a couple of weeks with Peter, eventually my mind started to wander, and I started thinking about *him* more and more.

He'd be scooting about Williamsburg, free as a bird, and I knew what he'd be doing with his time. He was not the sort of man to resist temptation. Whenever an opportunity presented itself, he always took it. It was what I liked about him. His greediness. But the more I thought of him sitting in some bar with some lithe young thing wrapped around him, the more I wanted to jump in the car and drive full speed down the highway and back to the city. I wanted to drag him from that barstool and carry him home with me.

Because I wanted him to touch me. I wanted him to kiss me. I wanted him to undress me. I wanted him.

Most of all, I wanted the validation. The little jolt of joy I felt when he noticed me. That I could still draw his eye away from all those girls, that I had not lost the power to attract; I needed to feel that more than I cared to admit.

And maybe I should be ashamed to say it—especially now she's dead—but sometimes, watching Isa as she goofed about on the beach, so young and fresh and beautiful, I felt jealous. Or perhaps unhappy is a better way of putting it. Unhappy and a little mournful that I would never be like that again. Young, beautiful, free. I looked at her and I saw myself as I was at that age. Brazen, assertive, unashamed. Everything a girl was not supposed to be. Every time I saw her preen and pose and flirt, I couldn't help it, I thought, *Good for you, enjoy yourself.*

I wished Katie had a little of Isa's attitude. Just take what you want and don't apologize. Enjoy the rush that came with feeling wanted and adored. Get out there and be too noisy, be too brash, be too wild. Because it was over before you knew it.

When had I last felt wanted and adored? With him, I suppose. He wanted me, didn't he? Adored would be pushing it. But desired, I could say that, couldn't I?

And I wanted him more than ever then. I had to get back to town. I had to see him. I couldn't sit here mooching around much longer. The summer would be unbearable if I did. No, I needed a release, and he was the only way I could let go of some of this restless energy. So, while the house was empty, I seized the moment and I called him.

He picked up on the second ring. He'd seen my name on the screen and answered immediately. Good, I thought. He's eager.

"Hey there," he said.

"Hey," I said, my voice more coquettish than I intended.

"Everything okay?" he asked.

"Yeah. Just a little bored is all. It's too quiet here. I think I need a little excitement."

And he laughed at that. "Sun, sea and sand not enough for you then?"

"Nowhere near," I said. "That's why I thought… maybe a little trip to Brooklyn?"

He paused before he spoke. Just a brief intake of breath, but it was enough to make me alert. "Right…" he said.

"What, don't you want me to pay you a little visit then?" I said, trying to hit the right note between teasing and playing it cool.

But my voice had a whiny quality to it that made it sound like I was pleading, and again, I heard him catch his breath.

"What's up?" I asked him.

"I'm just a bit busy at the moment is all."

"Really?"

"Yeah, work and stuff. You know how it is."

"Maybe you should come here then? A bit of sea air might help you relax. Take your mind off work and all that *stuff*."

"What? You don't seriously want me you come to Montauk? Don't you have the whole family up there with you or something?"

"I do, but I know all the nooks and crannies here, there'd be no need to introduce you or anything."

He laughed and I knew that if I was in the room with him, I'd be touching him then. Caressing his arm and catching his eye. Pushing him to say yes. I imagined it even, while I waited for him to reply. I closed my eyes and felt his skin on my fingertips, the goose bumps as he responded to my touch. I felt his breath on my cheek and saw the gentle thump of his pulse in the veins of his wrist as his heart rate increased. I felt my spine arch a little in anticipation. Then he spoke and the fantasy shattered.

"Listen, Louise," he said, "I don't think I'm in the mood to be sneaking about."

"Sorry, what?" I said.

"I mean, I just don't think it's good idea is all. Montauk. It's a small town and… honestly, Louise, I really am kinda busy right now."

"Kinda busy? Gee, sorry I interrupted you."

"Hey, come on, don't be like that."

"Then let's meet up in NYC. We could make a night of it. Check in to the Plaza and spoil ourselves. What do you say?"

"Sounds great…"

"It is."

"Some other time though. Sorry, I really can't right now."

I think we hung on the line in silence for close to a minute. I didn't know how to respond and neither did he. He just waited for me to say something. But I couldn't. I felt snubbed and jilted and destroyed. Unwanted. And definitely not adored.

"Louise…?"

"Hmm?"

"Are you okay?"

"Yeah. Disappointed is all."

"Sorry. I'll make it up to you. I promise."

"No, it's okay. Listen, I better go. I don't want to keep you any longer if you've got so much stuff to attend to."

And before he could reply, I hung up, then threw the phone across the porch where it clattered around before coming to a halt under the hammock.

It swung a little in the breeze, and I could see the indent there from where Isa had been lounging in it earlier that morning. And again, I found myself fighting the urge to scream at her and every other bright young thing. And I couldn't stop my thoughts from running ahead of me. *I bet if a girl like Isa had called him, he'd never have turned her down.* And that was enough to make me snap.

"Oh, don't be so fucking pathetic, Louise," I screamed. "Get a grip."

A guy like that. He wasn't worth it. I knew that. But my body still held traces of him. My muscles were taut and tense just thinking about him. I had no grip. All I had was this pathetic longing I couldn't satisfy. And two more weeks to fill in which I was going to have to stop myself from going mad.

CHAPTER NINE

Katie

Isa rolled in just before dinner, and I could see the change in her immediately. Something about the way she walked. It was in her shoulders, the sort of grace and elegance a dancer would have. Confident in her body, assured and completely at ease with herself. The trace of a smile on her lips, like the cat that got the cream.

When she saw me though, she tried to hide it, her smile meek and a little awkward at first, as if she knew what she'd done but felt too weak to resist the temptation of gloating about it.

"Hey, Isa," I said. "Where did you get to?"

"Oh, just hanging out on the beach."

"With Luka?"

And there was a hesitation there at first. A glimmer of understanding that whatever she said next would matter and that she had to get it right. Lie, or tell the truth.

When she opted for the truth it was a relief, of sorts. After a pause she came clean.

"Yeah."

"He's a nice guy," was all I could manage.

She came and sat on the bed beside me, tucked her hands under her legs, defensive in a way, as if she didn't want me to see the slivers of skin she had picked away around her fingernails. But I had seen the flecks of blood there, understood immediately how it must have been for her on that walk home. Thinking about what she would say, going over it to get her story straight. Two stories even—one lie, one truth. Deciding to leave it to chance. She'd take her measure of me when she walked in the door, and then decide which story would prevail. Isa was always the girl with options.

It made me wonder how I must have looked at that moment, sat on the bed, apparently deflated, defeated, and resigned to it all. Not someone who would put up a fight, or complain, or put our friendship on the line because of it, I imagined.

And maybe that was the truth. I couldn't do a damn thing about it. All I could do was make a choice myself. Take it or leave it.

"Are you okay?" Isa asked me.

"Yeah, I'm fine," I lied. "I think I just imagined the summer turning out a little differently is all."

"You and Luka…"

And now it was my turn to decide. Tell the truth, or lie? I opted for the lie.

"There is no me and Luka. I told you, we're just friends. That's all."

"Honestly?"

"Hey, you don't need to take my word for it. Ask him yourself."

And perhaps there was a little tinge of bitterness or disappointment there in my tone.

"You know that's not what I was getting at, Katie. I know you like him."

"Yeah, well… he's never looked at me that way, Isa, and he never will. And that's okay. I swear it is. I got used to the idea a long time ago, believe me."

"Honestly?"

"Honestly."

"So, me and Luka? You're okay with that?"

She knew I wasn't. But I didn't want to give her the satisfaction of hearing me say it, so I lied.

"Yeah, I told you already. I'm fine."

She smiled at me, then got up from the bed and pulled off her dress, slipping out of her bikini on the way to the shower.

"Okay, if you say so. Anyway, time to wash it all off," she said.

Typical Isa, that abrupt way she had of ending a conversation once she had gotten what she wanted. Perhaps she sensed there was a risk that things would take a different turn if she pushed it any further.

I've given her a way out, I thought. But it didn't feel graceful or good. It felt as bad as I knew it would. A torment, that's what it was. A torment that was only going to get worse when I watched them hang out together.

Together. Isa and Luka, an item now. Something I had just given Isa permission for. Though I laughed at that. As if I had any control over those things, as if Luka was mine to give away, or keep for myself.

From the bed, I could hear Isa humming away again in the shower, lost in a steamy world of her own.

When her phone buzzed, my first thought wasn't to check it, or sneak a peek at her messages. I simply looked in the direction of the noise and then noticed the name on the screen. The photograph.

Luka.

Isa had a message from Luka.

I leaned across the bed and picked up the phone, listened to Isa in the shower. The zesty smell of her shampoo had yet to fill the room. She'd be in there a while yet.

And the temptation, who could resist? I knew Isa's password. Isa wasn't discreet or that clever. The eight numbers of her birthday. Silly really, to be so obvious, it was almost an open invitation for prying eyes.

I swiped the screen and keyed in the code, the phone buzzing to life in my hand.

Don't think, Katie. Just do it.

I opened the message folder and read the latest message.

Did you tell Katie yet?

So, he knew how I felt about him after all. And it was almost enough to make me send a reply: *Yes, I did and she's so mad and so upset and, sorry, but I just can't do this to her, Luka, she's my best friend. Sorry, I can't see you anymore.*

Then a buzz again. A new message. A smile emoji and a photo.

The two of them tangled together and smiling. I could see from the way their skin glistened, from the pink flush of Isa's cheeks, that they were taken after all the exertion. Isa looked satisfied. That was a corny way to put it, but it was true, that was what she looked like—sated and tired and lazy with the pleasure of it all.

I hadn't realized until then that this was all I wanted too. To tingle, all salty and sweaty and exhausted with pleasure. And that I wanted to feel it with Luka.

Just in time I heard the water turn off and heard Isa fumbling with the shower door and grabbing a towel from the drawer.

When she walked back into the bedroom, all glowing and pink, the phone lay face down on the bed half obscured by cushions, Luka's message deleted.

Isa flopped down beside me and checked it casually, but seeing no new messages tossed it aside and turned to face me.

And maybe my face gave me away, some sort of curiosity I couldn't hide, because Isa put her hand on my thigh, patted it, like I was a pet dog in need of comfort or something.

"We need to do something about you, Katie," she said.

"Me? What do you mean?"

And she laughed a little.

"Oh Katie," she said. "I mean sex. I mean we need to wipe that gloomy frown off your face and put a great big smile there instead."

"Like yours, you mean?"

And she laughed again, louder this time, a real head back boom of a laugh.

"Yeah, exactly like me. Hell, wider, if you're lucky!"

Go along with it, I thought. Don't let her see what she's done.

"You've seen the boys around here, Isa. Luka aside, there isn't one of them you'd even give a second look, and you know it, so don't try and fob me off with any of them, not when you wouldn't go there yourself."

"True," she conceded. "But…" And she sat up straight then, turned to face me, legs crossed, with a determined glint. "Okay, just hear me out," she said.

I thought about stopping her, but it was impossible, once Isa got an idea into her head, then that was it.

"Here's the deal. For starters, you need to get any of that romantic stuff out of your head."

"Sorry, what? Romantic stuff? Since when have I been a romantic? Isa, what the fuck are you on about?"

"Just let me finish, will you?" And she cocked her head and smirked a little as if she knew way more about everything than I ever would.

"What I was trying to say was, it's just for the summer. It's just a bit of fun, okay?"

"Not really," I replied.

"What I mean is—it doesn't really matter who it is, Katie. It's just about getting it over with. And it's not as if you'll ever see them again, so…"

"Getting it over with?" I replied.

Even Isa could see how ridiculous that sounded.

"Oh, come on, Katie. Don't tell me you're going to wait for someone *special*?" Isa asked.

"Oh, fuck off, Isa! I just want it to happen when it happens, that's all. To feel no pressure about it. Is that so bad?"

"I never really thought of it like that. I mean, it's up to you, of course. I just thought it would be a bit of fun, shake things up over the summer, you know?"

"I don't need shaking up, if that's okay with you. It's my fucking body, in case you hadn't noticed. So, I'm just going to take it as it comes. Okay?"

"Fair enough. Just as long as you don't stop the rest of us having fun, is all," and with that she was up off the bed and heading to the door. "I'm going to see if James is sneaking a beer on the balcony. You coming?"

"In a minute, I just want to have a shower first."

"Okay. See you downstairs then."

And off she went. As if the conversation we just had was so instantly forgettable. As if nothing we had talked about meant a damn thing.

But I wondered about it, as soon as Isa said it.

Just a bit of fun, for the summer. Is that all Luka meant to her?

And what about me? I wondered. What did I mean to him? Not so much, it seemed. And I stared at the dress, lying crumpled on the floor, tossed there by Isa, so casually, because it meant nothing to her. It was just a dress, not a carefully chosen present. It was just something she decided she wanted and had then taken. And I picked it up and smelled it, grains of sand scattering on the floor as I held it to my face and breathed in the sea and the sweat and the sunscreen. The scent of Isa.

And I don't know why, but I felt I needed to reclaim it, to make it mine, and so I peeled off my clothes and pulled the yellow dress over my head, smoothing it down just as Isa had done. Then I walked over to the mirror to take a look.

But the girl in the mirror wasn't Isa. The girl in the mirror was a poor substitute. Her dark hair, dull and dry from the sun and the sea water. Her skin red and tender where the sun had burned her. Her eyes, soft and brown but full of self-pity. Because the dress, the dress which looked so good on Isa, did not quite fit her. The small, round, swell of her stomach, her fuller, rounder thighs, made it too tight and where Isa was all agile, feline limbs, this girl was clumsy-looking, the soft curves of her body infantile still, for some reason. She was "cute," that's what people said. And on a good day she could understand that to mean pretty; on a good day, she could take it as a compliment. But today, standing in front of that mirror, she understood the other meaning, all the things that word didn't contain. And what was it, exactly? Insouciance? Allure? Beauty? Whatever it was she understood it was something she lacked. Some missing element. An element Isa had in abundance.

And I remembered Isa then, on that morning when she had first tried on the dress. How radiant she had looked, how the shape of her hips had seemed so feminine, so much like a woman's, the yellow of the fabric as bright and vibrant as Isa's confidence. And I stood there and looked at myself again and I laughed a little. At the idea that I could pull on a dress and be as beautiful as she was. *Who the hell was I kidding?* Then I pulled it over my head and headed to the shower hoping I could wash it all away.

I ran the water full blast and cranked the music in the radio all the way to ten. The steam damping down every sound, making the bathroom feel small and snug, and far away from everything and everyone.

"Fuck you, Isa! Seriously. Fuck you!" I yelled.

I could shout as loud as I wanted in here. No one would hear me.

So, I said it again, only softly this time.

"Fuck you, Isa Egberts."

I knew it was no good to go sneaking around like this, checking her messages, scrolling through her photos. But I knew I would do it again because when you've done it once there's not much point in stopping.

I squeezed a blob of shower gel onto my hand and lathered it up to a foam. It smelled grapefruity and zesty, just like Isa, and I rubbed it into my skin, my hands lingering over my belly, which was softening already after Dad's sugar rich breakfasts. I'd left my swimsuit back home because I really thought I wasn't going to need it. This was going to be the summer I stayed in my bikini.

And I needed to laugh at that. Laugh out loud into the heat and the steam; thrusting my head under the scalding water as it blasted through the shower head.

Yeah, right, Katie! As if!

"Oh, but fuck you, Isa," I screamed again. "I mean it, fuck you. And you know what? Luka, you idiot, fuck you too."

*

And so, the summer drifted, a slow progression of days that only served to heighten my disappointment. I had imagined something different, definitely something more exciting, but Isa had gone her own way, off with Luka most days, or hanging on the beach with James. And I was held at arm's length, the killjoy no one wanted around.

But what could I do about it? Brush it all aside and pretend it didn't matter? Explain it all away with the usual excuse? It's just Isa being Isa? I wasn't sure I wanted to. Because I'd grown tired of it, I realized. Tired of letting Isa get away with things. Of letting her hurt people and never face the consequences.

But as the days passed, I found myself relaxing, and to my surprise, even started to enjoy the solitude, though it had taken me a while to figure out why. All those months I'd been talking to Isa and worrying about her, thinking I had to look after her for some reason, taking on a responsibility that no one expected of me. To shake that off at last and just let Isa go was a relief of sorts. And I'd even started to imagine how things would change when we got back home. There would be a distance between us now which wasn't there before, and it was something to look forward to. The summer hadn't brought us closer together, it had pulled us further apart. But I was actually okay with that.

When I looked at Isa that summer, it was like watching her from afar, and the new distance provided a perspective, and allowed me to notice something I hadn't understood until then. That Isa wasn't a good friend. Friends didn't treat one another this way.

Some days it was as if I didn't exist. Isa off with Luka or James, a cursory invitation thrown my way whenever she felt like it. As if she was a queen bestowing favors.

"We're going to hang out over at Luka's place today, don't know if you fancy it?" Isa would ask. The expectation already contained within the question. *I'm not expecting you to say yes.* The hope even stronger. *God, please don't say yes.*

It was Isa's way of showing me she was in control, the fake sympathy treatment, and it usually resulted in me backing down, and trying to get back in Isa's good books.

It was probably what Isa was expecting too. No, I thought. Not this time, Isa. This time you need to know how it feels. How much it hurts. It's your turn to patch things up, for once.

But as the days rolled on, I wondered if it would ever happen, if Isa even had it in her to say such a thing. Sorry wasn't a word she used very often and hoping for it was a waste of time and energy.

Luka knew how to say it though. God, and if Isa knew he'd made the effort to apologize to me, she would have been so mad at him. But it was a small comfort at least, that he felt he needed to say it, even if it made no difference. He was still with Isa. It still hurt. Just a little less was all.

He caught up with me one afternoon as I headed home from the beach and called out my name.

"Hey, Katie!"

I had squinted into the sun, seeing only a shadow at first, not daring to believe that the voice I'd heard was really his, because he hadn't said a word to me in days. Shame had made him keep his distance, I reckoned.

"Luka? Hey," I'd said, and I'd watched him squirm a little and look away. At the ground, at the sea, wetting his lips in that nervous way he had when he didn't know how to start the conversation.

All of it endearing and irresistible.

"You okay?" I asked him, giving him a way in.

"Yeah, I'm okay. You?"

"Bored," I replied.

And he nodded and looked me in the eye at last.

"Can I walk back with you? Talk for a bit?"

"Depends," I said. "What do you want to talk about?"

"Can't you guess?"

"Isa?"

"Yeah, Isa. But also, you too. Where you've been the last few days? It's not the same without you."

"That's a longer walk than the ten minutes it takes to get home," I told him.

And he shuffled his feet and touched my arm.

"So, you're not ignoring me then?"

"No."

"You're not… you know? Angry? At me? At Isa?"

"I don't know. Sometimes, maybe. Oh, I don't know… anyway, what did you want to talk to me about?"

He knew I'd decided to deflect it. Not to talk to him about how I felt. And maybe a part of me had wanted him to push it. To ask me about it. But Luka never was the pushy type.

And so, instead, I'd found myself ambling along the beach path, through the dunes, listening to Luka as he tried to explain things, as he tried to apologize.

"I didn't mean for her to come between us," he explained.

And I had needed to think about that. What it meant. That he had noticed Isa had driven a wedge between us and that he had not only allowed it to happen, but had decided that Isa was worth more, in the end, than our friendship. And now, there he was, apologizing for it, but not yet saying he had made a mistake. Isa was still there, and he wasn't letting her go.

"Three's a crowd though, eh?" I'd said. The glibness of my comment causing him to stop walking.

"It doesn't have to be, you know."

"Luka, that's not up to me. Isa doesn't want me around, so what can I do about it?"

"Oh, come on, that's not true. She does. She asks you all the time to come with us. Why don't you?"

"She doesn't mean it, Luka. She just knows she has to ask. Trust me, Isa and I have been here before."

"No, Katie, you've got it wrong. And anyway, even if it's true, *I'm* asking you. *I* want you to come along. Please? I want us to stay friends. I really do. And besides, it will be fun, you know, if you were there too."

I had shrugged, not sure if I wanted to tell him just how much I had wanted to tag along. How crap it made me feel that I had missed out. And now there was Luka inviting me to join them and, as sweet as it was that he asked, I had to wonder what the point of it was. Did he not realize the thought of watching him hanging around with Isa was too much? Surely he wasn't that stupid.

But it must have taken a touch of courage for him to catch up with me and start talking, I understood that. Knew, too, that it would be petty to simply dismiss him.

"We're still friends, Luka. Always," I told him. "If I've not been hanging around then it's just because I don't fancy it is all. It's nothing you've said or done, okay?"

And I had seen the relief spill across his face and break into a bright, wide smile.

"Honestly?" he'd asked.

"Yeah, honestly."

"Still though, Katie. I'm sorry," he said. "You know, about me and Isa. I didn't mean—"

And I had stopped him because, now that it was there, now that he was saying it, I realized it wasn't an apology I needed to hear from him.

"Hey, don't be sorry. No one can help who they fall for, right?"

"Right. It's just…"

"Hey," I told him. "We're good, okay?"

"So, see you around then?"

"Yeah."

"Promise?"

"Promise."

"Okay, Katie Lindeman. I'm going to hold you to that. If you're not at the end of summer beach party, I'm going to come and drag you there myself. Okay?"

"Sure, Luka. Okay."

And as he'd walked away, I could see the lightness in his step, as if the whole conversation had lifted him. Lifted him the way it had burdened me. Because when I thought about it, I felt it more acutely.

Isa. You could have done this too. For once, you could have said you were sorry. But it was never going to happen, I was more certain of that than ever. Isa was going to do whatever she wanted to do. It was always like that. Isa would never change or do the right thing.

So, stop waiting for Isa to change, Katie, I thought. Stop hoping for something that's never going to happen, and just get on with the summer. Go to the parties, hang out at the beach. Get drunk and wasted with the rest of them. Dance the rest of the summer away and figure out all the other shit later, when the summer's over and it's time to go home. Have the summer you were looking forward to, and to hell with Isa.

*

When Isa threw the invitation my way, it was another half-hearted, throwaway remark. I was already down the porch steps and headed to the beach.

"Don't suppose you'll be joining us this evening," was all Isa had said.

And James had laughed and joined in. "Yeah, come on, Katie. Don't miss all the fun, *again*."

But this time I was ready to surprise them and when I said, "Sure, why not?" Isa had stopped and stared at me as if she couldn't believe what she had just heard. She looked aghast. Somewhere between shock and disappointment.

It was James who broke the silence. "Yes! Finally!" he yelped.

His whisper in my ear as we left, the only thing which made me hesitate. "Forget about Isa and Luka. It's not worth it, Katie."

It hadn't occurred to me that he had noticed. My kid brother, so much more astute and caring than I realized, and I had held him tighter then, and tried to absorb the impact of it. Had fought off the tears and the urge to turn around and run back home.

"You think so?" I had asked him.

"I do. I think they're both assholes for doing this to you."

And I had wanted to reply but couldn't find the words. I didn't know if I should be mad at him for hanging out with them despite it all, or happy he had noticed what was going on and had comforted me.

And he sensed my confusion and had kissed the top of my head and said, "So, what do you think? We can go together after the beach."

And all I could do was nod. "Yeah, fuck it," I said. "Let's go."

But the party had been too loud, everyone spilling around by the end of the night, Isa and Luka locked together the whole time and barely noticing I was there. Just a quick, "Hey, look who's here!" from Isa, when I arrived with James, and a shy smile from Luka. That was it. I had spent the night sitting on the porch talking to a bunch of guys I didn't know, watching everyone get progressively more drunk and more stoned, the music getting louder, the dancing looser, the laughter more raucous. I had thought about Sarah and Willem, what they would do if they could see the state of their daughter. They probably wouldn't have recognized her.

After a while I had had enough. *What the fuck am I doing here?* I wondered. And I'd walked back home, alone, no one even noticing I was gone.

CHAPTER TEN

Louise

Teenage girls. They tell you nothing and think you won't notice they are hiding something, unaware that their every move, their every gesture reveals so much.

I'd found Katie lounging on the porch, alone. Isa and James off at the beach again without her. It was obvious what was troubling her. I'd seen Isa and Luka together and knew how much it had upset her.

"You want to talk about it?" I said, hoping, I suppose, that she'd respond to my opening. But all I got was a shrug, a mumble, then a turned back. "I mean it, if you want to talk to me then I'm here. I know how much you like Luka and seeing him with Isa… Well, it must be horrendous."

And I could have been a little more delicate in my phrasing, less intrusive, but the heat of the day had left me restless, and the wine had fuzzed up my head in such a way, that the words slipped out before my brain was able to reformulate them.

But I had to say something about it. The way she'd been recently, so forlorn and disappointed and alone, it was unbearable to watch her. I couldn't sit around much longer and say nothing.

I had seen how oblivious Luka was to everything and everyone when Isa was around. How Katie had been rendered invisible and humiliated by the blow of rejection.

"Sorry, that didn't quite come out the way I intended," I said. "I just mean—"

"I don't need to talk about it, Mom, okay? I'm fine, so don't keep asking me about it. It is 'horrendous.' But so what?"

"I'm just disappointed is all."

And I got Katie's attention then.

"Disappointed? Why? What have I done?"

"I mean with Isa. Not you."

"Oh, I see."

I let the pause linger and waited for Katie's curiosity to get the better of her. Ten seconds was all it took for the question to come.

"Why would she disappoint you?"

"Because I thought she was your friend."

When Katie turned around and took a seat in the lounger beside me, I knew I had broken through.

"You mean a friend wouldn't have made a move on Luka?" she asked me.

"Well, they wouldn't, would they? A true friend would never do a thing like that."

"She can't help who she likes though, can she? Or who likes her back."

"No, I know that. It's just…"

And I needed to pause there, because I didn't know what I was trying to say. Why it was I thought loyalty and friendship should take precedence over attraction. Katie was right, no one could ever really be blamed for falling for someone. So, what was it? I wondered. What was it about Isa and Luka that felt different?

"She just shouldn't parade it. That's what you mean," Katie replied.

"Yes, that's part of it I suppose."

"Yeah, well, what do you want me to do about it?"

"I don't know, Katie. I guess there's not much to be done, is there? I hope talking about it helps a little though."

"Yeah, maybe. I dunno…"

The little sigh at the end a cue I was familiar with. Keep going, keep talking, keep asking.

"If I thought Isa was taking it seriously, this Luka business, then maybe it wouldn't upset me so much."

And Katie turned to face me then, surprised by my observation.

"You know what she told me?" Katie said. "That it's just a summer fling. After the summer, she'll pretty much forget all about Luka."

"I thought as much."

"Yeah, the trouble is, Luka doesn't get it. I think he thinks it's something else, that after the summer, they'll carry on."

"Oh, that's not so great…"

"Yeah, I know. She's going to hurt him, Mom. She's going to really hurt him, and all I can do is watch it happen."

"Or tell him," I suggested. "You could tell him."

"Yeah, and he'd listen, of course. I mean he'd be wide open to hearing me tell him that."

"Sorry, that was a stupid suggestion. Love is blind, eh?"

"Yeah. Deaf too."

"He's got a good friend in you, Katie. I hope he appreciates that."

"So, you think I should be there to pick up the pieces then? Is that it?"

And I had laughed and said, "Well, you know, sometimes guys just need to learn the hard way who it is that has their backs."

"Yeah? I don't know. Maybe. To be honest, after this, I'm not sure I want to have anyone's back. I mean, why should I care? If people are such shits, if even your best friend… Ach, I don't know what I mean… I guess I just don't care anymore. Yeah, that's it. I don't give a fuck."

"What I don't understand is what happened to Isa," I said. "When did she get so careless with other people?"

"Oh boy," Katie laughed. "Trust me, you don't want to know."

And she stood up then and walked into the kitchen, not waiting for me to reply. But the sigh, the flick of the wrist as she attempted to casually dismiss the whole thing, left me unexpectedly anxious and angrier with Isa than I wanted to be.

Oh, Katie, I thought. *You care way more than you realize.*

I could see the heartbreak and the arguments that were looming on the horizon and hoped we would at least be spared the worst of the drama while we were at the beach house. All I wanted was some rest and relaxation over the summer, was that too much to ask?

I'd keep an eye on them though, was what I thought, make sure it didn't get too out of hand and too teary—forgetting how it felt to be seventeen, to be the one who is ignored, the unwanted one. It was an anguish that seemed impossible to bear. The whole world was unfair and unacceptable. Drama and tears were inevitable, and I should never have imagined we could avoid them.

CHAPTER ELEVEN

Katie

Sometimes things are set in motion without anybody realizing it. Small decisions are made, things are said in passing, and it's only later you come to realize their importance.

It was a lazy sort of day, the day Isa died. We'd all headed to the beach as usual, none of us saying very much, because the novelty of it all had already worn thin. The end of summer was the only thing we were looking forward to. In a few days, we'd all be back home, and I was surprised how much I wanted the summer to be over.

At the beach I managed to keep myself together when I saw Luka with his friends, and I ignored Isa as she made a show of sauntering over to him and wrapping her arms around his neck, letting her fingers tickle down his spine as she planted a kiss on his lips.

I knew Isa wanted me to watch, but I turned away, started laying out my things on the sand, pulled out my phone, plugged in my headphones and drowned everything out with music. Then I let the morning slip lazily into early afternoon. I was half asleep when I felt a tap on my shoulder and looked across to see Luka there, miming to me to pull out my headphones.

"Hey, Katie," he said. "Can I talk to you for a bit?"

"Sure," I said.

"Fancy a walk?"

I'd looked around and noticed James and Isa weren't there.

"They've gone off to buy some drinks," Luka told me.

"Oh, okay," I replied.

And that was it. We'd set off down the beach then headed up on to the coastal path, neither of us saying much. I could sense how nervous Luka seemed, but I didn't know how to put him at ease. Whatever it was that was bugging him, it had to be something about Isa though; that much was obvious. Nothing else would make him this fidgety.

At first, I'd tried to make light of it.

"Listen, whatever it is Isa's done now, I don't want to know," I told him.

And I couldn't fail to spot the disappointment on Luka's face, an embarrassed sort of frown that wrinkled his brow as he looked away for a split second. Just long enough to absorb what I had said.

"You say that as if you're not surprised. As if she gets up to all kinds of shit all the time."

I said nothing, just looked at him and shrugged a little. Nodded as if to say, *Yeah, she does.* Then found myself defending Isa, in the hope it would push him to tell me what he really thought of her.

"Listen," I told him. "Isa's just been letting go for the summer is all. She's had a hard time lately, at home. So maybe just cut her some slack. She's okay really. Deep down I mean."

"Is she? I'm beginning to wonder."

"She's my friend, Luka. My best friend. What do you want me to say about her?"

"We're friends too though, I hope?"

"Yeah, we are. I told you that already and I meant it. We are. And we always will be. It's just, well, you know?"

"You girls have secrets, is that it?"

"Secrets? No, not really."

"Alex, I mean."

And he knew it was going to take me aback to hear that name. To hear him say it. Because how could he know about Alex? About a stupid affair that had only lasted a few months and had left Isa mooching about for a few weeks and feeling sorry for herself.

"Alex," I had replied. "How do you know about Alex?"

"So, you know about him too then? Fuck, Katie. Why didn't you tell me? You let me make a total idiot of myself all summer and never thought to tell me about him?"

He walked off and I had needed to run after him, grab his arm, turn him towards me so I could talk to him.

"Wait a minute, Luka. What are you talking about? Alex is old news. Why would I need to tell you about him?"

"Really? Old news. Is that what Isa told you?"

"Yes, they stopped seeing one another months ago. Shit, I've had an earful of Isa moaning, for months, ever since they split up. I was sick of hearing her talking about him and moaning about how he broke up with her."

There was a bench on the path and Luka slumped down on to it and sat there for a while, a little hangdog and forlorn. I sat beside him and touched his arm.

"Hey, come on, Luka. Tell me you don't think I'd keep a thing like that from you. Honestly, if Isa was still seeing Alex, do you really think I wouldn't have told you by now? That I wouldn't have said something from the start?"

And he looked at me and draped his arm over my shoulders, and I couldn't stop the tingle that shivered down my spine, the goose bumps that sprang to life on my skin.

"Shit, sorry, Katie," he said. "No, of course I don't think that. I'm just so angry with myself."

"What? Why?"

And he let his head fall on my shoulder, a small gesture that almost made me get up and leave, because the weight of his head there, even though it was only in friendship, even though it was only through sadness and the need to talk to me, it was too close, too intimate. It brought back too many feelings I had worked so hard to dampen down.

Don't read anything into this, I thought. *Don't keep doing that to yourself.*

Though the revelation about Alex made me want to wrap my arms around him and let him see that he had chosen the wrong girl. I wanted to claim what was mine. What Isa had stolen from me. Even though I knew that was a stupid fantasy. Luka was not mine, no matter how much I wanted him to be.

"I asked Isa about after the summer. About what would happen to us," he said. Then he laughed a little. Annoyed with himself again that he had been so stupid, so optimistic, so naïve. "I guess I was hoping we could carry on. Work out some way to see each other. In the weekends or something like that, you know? I could have come to New York on the train. Or she could have come to Scarsdale. Easy, that's what I thought."

And I agreed. "Yeah, it's not so far, that could work."

"That's what I thought. Trouble is, Isa didn't think the same."

"Alex?"

"Yeah, Alex. She said she had a boyfriend in New York. Said she thought I realized this was all just a summer fling. Just a bit of fun. She actually held my hand and walked along as if it was the most normal thing in the world to tell me about it."

"Sorry, wait a minute. Isa said she was still seeing Alex?"

"Yeah."

"But that's not true. They split up."

"Yeah, well that's not what Isa says."

"No, she would have told me if they'd gotten back together. Honestly, Luka, that's not something Isa would have kept secret from me."

"But she did though, Katie. She did. How else would I know about Alex if Isa hadn't told me? Huh? Think about it."

And he had me there. It was true. He could only have known because Isa had told him.

"Fuck," was all I could say. "I had no idea."

"Yeah, well. Seems Isa hasn't been too honest with any of us then, doesn't it?"

"What are you going to do?" I asked him.

"Do? What can I do? I mean, this is it then, isn't it? I mean, now that I know it's true, what can I do? Isa has had her fun, and, in a few days, we all go home, and she can forget all about me, her summer fling."

"I'm sorry, Luka. Really. I'm sorry."

"You don't need to be sorry, Katie. What did you do?"

"I brought her along with us. Introduced you to her," I replied.

"Yeah, well, you could hardly have known…"

"So, what will you do now then?" I'd asked him.

"I don't know. Talk to Isa, I suppose. Tell her it's over. Shit, you know she actually thought I'd go with her to the beach party. Can you believe that?"

All I could say was, "Sorry." It didn't feel like enough. But I had nothing else to give him at that moment. Save a hug and a gentle kiss on the cheek.

"You're still going to go though, aren't you?" I asked him.

"I don't know if I fancy it now, to be honest."

"Hey, come on. We're not going to let Isa ruin the end of summer for us, are we? Let's just go and show her what we're made of, huh? Have a good time despite her."

And he'd tried to smile, had nodded a noncommittal sort of yes, and we had left it at that. What more was there to say? I had watched him saunter off down the path and then head back down to the beach, off to tell Isa he was done with her.

And if he hadn't have looked so forlorn, I'd have smiled. If he hadn't have looked so sad, I'd have laughed. I'd have felt happy that Isa was finally getting her comeuppance at last.

Why did you have to do this to him, Isa? I thought as I watched Luka's figure get smaller and smaller then become lost among the crowds on the beach. Why do you always do this sort of shit to people?

*

Alex. I could never figure it out, what the allure was. Not at first. A guy of thirty-five, what did he want with a teenage girl? More to the point, what did Isa want with him?

I remember the day she told me about him. She had been itching to reveal her secret.

"I bought this book today."

I had glanced at the paperback Isa had tossed on the table. *L'Étranger*, the cover said. And I'd laughed, then quoted the first line by way of a reply.

And Isa had laughed too. "A bit cliché?"

"It's maybe just a *little bit* pretentious," I laughed.

"Ha! Yeah, well," Isa continued. "To be honest, I didn't really look at what I was buying. It was just what happened to be on the top of the pile."

And I had looked at her with a little frown of confusion.

"Eh? You bought a book without looking at what you were buying?"

"Yeah," Isa replied. "But trust me, if you'd seen the guy in the shop, you wouldn't have paid attention to the books either."

And, again, I had laughed and told Isa she was crazy.

"Although, I say guy," Isa continued. "But I guess he's more of a man."

"A man?"

"Yeah. Definitely."

"French?" I had asked.

"No, he's from Brooklyn. But you know, he can give those French guys a run for their money, believe me."

And I had asked her how she could possibly know that.

"He asked me out."

"What? Shit, wait a minute, Isa. How old is he?"

"Thirty something. Why?"

"What do you mean, why? Isn't it obvious?"

Isa had pulled out her phone then and swiped up a photo.

"Here," she said. "This is him."

I looked at the screen. Two blue eyes stared back at me. They were that grey shade of blue you sometimes encounter where little flecks of indigo sparkle in a certain light. Gentle eyes, more feminine than masculine, and framed with a sweep of dark hair and just a shadow of stubble on the jaw and chin. He was smiling. The kind of smile that holds a touch of laughter in it. I could almost hear him. A deep timbre. Something irresistible. Something dangerous.

I looked at the phone and felt an unfamiliar contraction pull in the muscles of my spine. A fear that felt too much like pleasure.

"Good-looking," was all I could say.

"He really is," she replied. "Even better in real life."

"Isa," I asked her, "you're not going to go, are you?"

And Isa had looked surprised.

"Katie, look at the guy. Of course I'm going."

Six months it lasted—autumn through to spring. Isa skipping track meets to head into town and spend the afternoon with him. Once, I had gone over to Brooklyn and walked by the bookshop, hoping to pop inside and take a look at him for myself, but the sign on the door said closed. It was only later that I realized why a bookshop in the hipster heart of Williamsburg would be closed on a Friday afternoon. I'd texted Isa all the same, just to check.

Hey! Fancy doing something? I'm in town.

Love to, but I'm with Alex. Later maybe?

Later, always the same, a gushing update on the wonderful, incomparable, "*utterly delicious*" Alex. There was nothing I could say to get Isa to dial back her enthusiasm. Though I tried.

"Don't you think it's a bit off? You know, a guy his age, hooking up with a teenager."

Isa had simply shrugged. "Do you see me complaining?"

"No, it's just—"

"Then let's just leave it at that, yeah?"

And there were times, as I listened to Isa talking about him, when I understood what it must be like to have a guy like that take an interest in you.

Those afternoons when he would read to her, in bed. The two of them lying there in his attic room listening to the rain hit the skylight, limbs wrapped around one another, his voice filling the air like cigarette smoke. I'd dreamed that scene many times. Had woken some mornings with a shiver in my legs, Alex's imagined touch still there on my skin.

I couldn't blame Isa for getting caught up in it all. Because it was true—Alex, in the flesh, really was stunning. Something about the way he looked at you seemed to linger. The tilt of his head as he listened made you believe you were the most important person in the room, the most interesting, the most beautiful. Who wouldn't want that?

It took me a long while to realize that it was just a technique. A tried and tested trick to get what he wanted. A guy like that, he'd hold your gaze, smile a small, gentle sort of smile, and then wait. He knew what that sort of attention could do to a girl like Isa. Young, pretty and more naïve than she believed herself to be.

And Isa was definitely not going to be told anything, not when it came to Alex. The excitement of it, the fact that it was so inappropriate, that it was something illicit, it was just too tempting, too exhilarating. The attention, too flattering. She was never going to listen to anyone who tried to explain to her that, maybe a thirty-five-year-old guy hanging out with a teenage girl, even if she was almost eighteen, was more than a little creepy.

But I'd been an idiot to ask Isa what she saw in Alex.

"Sex," Isa had explained.

And there was no way for me to stop it, the blush that turned my cheeks crimson. Isa had seen the color rise in my cheeks and had laughed.

"You've got no idea, have you? How powerful it is to have someone look at you that way? Touch you that way?"

And I could have handled the comment on its own, could have brushed it aside as Isa being silly, were it not for the little smile. Smug and self-satisfied, and delivered with the intention to belittle me. To make me shrink in the face of the simple truth. That Isa understood more than I did. And that she was somehow better than me because of it.

I'd tried to stand my ground though.

"True, I don't," I replied. "But that doesn't make my question less relevant."

"What question?"

"Alex. What you see in him. Why you don't think his attention is wrong."

"You've met him, Katie, I'd have thought it was obvious."

"Yeah? Well, it's not. Sure, he's good-looking, sure he's smart, and fun to be around. But he's also thirty-five and, well, I mean, what's he got against women his own age?"

And Isa had laughed.

"I dunno. Wrinkles, maybe? Cellulite?"

"I'm serious, Isa."

"Yeah, and so am I."

"Maybe he's just scared of them, did you think of that?"

"What?"

"Think about it. He wants someone younger, someone he can control. Someone unsullied by life."

"Unsullied? Katie, what the fuck are you going on about? Jesus! You're so fucking prissy sometimes."

"I just think it's weird is all. I just think—"

"No one can help who they're attracted to, Katie. That's just the way it is. Wait and see what happens to you first, before you go judging other people, okay?"

"I'm not judging you."

"Oh, but you are, Katie. Trust me, you are."

And we had never spoken about it again. Alex became off limits, and all I could do was watch and wait.

Because I knew it was coming, even if Isa didn't—the day when Alex would tire of it all. I'd noticed it pretty quickly, the way his attention had wandered since he'd got what he wanted. The way he'd always be looking around the room when you were with him, as if you were only worthy of half of his attention, if that.

At first, when I had joined them on the odd occasion for a coffee in town, I'd assumed it was because he was nervous. That the furtive glances came from a desire not to be seen sitting at a café table, sipping coffee with girls who were so much younger than him it almost verged on being illegal. He knew what it must have looked like to some people, not just me, the older guy with the giggling girls. I'd seen him brush Isa's hand away when she reached out to hold it in public. Had seen Isa glance quickly in my direction when it happened, hoping I hadn't caught it.

It was only after a few of these meet-ups that I started to realize it was something else. Not shame or embarrassment: Isa was actually right about that; Alex wasn't ashamed of their relationship. Shame wasn't what drove him to sweep the room every time they entered a café. No, it was something else that was driving him. He was taking the room in, checking everyone out. Looking to see who else was there, who else caught his eye, and took his fancy.

I'd joked about it with him once, when Isa got up to use the bathroom.

"Pretty good-looking clientele they've got here, eh?"

And he'd looked me in the eye as if it was nothing and smiled at me and said, so nonchalantly it shocks me still to think about it, "Guys want what they want, Katie. That's just how it is."

And a stronger person, an older person, someone with a bit of courage and nerve, would have stood up to him then. Picked up a glass of water and thrown it in his face, yelled out that he was an asshole, let the whole room know that he was fucking a girl eighteen years younger than him.

A braver person would have said something. Not sat there stunned and dumbfounded and close to tears. A stronger person would have stood up and said, "Hey, Isa, have you got a minute?" instead of sitting there at the table watching as Alex threw down a hundred-dollar bill, and told me, "Settle up, will you, Katie? Isa and I have to go now." A stronger person would have stood their ground and not simply watched as Isa shrugged and smiled and giggled, then wrapped her arms around Alex and sauntered out of the café and back to his apartment.

I had felt the anger rise in me, too late. I had settled the bill and then left the café in a daze. It took a good hour of walking for me to calm down and realize what I knew for certain now.

Alex was an asshole. A complete and utter asshole. And whatever happened I was never going to let him hurt Isa.

And maybe Isa felt it, because for a couple of days she let my calls go unanswered, ignored my text messages, posted no updates on Facebook or Instagram. She put herself deliberately out of reach. I could almost hear her sneering, "I'm not in the mood, Katie. Whatever you think about Alex and me, just keep it to yourself."

It was a way to torment me as well. Isa knew I would be sitting there in my bedroom wondering what she was doing with Alex. Imagining the two of them together in cafés, at the cinema, in his apartment. Isa knew, the longer she stayed silent, the more vivid my imaginings would become. The more desperate I would be to know what was happening.

When she finally answered the phone after two days of silence, she sounded coy, as if she half expected me to blurt out immediately, "Isa! Where have you been? What have you been up to?" Like an anxious parent, angry and relieved, and not fully sure if they really wanted an answer to their questions.

I had tried to cover up my relief with a breezy, "Hey, Isa! There you are!" Careful not to sound too eager, careful to hide any hint of curiosity, any neediness.

We chatted and laughed as if we'd only just spoken that morning, as if there was no argument between us. And when Isa had agreed to come over and hang out, it felt as if something had been resolved, without either of us having to speak about it directly.

"You must have shit loads to tell me," I had asked her.

"Nah," Isa replied. "Nothing much. Nothing you'd want to hear about in any case."

Maybe that should have alerted me to the truth. The snide remark, disguised as something offhand, as if the last few days had been boring and uneventful, as if that was the reason she hadn't called or returned any of my messages. No, I wasn't forgiven yet.

But I didn't want to believe it. I just wanted to see Isa. To hang around for a bit and gossip and giggle. I'd need to wait for the right moment to bring it up again. Because I would have to say something. I couldn't just stand by and let Alex hurt my best friend.

So, I thought. *Smooth things over first then find the right moment.*

And I would have done it. I would have said nothing, asked no questions, let Isa do the talking if that was what she wanted. That was the idea. Easy.

But I hadn't reckoned with Isa. The sight of her when I opened the door and saw her standing there. She looked grey and tired and rumpled. As if sleep was something she hadn't indulged in for days. She had the hood of her sweatshirt pulled over her hair, but I could see she hadn't washed it and had scraped it tight into a ponytail in an attempt to make it look at least half respectable. There was a hollowness too, to her cheeks, as if she hadn't eaten properly for a while.

I had gasped when I saw her, unable to hold it in. Had found myself apologizing when I saw Isa wince a little and make to walk away.

"Sorry," I said. "It's just, well, you look a bit rough is all."

And Isa had smiled and shrugged and almost in a whisper admitted that she did "feel a bit green about the gills."

And I should have held back. I knew that. I should have kept her calm, played it down, pretended not to notice. And if it wasn't for that name in my head, I might have been able to do it, too. But there it was, spinning about in my mind as we rushed up the stairs to my bedroom before Mom had a chance to notice Isa was there. Alex. Alex. Alex. Whatever had happened to Isa, Alex was responsible. Because I'd never seen Isa in such a state. So grey and bewildered and rough-looking.

Isa had flopped on the bed as soon as the bedroom door was shut, pulling her hoodie off and mussing up her hair.

I had just stood by the bed looking down at her and not knowing what to say. Because, despite her appearance, she seemed okay. As relaxed and calm as ever. Lying there punching at the bed cushions and making herself comfortable, kicking off her Vans and letting out a little sigh of happiness, as if she was glad to finally be back here again, in the sanctuary of my room.

"You okay?" I asked her.

"Me? Yeah, just a bit tired is all. You know…"

"I missed you at school this week."

"Oh? Why, did anything happen then?"

"No, just the usual. Just school."

"The same boring shit you mean?"

"You know the principal is going to call your parents soon enough if you keep this up. And then you're going to be in deep shit."

"Oh well," she sighed. "Whatever."

"Isa?"

"Yeah."

"Where were you?"

And Isa had laughed and flopped back on the bed and closed her eyes.

"You don't really need to ask me that, Katie. Do you?"

"It's just… well, you really do look rough."

And Isa had lifted herself off the bed then and walked over to the mirror next to the wardrobe and examined herself in the mirror. Pulling at her eyes and checking how red they were, smoothing away imagined blemishes on her cheek, stepping back to take in the full-length view.

"True," she said. "I've definitely looked better."

"Do you not think maybe you should calm down a bit?"

"What do you mean?"

"I mean, with Alex. Going out all the time when it's a school night."

"Geez, Katie. You sound just like my mom. Or you would, if she paid any fucking attention."

"Don't they know where you are then? Who you're with?"

"What do you think?"

And it made me nervous to hear that. To know that Isa was out there at night, in the bars and cafés of Williamsburg, and Willem and Sarah were oblivious. That they didn't look at Isa and see the same thing, the grey skin, the dark circles under her eyes, the weight loss, seemed impossible. How could they fail to notice that?

"Come on, they must know where you are, Isa."

"They've got other stuff on their minds at the moment, I guess. More important stuff."

"Shit."

"Yeah, they are. Both of them. A pair of shits."

"That's not what I meant."

"No? So, you think it's okay that they don't have a clue what I'm up to?"

"No, you know I don't. I just mean, why take it out on me when I bother to ask? Seriously, every time I ask if you're okay you snap at me and tell me to shut up and mind my own business. But you can't have it both ways, Isa. You can't want people to care about you and then spit at them when they ask how you're doing."

"Fair enough, I suppose."

"And, Isa…"

"What?"

"Alex—"

"No. Stop it, Katie. Alex is off limits, okay? There's a difference between caring and interfering, okay?"

"What? Isa, come on, that's not fair. Why should Alex be off limits?"

"What? Are you serious?"

"Yes. I mean, he's the reason you look like shit. He's the reason you're not at school. He's the reason I never see you anymore."

"Listen, Katie. You don't know him. So just leave it, okay?"

"I know him well enough."

"Oh yeah? What is it you know then, huh? No, don't answer. Let me tell you. You look at Alex and all you see is an older guy and a younger girl. All you see is something that feels, what? A little 'off'? Something wrong, in any case. Something sleazy. You think he should back off and leave me alone. You think he's harming me. Taking me out, showing me stuff. Taking me places I shouldn't be. Doing things with me, I shouldn't do. And you know, maybe you're right. But here's the thing. I feel okay. I feel happy. I feel, I don't know, *good* about things. And there's not a lot of that about, at the moment. I mean, it's all shit, if you must know. At home

I mean. My mom and dad, and all their crap. So, this, Alex, this one good thing. Katie, just let me have it, okay? Just let it go."

And what could I say? All I could do was wait until it blew over, until Isa saw Alex for who he was. All I could do was wait for Alex to hurt her and be there to pick up the pieces.

God, the mess it had all been. The mess Isa had been. I thought all that crap was over. I thought Isa had sorted herself out. Gotten over Alex. That she had finally figured out he was no good for her. Accepted that it was finished, her stupid little fling.

But that was just another lie. If what Luka was telling me was true, it wasn't over. Alex was still there. We'd head home after the summer, and it would start all over again.

And I could feel the disappointment quickly turning to anger, the more I thought about it.

You idiot, Isa, I thought. *You stupid, reckless idiot. If you think I'm going through all that again you've got another thing coming.*

*

But while I was worrying about Luka, Isa was busy making plans.

I found out all about it later in the afternoon when she came tumbling home. Something about her seemed different. Disheveled, and, I thought, slightly smug. As if telling Luka all about Alex was some sort of a joke. Something to take lightly.

"Where were you?" I asked her. "I was looking for you, down at the beach, but couldn't find you."

"Just out and about. Why?"

"I wanted to talk to you about something was all."

Isa anticipating what it was about then.

"You mean, you wanted to give me crap about Luka, is that it?"

And the flippant way she said it, again, as if playing with people's feelings was no big deal. For the first time in my life, I felt like lashing out. Just slapping her across the cheek. I had to control the urge to do so and felt my nails digging into the soft flesh of my palms as I counted to ten and waited for the edge to be taken off my anger just long enough that I could speak.

"It's not *crap* to let you know you hurt him, Isa."

"Yeah, and you'd believe me if I told you it wasn't my intention, is that it?"

"Not your intention? How do you figure that one out?"

"Huh?"

"I mean, Alex, Isa."

"Oh, God. I should have known. Alex, Alex, Alex, here we go again."

"Isa, listen to me, damn it. You said it was all over with you and Alex. Why did you lie to me about that?"

"I didn't. It was over."

"Yeah? Then how come you're telling Luka something different then? How come he told me earlier that you'd dumped him because of Alex?"

"Okay, so that was a bit thoughtless of me. But I was just trying to be honest with him. I mean, how was I to know Alex was going to show up here and lure me away again?"

"What? What do you mean?"

"Alex, he was here this afternoon. Popped by to say hello. I think all those photos must have done for him in the end. You know how he is, Katie. He's not one for missing out."

"Alex came here?"

"Yes, this afternoon and, you know how it is. One thing leads to another and, yeah, we're an item again."

"Fucking hell, Isa."

"Hey, I told Luka about it immediately. As soon as I knew what was going on, I told him. I'm not the absolute shit you sometimes think I am, Katie. I do have some idea about other people's feelings you know."

"Right. Sorry. I, just… when Luka told me, he was so upset and so hurt. I felt sorry for him."

"Yeah, and it sucks. I know. But what do you want me to do? String him along?"

"No, I guess not. It's just a bit sudden is all."

"Yeah, I know. And…"

"What?"

"Alex, I was thinking of bringing him along to the party tonight. What do you think?"

"What do I think? Oh, come on, Isa, you have got to be kidding me. That's going too far. If you want to hang out with Alex, then fine. Be my guest. You know what I think about him. But go do it someplace else. Leave Luka out of it. At least then he might have a chance of enjoying the last night of the summer."

"I suppose."

"And anyway, are you sure Alex would come? To a beach party with a load of teenagers? Seriously? That's not exactly his style, is it?"

"Why not?"

"Because… Oh, forget it. Just promise me something, Isa. If Alex does show up tonight. Will you go somewhere else? Please?"

"Okay, okay. God, you don't have to get so worked up about it."

And with that she headed to the shower.

"I'm going to get ready for tonight. Whatever happens, I've got to look my best, right?"

But I wasn't listening anymore. Isa had pushed me to the point where I simply didn't care. There was nothing anyone could tell her. She would never listen. I had tried, many times, especially where Alex was concerned. But it was clear to me now, there was no point in arguing with Isa about it. When it came to Alex, Isa was beyond reason.

Fine, I thought. Go your own way then, Isa. Just know, you're on your own. Whatever happens to you from now on, I honestly don't give a fuck.

CHAPTER TWELVE

Louise

That last evening. The strangest thing about it is that it was so perfect. There was no hint of what was to come, no sense that it would end in tragedy. It was simply a nice summer evening and I remember being surprised that I had managed to shake off all the problems of the few weeks and finally relax into it.

I enjoyed a long, lazy dinner with Peter, the evening tinged with that unique mood that comes with every summer's end, a mix of happiness and melancholy. We stumbled home from the restaurant, tipsy and tired, and I remember feeling looser than I had all year, because some of the tension between us had gone, and whether it was the wine, or the dinner, or the walk home through the dunes, I didn't care. I'd agreed with Peter that we would turn a blind eye to whatever the kids got up to. We knew all about the all-night beach party, and my initial reaction was to insist they came home rather than stay out all night on the beach.

"Let them sneak out to their party, Louise," Peter had said. "One last blowout before the summer ends. They're seventeen after all."

"James isn't."

"No, but Katie will look after him."

"Yeah, I suppose she will."

"And she deserves a bit of fun, don't you think? It's not been the greatest summer for her really, has it?"

That was true. It hadn't been much fun for her. And the vacation was about to come to an end and then real life would kick in again. No one was ready for it. No one wanted it. So, one last chance to party, why not?

But as the night wore on, sleep didn't come, and the relaxed post-dinner mood faded. I had lain in bed and imagined them all at the beach, sitting round the fire, music playing, people laughing. The sound of the sea as the waves lapped the shore. The warm breeze of the summer night on their skin. And I remember I wished, just for a moment, that I was seventeen again.

Then, from outside, I heard James whispering and Isa giggling, the clink of bottles as they walked away. I got out of bed, careful not to waken Peter. Just gone midnight and he was already sprawled across the bed, languid as a cat, post-coital and dead to the world.

I lifted back the veil of curtain and looked outside. Isa and James were already on the path heading to the dunes, arm in arm with their bag of bottles slung over their shoulders.

I wondered why Katie wasn't with them. Perhaps the argument earlier had made her change her mind, the idea of a final blowout party with her friends not something she could think about now.

Then the front door creaked open, and Katie appeared in the dim evening light. No bag over her shoulder, just a sweater. It was only as she started to jog slowly in the direction of Isa and James that I noticed the bottle dangling from her hand. Every few steps, she'd stop to take a long drink from it before stumbling on ahead again. Already a little drunk, apparently. And in no state to look out for James, I thought.

"Watch out, Katie," I whispered. Only then realizing I had woken Peter after all.

"Hey," he said, half-asleep. "Don't go worrying about them. Let them have their party."

I turned to face him, and he parted back the sheet.

"Come back to bed."

"In a minute. I think I might go drink a glass of wine, sit on the porch for a while."

I was relieved when he didn't come and join me, because I wanted to sit and think about the conversation I'd had with Katie that afternoon. Over dinner, I'd managed to forget about it, and let the wine and mellow mood distract me. But in the silence of the bedroom it had come back to me and it had left me restless and feeling that I needed to do something. I just didn't know what.

I'd heard her arguing with Isa and just assumed it was about Luka, but the more I listened, the more I realized they were arguing about someone else.

When Isa left, I had gone upstairs and knocked on the bedroom door but had not waited for a reply. Just cracked it open and asked if I could come in. When Katie saw me standing in the doorway, she'd flopped back on the bed.

"Oh God, Mom, what do you want?"

"I just wanted to check you were okay."

"Why would I not be okay?"

"It's just, I couldn't help hearing you and Isa arguing."

"We weren't arguing."

"No? You sounded quite upset."

"It's nothing, okay? Please, Mom, just leave it will you?"

"I thought maybe you were talking about Luka, but it wasn't about him, was it?"

Katie sat up in bed then and stared at me, and I saw the flicker of doubt in her eyes as she tried to make a decision: tell me the truth or try and fob me off with a lie. Betray Isa's secret or keep quiet. When she decided to talk to me, it was such a relief to know she trusted me, it left me wanting to hug her.

"No," she admitted. "It wasn't about Luka."

"Is Isa in trouble, Katie? You know you can talk to me if you need to."

"There's this guy," she said. And then she hesitated again, unsure if she really should carry on.

"Another boy?" I asked her.

"No, not a boy."

And she saw the confused look on my face.

"His name's Alex. She knows him from back home."

"Alex? You've never mentioned him before."

"Yeah, well. He's sort of Isa's little secret."

"What do you mean?"

And she hesitated, unsure if she should betray her friend. But maybe she saw the concern in my eyes, because she relented.

"She was seeing him for a while, a few months ago. You know all that time she never came to hang out with me? When she was flunking pretty much everything at school? Well, that was all because of Alex. And he's not a boy. He's thirty-five or something. And I swear to God, I wish she'd never met him."

It made my stomach lurch to hear it. I should have been told all about him before I agreed to let Isa come with us.

"Katie, damn it, why didn't you tell me? Thirty-five? Are you sure? I mean, he's got to be twice her age."

"Yup."

"And he's been seeing Isa?"

"Yeah, for quite a while now. I'm sorry, I should have said something, it's just, I don't know, Isa is my friend and…?"

"No, it's okay. It's just, a thirty-five-year-old man, that's so…"

"Creepy? A guy his age sleeping with a teenager? Tell me about it."

"Well, yes it's… Do Sarah and Willem know?"

"No. Honestly, Mom, I thought they had stopped seeing one another. Isa told me they had. And then, today. Who pops up? Alex. And worse, she had actually called him and asked him to come over. To come to the party tonight."

"He was here?"

"Yeah."

"And he's going to come to the party tonight?"

"Apparently."

"But why?" I asked. "Why invite him?"

"Ha! You really don't know Isa, do you? She's a show-off. It's as simple as that."

"But, why would Alex agree? If they're not friends anymore then why would he come?"

"God, Mom, are you really so dense?"

And Katie pulled put her phone then and swiped through to Instagram. There on the screen was Isa in a series of provocative poses.

"These? All these photos? Who do you think they were for then? It was a tease, you know? A way to remind him of what he was missing. I suppose it must have worked."

I looked at the photos and felt a wave of nausea hit me. The realization that Isa was sophisticated enough to manipulate a grown man like this was too much for me to handle at that moment. And that he'd fallen for it too, that he'd been unable to resist her. It made me feel sick. A man his age should have more self-control.

"The worst of it is," Katie continued, "that Luka really liked her, and she knew it, but she hurt him all the same."

"And now she's going to take Alex to the party tonight and rub salt into the wound. Is that what you two were arguing about?"

"I think she really just wants to be with Alex and Luka was just a bit of fun for the summer. I don't think she thought she was doing anyone any harm."

I hadn't expected her to defend Isa and it took me a moment to absorb what she had just said, before I could reply.

"Still, she shouldn't have done that to Luka. It was callous, don't you think?"

"It's just Isa being Isa."

"That's not much of an excuse though, is it?"

No reply, so I tried to coax a little more detail from her about Isa and Alex.

"But, this man, Alex. He's so much older than her. I just don't think it's right. I mean I don't understand how…"

"Like I said, it's creepy. I've told her that a million times, believe me. But she won't listen to me. She's obsessed with him. No matter what he does to her, no matter how much trouble he gets her into, she won't hear a bad word against him."

"Right, that's it. I'm going to call Sarah, this is just ridiculous. A grown man should not—"

"No! Mom, stop! Isa can't be told when it comes to Alex, okay? Believe me, I've tried and she's not listening. And anyway, we've only got a couple of days left here and Sarah and Willem are miles away so what's the point? Do they need to know? I know I'm not going to tell them, and I know Isa isn't. So, why get involved? It will just cause a load of hassle and arguments and…"

"You think so?"

"Trust me. Stay out of it. This is Isa's mess. Let her clear it up."

Stay out of it. If only it was that easy. Even with a second glass of wine inside me, I still couldn't shake off my nerves. Something about it all made me anxious. The idea of Isa, out there, at night, on the beach with a thirty-five-year-old man. It was my responsibility to make sure Isa stayed out of trouble. And this was exactly the sort of trouble Sarah would be counting on me to keep Isa away from. But every time I tried to think of a way to step in, the impossibility of it all overwhelmed me. What was it Katie had said? When it came to Alex, Isa never listened. So what chance did I have of convincing her?

From the porch, I could hear the sea in the distance, and I thought I caught the sound of a guitar floating through. The kids down on the beach, enjoying the end of summer.

Just go there and see what happens, I thought.

If I took the path through the dunes, I could drop down onto the beach and take a look. Just make sure everything was okay. Check that Katie and James were with Isa. I could keep my distance, no one would notice me there, in the dark. And if they did spot a figure walking alone on the beach, they would think nothing of it. Just a walker out on a beautiful night. All of them too happy and drunk, too young and alive, to notice or care very much.

Yes, it was a good plan. And I drank the last sip of wine and pulled on my sandals and sweater and headed to the beach.

*

And then a new day dawned, and Isa was gone. That was how sudden it felt.

In the morning I sat on the porch drinking coffee and watched James and Katie come over the top of the dunes and stumble back home together, looking exhausted and disheveled and more than a little the worse for wear. When they saw me, they slowed down to a shuffle and I could see them whispering to one another and trying to get their stories straight. They clearly hadn't figured anyone would be up and about by the time they stumbled back home.

"Morning," I said to them as they climbed the steps to the porch. "I take it you both had a good night?"

James shuffled and scuffed his feet on the wooden planks, scratching the sand underfoot. And Katie tried to look me in the eye but found she had no stomach for a confrontation.

Neither did I. The night had been too long and too restless and had left me with little energy for anything.

"Why don't you both go get a rest. You look terrible."

And they'd both looked at me then, relieved and surprised and a little sheepish.

"I thought you'd be mad at us," Katie said.

"Yes, well, go and get some sleep," I told them.

They'd nodded and headed into the house.

"Where's Isa?" I asked them, more as an afterthought than anything else.

"Dunno," James replied. "Probably still at the beach, I suppose."

He headed inside and Katie hung back as if she wanted to talk to me but didn't know how to start.

"Thanks for looking after him," I told her. "I was worried about you guys."

And she nodded and smiled, then followed him inside.

I sat on the porch with my coffee and let the day begin, enjoying the early morning sun. At 11 a.m. Peter came home from his morning run and asked me if the kids were back yet.

"Yes," I told him. "Well, save for Isa."

"Oh, shit," he said. "Did she not come back with Katie and James?"

"No."

"But where is she?"

"Probably sleeping it off on the beach. It seems like they had quite a night of it, if the state of Katie and James is anything to go by."

"Right." He laughed. "Well, she'll show up soon enough, I suppose."

But when the hours passed and there was still no sign of her, I began to feel the panic squeeze my throat, despite my efforts to swallow it down. Every minute felt like a step closer to something grim. And when the wait grew unbearable, I woke Katie and James and we headed out to the beach to look for her, Peter holding me back for a moment as we headed out the door.

"We're going to have to tell Willem and Sarah about this, Louise. Seriously, they're going to have to sort her out when she gets home."

Home. She never made it.

For hours, we scoured the dunes searching for her, calling out her name, "Isa! Isa!" Other people on the beach joining in to help once they heard what had happened. Until, one by one, we had all fallen silent, because we knew it was pointless. There would be no reply. And when word filtered through that she'd been found, and our worst fears confirmed, it all seemed horribly inevitable.

I sat on the beach with Katie afterwards and watched her scroll through a summer's worth of photos on her phone, hundreds of pictures, and in every one of them, there was Isa, all smiles and laughter and seventeen forever. Katie staring at them and shaking her head in disbelief.

"How can she be dead?"

And I had no answer, all I could do was hug her close and tell her, "I don't know, Katie. I don't know."

Though the image on the phone was an answer of sorts. Isa on the beach in her bikini, hands on hips, left leg tilted, chest out, the pose flirtatious and strangely defiant. I was amazed I'd never really noticed it before, because anyone looking at those photos would see it: she was trouble, that girl, nothing but trouble.

CHAPTER THIRTEEN

Katie

The beach party was a blur in the end. When it was over, the only thing that remained was a hangover and an exhaustion like I'd never known before.

I'd come home in the morning and was relieved that Mom had let it go, just sent us upstairs to sleep it off. I'd fallen asleep almost immediately. Figured I would wake up and see Isa there on the bed opposite me, as tired and disheveled as I was. A little pissed off that I had headed home without her.

Instead, what I woke to was my mom, shaking me.

"Katie, wake up."

I'd blinked awake and tried to speak, but only a garbled, "What?" came out.

"Where's Isa?" she asked me. "Katie, did you hear me? Where's Isa?"

The panic in her voice frightening me, so I couldn't think straight. I kept looking over at her empty bed and trying to figure it out. Where was she? I had no idea.

Even as I sat in the kitchen listening to Mom explain that we were going to have to go the beach and look for her, I couldn't quite get to grips with any of it. All I could do was drink cup after cup of coffee in an attempt to sharpen my wits and sober up from the night before; I couldn't get my head round what she was telling me. That Isa was missing. It was ridiculous. She'd stumble home soon enough. They were all panicking for no reason.

"Listen, Katie. I need you to tell me the last time you saw Isa. Where was she?"

"I don't know… at the beach… yeah… I think…"

"At the beach? Who was she with? Was she with that man? Was she with Alex?"

"Alex? No. He never showed up."

And I saw the relief wash over her face, a little ripple of hope that Isa was maybe okay after all.

"When did you last see her then?"

"I don't know. But she was okay, she was fine, I…"

"Listen, Katie, you need to pull yourself together and help us find her."

"Why? She'll be back soon. It's just Isa. Honestly, why the fuss?"

"No, Katie. Something's happened. No one's seen her all morning."

"But… why? What time is it?"

"Late. Now come on, we need to find her before it's too late."

"Too late?"

The statement so outlandish, so horrific, I had a hard time focusing on it. When I tried to think of Isa, nothing came into focus. All I could think of was that phrase: too late. Too late for what? What did she mean?

But when I looked her in the eye, I understood without her having to tell me. Too late meant something had happened to Isa. Too late meant we could do nothing about it. Too late meant she thought there was no point in searching—Isa was already gone.

But it seemed too surreal. Not the kind of thing that happened in a small Long Island beach town filled to the brim with people too comfortable to ever worry about a damn thing. Not something anyone would have to sit around the kitchen table and worry about.

"Katie," she kept saying to me. "Katie, you have to remember. When did you last see Isa? What the hell happened last night?"

And I nodded and said, "I know, Mom. I know. Just give me a minute so I can think."

Remember, Katie. Remember. As if was that easy. All I had were vague recollections that kept coming at me in some sort of random order and none of it made sense or had any focus. The beach party, when I tried to remember it, was just hazy pictures in my head.

I was at the bonfire. Isa was there. James was there. Luka and the gang were there too, though Luka didn't really speak to me the whole night. I remembered that. How he had gone out of his way to ignore Isa. How angry he was with her still. All he had done was nod a small hello to me and left it at that.

And Alex. There was no sign of him. He hadn't come. I'd wanted to laugh so hard at that. To just walk over to Isa and ask her straight out, "Ha! So, he ditched you again then, did he?" But it had been enough to simply sit there and watch Isa looking sorry for herself.

Good, I remember thinking. *You deserve a taste of your own medicine.*

And then? Nothing much. Just the drunken grogginess of it all. I sat and watched Isa sulking and drank the wine I had pilfered from the kitchen. My head was nice and woozy and loose, and it felt good, better than just being drunk, because it felt like I could finally just stop watching everyone, stop thinking about everyone. Just be.

I remembered how I sat and stared at the bonfire for a long time. I knew that much. Remembered that much. How everything became a blur of orange, then just a blur, then nothing. From somewhere, the sound of a guitar and someone singing "Hey Jude," and slowly the chorus picking up and everyone humming along, laaa-la-la-lalalalaa.

At some point James was beside me, cracking open beers and handing one to me. Leaning against me with his full weight so

I didn't know if he was simply sleepy or dead, dead, drunk. He passed me a pill. Did I take it? No, I didn't. Though James did. I remember he slipped it under his tongue and took a sip of beer to wash it down. I remember thinking I had to watch over him and take care of him. Alcohol and pills, it was not good. Try and keep a clear head, I thought. As if that was even remotely possible. That was the point I stopped drinking. As if I knew, even in my hazy state, that I needed to look out for my kid brother. One of us would need to sober up a little and it looked like it was going to be me.

What else? James repeating a question. It came back to me slowly what it was.

"Hey, have you seen Isa?" At least four, maybe five times he asked me. Until it got on my nerves and I told him to just shut up and, "Go find her yourself if it's so important."

And at some point, that must have been what he did, because he was not there beside me anymore. I looked up and saw him stumbling off into the dunes. It took me a moment before I realized that he was going to look for Isa. When I realized he was also headed to the beach and to the water, I panicked and headed off after him. He was just stupid enough to go into the water, just drunk enough not to be able to assess the situation. I could almost hear my Mom's voice admonishing me: "You said you'd look after him."

And I did look after him. Despite everything that happened, I can say that, at least. I took care of James. I made sure he came back to the safety of the bonfire. I got him away from the sea and away from danger. It's about the only consolation I have—that I made good on my promise to Mom. I looked after him. I took him back and laid him down by the warmth of the fire. He was half-asleep already, cold from the water and ready to sleep it off. I placed his sweater over him and watched as he closed his eyes. Then I sat and watched the flames flicker and listened to the music and the laughter.

And then, he was beside me. The guy with the guitar, and he was offering me a cigarette, which I took and smoked as if it was something I did all the time. He smiled at me and I smiled back, and he strummed a tune and asked me if I wanted him to play anything special.

"No," I told him. "Just keep doing what you're doing." And he laughed at that and laid the guitar in the sand and said, "I'm Ben."

"Katie," I replied as he leaned towards me and kissed me. Introductions were over. He stroked my arm and nudged me on to my back then kissed me again and again and again.

I remember him saying, "Katie, hey, Katie, c'mon, let's go somewhere more private."

Into the dunes, I suppose, because that's where I woke up in the morning, Ben, there beside me, asleep. Towels wrapped around our naked bodies, our clothes strewn in the sand. Half dead from lack of sleep, I stared at them a while and took in what it meant and tried to piece together the events from the night before, but all I remembered was the bonfire, the chorus, the stroke of his fingers on my thighs. The wine, the woozy spinning of my head as the alcohol hit with an unexpected dizziness.

I thought of Isa and what I would tell her. That this, apparently was it. The deed done. My entry into the hallowed group of adults now confirmed and irretrievable.

And I didn't know whether to laugh or cry. I looked at sleeping Ben. The sun-streaked blond of his hair, the polished sheen of his suntanned skin, the looseness of his lips as he slept, as he breathed. He looked beautiful. And the sight of him unsettled me. I should have been pleased. Pleased that a boy like this was mine. Even if it was only for one night. But he was too much, for some reason. Too golden. Too polished. Too angelic. And still, for all that, not Luka.

So, I left him there, alone in the dunes, and pulled on my clothes to head home.

He would wake alone and understand that this was it. No more Katie. And I didn't know if that made me happy or sad. But there was a weightiness there, coursing through me, that made me want to head to the sea, jump in and float a while, just long enough for it to lift.

When I got home, I remember Mom talking to me and James beside me, though where he appeared from, I had no idea. Suddenly he was there walking home with me and Mom was asking us a question. Something about Isa. Did we know where she was.

"On the beach still," James said. And I was so exhausted and felt so nauseous and dirty. All I wanted to do was head upstairs and sleep.

"She'll be back in a while," I told Mom. "She could be upstairs sleeping for all I know. Did you check?"

Mom admitted she hadn't looked in our room and when I headed upstairs, I half expected to see Isa there. But when I stepped inside, the room was empty. I crashed on my bed and couldn't even think about getting undressed. As I shifted in bed something fell from the pocket of my shorts, hitting the floor with a heavy thud. I picked it up.

My phone.

I turned it on and punched in the code. No messages. No calls.

I remembered thinking that was strange. Isa hadn't sent me a single message all night, which wasn't like her. Then I remembered the incessant ping that had followed me all summer. No way I was having that thing beep at me all morning. So, I turned it off and later Mom came to wake me.

*

And off we went, back to the beach, back to the sea, off on our ill-fated search for Isa.

Isa who was long lost. Isa who was beyond saving. Isa who was dead.

"They've found her! They've found her!"

I will never forget that.

I heard the words but could make no sense of them. I just stood there on the beach, my heart racing, my head thumping and I stared at my mother not understanding, not daring to believe it.

"No," was all I said. "No. No. No. No. No."

CHAPTER FOURTEEN

Louise

I had been dreading their arrival. The whole morning, as I waited for them to drive over from the airport, I had paced the house and struggled to stay calm.

"What am I supposed to tell them?" I asked Peter. "I mean, how do we explain this to them?"

But he had no answers either. Because there were no words. There were no explanations. We had no consolation to offer. Just the terrible fact that we had failed Sarah and Willem in the most awful way imaginable.

They'd left their daughter with us, their only child, and we hadn't protected her. That was all they would see when they looked at us—the way we had failed them. Because of us, they were sitting in the back of a police car on their way to identify their beautiful child.

There was nothing I could say to them, no consolation or explanation. All I could do was stand there and take it as they blamed us for what had happened. Because we would be blamed, I understood that. I could almost hear Sarah beseeching me: "Why didn't you do something, Louise? You should have done something."

But what? It was formless, this something. It was wishful thinking. It was trying to turn back time and undo the damage. But the truth was uncompromising. There was nothing we could have done. Absolutely nothing.

And I kept telling myself that: *This is not your fault.* Repeating it like a mantra as the day wore on. Those words in my head as Sarah and Willem walked through the door.

I remember Sarah stared at me for a long time as she stood in the hallway, and I didn't know what it was I saw there in her eyes.

Everything, I suppose. Pain. Grief. Terror. But also, confusion, and anger. She couldn't speak, she couldn't find the words, but she didn't need to. I knew what that look said.

"How could you have let this happen, Louise? How?"

"I'm sorry, Sarah," I told her. "I'm so, so sorry."

Then someone ushered her into the living room, some police agent or other, and she shuffled past me, but didn't meet my eye, didn't say a word and I felt a chill of panic ripple across my skin.

When Willem laid his hand on my shoulder and said, "Hey, Louise. You okay?" the fact he understood we were all shocked and affected by what had happened was some small consolation but not enough to dampen my fears.

For an hour, Sarah sat in the room, soundless, motionless, while we all tiptoed around her and whispered to one another. And then, without warning, she got up and walked upstairs to the room Isa shared with Katie. A few minutes later, a wail filled the air. Raw and caustic and animal. She was up there, I knew, surrounded by Isa's things. Surrounded by the detritus of her daughter's last days.

And I knew exactly what she was looking at, what she was touching, and caressing and smelling and longing for. All those traces of Isa so present still, so *alive* still. Making it all seem even more impossible.

How can she be gone? How can she be dead?

And when Sarah came downstairs later, her eyes were red with tears, her face ghostly pale with the horror of it all.

"What happened, Louise?" she asked me. "What happened to my daughter?"

And all I could say was that I didn't know. There'd been a party on the beach, and they had all been there. And then, when it became apparent that Isa wasn't coming home, we'd gone out looking for her.

All afternoon we had searched. Until she was found.

"But how could it happen, Louise? How?"

But I could only meet her question with a despondent silence. I had no answers for her.

*

I can't remember whose idea it was to walk to the beach. The whole morning had been one of numb disbelief, events experienced through a gauze of horror and whispered conversations. No one sure what to say, because none of it made sense. Two days ago, Isa had still been there, and signs of her still lay scattered around the house. A beach bag full of sand and smelling of sunscreen still sat on the porch, a half-read book lay open and face down on the living room table. A discarded sweatshirt flung over a kitchen chair, hung there as if it was waiting for Isa to walk through the door any minute, and pull it over her head, as she asked everyone: "Hey, what's up?"

Maybe it was this that left Sarah wanting to get out of the house and away from the growing realization that her daughter wasn't going to walk through the door and greet her.

"I need to go for a walk," Sarah had said.

At first, I didn't realize she wanted me to take her down to the beach to see where Isa had spent her last weeks.

If I'm honest, I wasn't sure if I could do it, but I found myself agreeing, because to deny Sarah anything seemed wrong.

On the walk to the beach we had said very little, Sarah simply commenting on how beautiful it was to walk through the dunes and shrubs and listen to the muffled sound of the sea.

When we climbed the path to the dunes, the sound grew clearer and louder until, at the top, there it was, the murky grey of the ocean flickering before us all the way to the horizon. And we had stopped there for a moment, gazing out over the water, as if the sight of it was too dumbfounding. The expanse of it, the beauty of it, the way the sun caught the ripples of the tide and glistened. It was all too beautiful to imagine it was also the place where Isa had died.

I knew this was what Sarah was thinking too, and I reached out for her hand, and took it in mine, and with a gentle squeeze said, "Come, let me show you."

There was no trace left. No police officers, no cordon, no flowers yet, no memorial to what had happened. Just the sea. Just the sand. Just the cry of gulls. The peacefulness of it all, enough to silence Sarah, it seemed, because she didn't cry or lean on me or gasp. She simply stood, taking it all in and nodding slightly.

"Are you okay?" I asked her after a few minutes had passed.

"Is this where they found her?" Sarah asked.

"Somewhere here, yes."

"Somewhere here?"

And I didn't know how to explain it, the way the sea can shift and push and move, the shoreline changing all the while, so you can never be sure where it lies. Every second, it changes and collapses in on itself, wave upon wave. As intimately as I knew this place, it could still disorient me sometimes. How often had I found myself walking along the beach only to realize I had walked further than I realized? Too many times.

And maybe Sarah understood it then too, as we stood there looking out at the horizon, neither of us wanting to stare too long at the rippled ridges of the sand at the shoreline, both of us trying to push away that image which haunted us: of Isa as she was buffeted back and forth among the waves, floating down the coastline, far from where anyone last remembered seeing her. Alone in the water, the night slowly brightening as a new day dawned, the first day without her.

There was something about the rhythm of the waves and the brush of the breeze that made it all seem too vivid, the reality of it, too harsh. Sarah wasn't ready for it yet, and neither was I. There was still a part of me that clung to the hope that a mistake had been made, that the girl they pulled from the water was some other poor soul; that Isa, badly behaved, rebellious Isa, was out there somewhere still, groggy and hungover and unaware of the drama unfolding close by.

When Sarah turned away from the shore and started to head back to the dunes, it was a relief. The grim thoughts disappearing immediately as I looked around and saw there were people there, just as there always were, brightly colored and laughing and alive and moving on with another summer day, the sad truth of what had happened there, yesterday's news already.

"You think that will ever be possible again?" Sarah had asked me.

"What?"

And Sarah had gestured to the people on the beach, already splayed out on beach towels, and setting up parasols and running into the water.

"This. You know, life?"

"I hope so," I replied.

"Hope? Yes, we can hope, I suppose. But I don't know if it is possible."

"Oh, Sarah, one day at a time, that's what they say."

"What happened here, Louise? What happened to my daughter?"

And all I had was repetition. The same things I had told Sarah already. Isa was happy and joking around and relaxed and looking forward to going home again. The summer romance that had already dwindled. The parties and the fun.

"You make it sound like she had a wild time of it."

"Do I? I don't mean it that way. It was just teenagers having fun was all, nothing out of hand."

"Save for the end."

And again, I had no answer to that, because the end couldn't be denied, the end couldn't be changed, or explained. So, all I could do was repeat myself, yet again.

"It was an accident, Sarah, and if I could change it, I would. If I could go back and have it turn out fine, I would."

"It's just when I hear you talk about Isa like that, I don't recognize her, Louise. Late night parties and summer romances. I keep listening to that, and I don't see Isa. I can't match the two things. What you're telling me, and the Isa I knew, the Isa who was my daughter. I mean, can you, Louise? Can you think of a reason why she would walk into the sea, at night, alone, drunk? Isa? She wouldn't do a thing like that. Oh, she was wild at times, I know that. I'm not stupid. I know what teenage girls get up to when they think their parents aren't paying attention. But I know she wasn't reckless, Louise. She wasn't. And that's the thing, I just can't understand. Why she did this. How it could have happened. I just…"

I had listened and nodded and searched for words which wouldn't come. I couldn't answer her question. Because how to tell her that the Isa I had seen over the summer was more reckless and wild than any of us could have imagined? How could I tell Sarah that she didn't know her own daughter? She would never believe me.

One day, I would have to talk to her about what went on here over the summer. One day I would have to show her the daughter she didn't know. I knew that. But just then, with Isa's death so raw, with the smell and the sound of the sea all around us and the immediacy of what had happened, still there in the air, it was impossible to explain to Sarah what I thought.

And what I thought was that there had been a terrible inevitability to it all. That Isa's accident was not so unimaginable. It was simply fate. A fate of Isa's own making.

CHAPTER FIFTEEN

Louise

I thought the funeral would mark the end of it all. But standing there at the graveside, watching them lower Isa into the ground, I should have known. Every end is also a beginning.

If I was being honest, I would admit I felt uneasy the whole morning. Filled with something close to dread, but I'd dismissed it as nothing more than the weight of sorrow, the shock of it all, and that terrible sense that none of this should have been happening. Above all else, that was the sense which gripped me—that our lives were not meant to pan out this way, that some sort of mistake had been made. But who had made it, I wondered—God? Was he responsible for such things?

It had left me dizzy and half hallucinating, and at the graveside I had stared at that hole in the ground and imagined myself floating free, and rising above the beech trees, where I hovered, and looked down at the mourners from above, taking it all in, the sad little scene below.

There was Sarah, draped on Willem's arm. Willem stood, erect and stony-faced, keeping his emotions in check, holding Sarah up, because he knew she would fall if he let her go, and she would fall willingly. He saw the hollow space at their feet and knew it was where Sarah wanted to be. Down there, with her daughter. He understood, too, that it was his job to keep her above ground, even though I knew it would hit him later, that there was no one there to hold on to him, that there was nothing to keep him from falling.

There was Katie, looking beyond them at something in the distance. Not daring to look at the earth, the coffin, the faces of the mourners all huddled together and dumbfounded by grief. Preferring instead to stare into the distance, and I wondered if perhaps she imagined she saw Isa waving at her from beyond the cemetery gates.

There was James, nails digging into the soft white of his palm, the taste of blood on his tongue from where he had bitten his lip in an attempt to stay silent, because he can feel the scream swelling his throat. A scream he has tried to contain from the moment they pulled Isa from the sea. A scream which contains more anger and pain than he can cope with.

There was Peter, hands clasped on James' shoulders. At first, I thought it was an act of consolation and comfort. It would only hit me, weeks later, when events took another hopeless turn, that Peter was actually holding on to him, that he was trying to protect his son. As if he knew, somehow, that this wasn't the end, that there was more to come. The instinct of fathers. It was stronger than I realized. Stronger than my own. My intuition failed me in the end. Twice.

And, where was I? I didn't see myself as I floated there above them. I was lost in the shadow of black around the grave. The mourners surrounding me, strangers mostly. This was the only moment we would ever share together.

And I closed my eyes then and tried to shake off the hallucination. Felt the weight of the day pressing down on me again, as I thought of Isa. Isa, who lay there, enclosed and waiting. Waiting once again to be pulled under.

The whole morning was so sad, so strange, as if the world had turned itself upside down. I had left the graveside in a daze and hoped the worst of it was over and tried to erase the image of us all huddled around that terrible hole in the ground. I didn't realize the interment was only the beginning. There was worse to come. The gathering afterwards, a macabre event, something I don't think I'll ever forget. Though perhaps I should have anticipated it. The funeral card had stated the service was to be "a celebration of Isa's short life."

I had frozen when I read it, and thought I'd got it wrong, but when I looked again, it was still there—"a celebration."

What was there to celebrate? I wondered. A *short life*. Did Willem and Sarah not realize how deeply sad those words were? How at odds they were with a *celebration*.

"What were they thinking?" I asked Peter.

And he had smiled and tried to make light of it. "Do you think tears will be permitted?"

But Katie and James seemed to think it was okay. They saw no reason why a funeral could not be a cause for celebration.

"Better than moping," was how James put it. "Isa never moped, so why should we stand around wailing? All she ever did was laugh. Or have you forgotten? She might be dead, but she's more than just the girl who drowned. She's still Isa."

And I knew what he meant. The sentiment of it was well intentioned, though I couldn't help but wonder if they'd all suffered a temporary loss of their senses, because there was no part of me which felt celebratory; the ache of grief, the nag of guilt made sure of that.

But it was Willem and Sarah's choice, and grief did strange things to people, so all any of us could do was go along with it and try not to appear too somber. But the whole afternoon was a blur of misplaced cheerfulness. Of music and speeches, even laughter, and I had struggled to connect the sadness of the morning with the cheerfulness of the afternoon. That grim gathering at the graveside, how had it transformed into something so festive? How did Sarah manage to laugh again so easily after her tears?

At the cemetery, we had waited so long for Sarah to say one final goodbye to Isa, that I had felt the tips of my fingers grow cold. As we walked away from the graveside, after the casket had been lowered, I had turned around and seen Sarah kneeling on the ground, whispering and crying, and I had wanted to rush over and comfort her, and help her to her feet, because it looked as if she would never be able to get up, as if all she wanted was to stay there with her daughter. Even Willem was too weakened by grief to do anything to help her.

For that moment to shift to this, to this "celebration," seemed impossible, absurd even.

And again, I had needed to ask Peter what he thought about it, because I couldn't be the only one who felt perplexed by it all.

"Don't you think this is all a little misplaced?" I'd asked him. "The laughter, I mean."

But he'd shrugged and looked over at Sarah and Willem.

"If it helps them get through it, then who am I to judge? And James is right. We should remember Isa for who she was, not how she died. And she was fun, and she did laugh all the time, so…"

And I supposed he was right. Sarah and Willem had a right to seek comfort wherever they could find it. Though if I had known what was coming next, I would have questioned their sanity again.

Gifts. Presents at a funeral.

At first, when Sarah made her way around the room, I assumed she was simply receiving condolences. There were the normal whispered conversations, the small, barely audible whimpers and tears, sadness creeping into the occasion at last, it seemed. I had steeled myself for the conversation and tried to think of what to say. How to console Sarah, how to apologize yet again, because I still felt apologies were necessary. Those words in my head again, like a drumbeat. *This was our fault, this was all our fault.*

We were huddled together, when Sarah and Willem approached us, and Peter took my hand and gave me a supportive squeeze.

"Sarah, Willem," Peter said as he shook Willem's hand then leaned forward to kiss Sarah on both cheeks.

"I'm so sorry, Sarah. I'm so, so sorry," I found myself saying.

"Thank you," Sarah replied, with a perfunctory nod, quiet and polite but nothing more. Then she turned to Katie and took her hands and said, "We have something for you, Katie. A little something of Isa's we thought you might like to keep. Just as a way of remembering her."

And as a gesture it wasn't so strange. Perhaps a bit soon to be considering such things, but it was a kind, thoughtful thing to do; that was what I thought when Sarah handed over the little velvet box.

I remember hoping it was a sign forgiveness was coming at last. Perhaps not immediately, but soon. It was on its way and this was the first indication that things would heal. That our friendship would somehow survive all this.

I watched as Katie opened the box and took out a silver locket, then stared at it, a little confused as Sarah explained to her what it was.

"Open it," Sarah told her. "Look, here, let me show you." And she took the locket from Katie and flicked it open. "This is how you open it, see?" And it sprang open to reveal the contents.

A memento mori. A lock of Isa's hair coiled there under glass and catching the light exactly the way it had on the beach that summer.

There was something so disturbing about it. Something so wrong, and I just looked at Sarah in disbelief and waited for some sort of an explanation.

Surely there must be some mistake? I thought. A memento like this, a piece of Isa, a piece of their daughter, surely that couldn't be something they would want to give away. And I thought of them, asking the mortuary to cut Isa's hair so they could make these sad, macabre trinkets. And the ghoulishness of the request left me feeling faint and desperate to leave the room.

But Katie seemed happy to receive it. She smiled and thanked Sarah and Willem. Hugs were exchanged, and more kisses, and consoling words.

And James, poor James. He stared at the hair in that locket and seemed transfixed. Even when Sarah spoke to him, and asked him how he was, he didn't hear her. The only thing which seemed to hold his attention was the locket, and that shining snip of golden hair.

He asked Katie if he could look at it, and I watched as he opened the box and took out the locket. Listened to the tiny click of the catch as he opened it and touched the lock of Isa's hair. Saw his eyes glaze over, then begin to fill with tears as Katie took it from his hands, snapped it shut and placed it back in the box.

The whole scene conducted in silence. Even James' tears. They slid across his cheeks, but he didn't sob, he didn't sniff. He just stood there staring into the distance.

It was only when Sarah moved towards him to give him a hug that he snapped back.

"She should never have been with us this summer," he told Sarah. "She would still be alive if she hadn't come with us, wouldn't she?"

And I saw it in Sarah's face. How it froze her. As if she couldn't be sure what James meant. Was it an accusation? That it was somehow Sarah's fault for letting Isa go with us to the beach house? That her selfishness in insisting on a reconciliation with Willem had brought all this about? Or was it something else? Some appropriation of blame in the other direction? This was our fault, he seemed to suggest. Isa was with us and we didn't look out for her, and now she was dead.

The whole moment seemed to hover, as if time had stalled, until Sarah started to cry and someone, Peter I suppose, pulled James away and hurried him out the door and back home.

But James was right, was what I thought. Isa should never have joined us for the summer. That had been the fatal mistake. We all knew it.

*

Since the funeral, there had only been silence. No matter how often I called, I was met with the cold shoulder of Sarah's voicemail kicking in.

Pick up the phone, Sarah. Please, pick up the phone. Just talk to me.

Nothing. Sarah was avoiding me. Sometimes I dialed knowing there would be no answer, but just wanting to hear Sarah's voice. I never left a message, just listened to the voicemail at the other end of the line and imagined Sarah sitting there, staring at the name on the screen, "Louise," and waiting for the ringing to stop.

"Talk to me, Sarah," I whispered when I was cut off. "Please. Talk to me."

The silence in those first weeks was more difficult to cope with than I imagined it would be. The powerlessness of it. I don't think I've ever felt so helpless.

It surprised me how much I missed Sarah, how much I wanted to talk to her, not just about Isa and everything that had happened, but all the small day-to-day things too. The easy chitchat. Ours had never been a deep friendship. It was one of those superficial things, built on coffee mornings and shopping trips and banal dinner parties where the conversation never strayed further than the next family trip or problems at school or the office or the recommendations for a new family car. Everything so polite and unthreatening and nice. But now that it was gone, I felt shunned. I felt unwanted and unwelcome. And in those still moments, when the house was emptied and quiet, I felt something else, something worse. That persistent feeling, that Sarah's silence was also an accusation.

I first felt it during the funeral, the way Sarah's gaze failed to meet mine. Every time I tried to seek Sarah out, to offer sympathy or consolation, Sarah turned away from me as if she couldn't bear to look at me.

"Don't read too much into it," Peter had told me. "All this—Isa, the funeral, whatever it is that comes after—it's a lot to bear. I don't think either of them know what to do right now."

And in those early days, it was possible to believe that it was simply grief and the shock of all that had happened. It disoriented everyone. And it was going to take a long time before any of us resurfaced and felt capable of facing things with any degree of clarity.

But through all of it, I had never once questioned whether our friendship would survive. As superficial as it was, I thought it was strong enough to withstand all of this.

It was only after a few weeks had gone by and Sarah still hadn't called me or returned any of my calls, that I started to worry. That feeling returning again, that there was something lurking there under the surface. Some unspoken accusation: *This is all your fault, Louise.*

It had stunned me the way an idea like that could take hold. I thought the years we had spent together, the intimacy that always develops between people when they watch each other's children grow, would be enough to get us through it. I thought a trust existed between us. An unbreakable trust.

But with every day that passed, without any word from Sarah, I needed to convince myself that I hadn't imagined it. Our friendship was real, and it did mean something, didn't it? We trusted one another still, didn't we?

*

It had started one winter day in Central Park. I had taken to walking there in the mornings with Katie because the days could feel interminable and it was a nice way to pass a few hours. We would feed the ducks, play on the swings, then go and eat cake in the Loeb Boathouse café.

I was glad to have a rhythm to the day and would head to the park even in the worst of weather, wrapping Katie up against the wind and the rain and the cold, anything to get out of the house and be some place where there were people around who were noisy and busy, and fun and young. I needed to know that New York was out there and that I was a part of it still because the isolation motherhood had brought with it was something I had not anticipated in those optimistic months before Katie's arrival.

For the first time since moving to New York, I felt I didn't really belong and, worse, that I never would. The ambitious girl who'd made her way from Blairsville, Pennsylvania and had managed to transform herself into a passable version of a New Yorker, had somehow disappeared in the demands of motherhood, and I had no idea how to get her back.

At get-togethers I found the conversation floundering as I tried to keep up with what was going on. The world seemed to have carried on without me, while I sat at home and figured out how to be a mother. If I'd been back home, I would at least have had family to help me out, people I could rely on and who I could be myself around, people who didn't mind that I was now a little less smart, a little less accomplished and far from confident. Who didn't care that my wardrobe was out of season and in need of replacement or that I hadn't read the latest book or seen the fascinating new play at the Shubert Theatre. I felt overwhelmed and in need of friendship. And so, that winter day in the park, the sound of a small child laughing was something welcoming and comforting, and I'd looked around and there was Sarah, with her tiny daughter, and it was like looking in a mirror.

They were skimming stones over the lake which had frozen over, trying to see who could get their stone to slide the furthest and I had walked over to them and said, "Hey, looks like fun. Do you mind if we join in?" And Sarah had smiled and said, "Of course!"

We'd spent the next half hour laughing and skimming stones, then headed to the Boathouse café for coffees and hot chocolates, Katie and Isa holding hands and skittering about on the frozen puddles, and communicating easily, the way toddlers do, with whoops and smiles and gurgling wails.

We recognized ourselves in one another, of course. Shared the same frustrations, the same befuddlement that new motherhood always brings. The longing for excitement and mental stimulation, which we tried to suppress, but never really kept at bay.

"Now that I know the reality of all this," Sarah had told me, looking at Isa, "I feel a little claustrophobic. As if some opportunity has been taken away from me. The chance to be someone else, I guess. Oh, I know we're not supposed to say such things, but it's the truth, isn't it?"

I had been surprised at her frankness and impressed by her eloquence. It was as if Sarah had been able to explain to me what it was that had been troubling me since Katie's birth. Like gaining a diagnosis for some hitherto unexplained illness, it was a relief of sorts. And we had talked all morning and into the afternoon, as if we had known one another for years. That easy flow of conversation that can sometimes arise when you assume you will never see the other person again.

And that day, I really thought we would never see one another again. The differences between us were too noticeable, once you scratched the surface. Sarah's social credentials, and her well-heeled upbringing, something which set us apart.

"How did you end up in New York?" Sarah had asked me after we'd been talking for around a half hour. The question was polite, but it contained a hidden suggestion I was well aware of. She could see past my adopted persona to the person I really was. The slight inflection in my accent, and the tired little slouch in my shoulders, couldn't be disguised by a Max Mara coat and some Jil Sander earrings. I decided to skip the childhood part and go straight to recent history.

"I was working at Belmont and Adams Capital," I explained. "I met my husband there and well, here I am, seven years later. You?"

"Oh, I've known my husband's family since childhood. New York can be quite intimate in that regard sometimes. But we only really got to know one another when we were both at Columbia and, well, that was that. You know how it is, just your typical Upper West Side story," she laughed.

I didn't know and could only shrug, and I found myself wondering where that habit of naming a borough came from. This assumption that everyone knew there was a distinction and why it was important. Upper West Side, not New York; and she noticed my hesitation and smiled, then said, "So, where is it you're from then? Upstate some place?"

"No, Pennsylvania," I replied. There was no point in naming the town, she would never have heard of it.

"Oh," she nodded. And then, without skipping a beat. "Do you ever think of moving back there?"

"No," I told her. And I made sure my voice was firm and my expression assertive. "I've lived here so long now it feels like home. I don't belong in Pennsylvania anymore."

I pretended not to notice the small frown that creased her forehead and the slight downward slant of her mouth as she considered this, as if she was trying to decide whether New York was a city I should be able to consider home. I remember how she nodded at me in a way that left me feeling strangely diminished, as if she thought I'd stepped beyond my limits.

I could tell she was wondering what would have happened if we'd met someplace else. If we'd been introduced at some event or other. Would we even have spoken to one another beyond the polite introductions? The differences between us would probably have ensured we never went beyond a brief hello.

And if I'm honest, I thought it would go that way, that we would never share more than a passing familiarity with one another. That the kids would maybe bring us together on the odd occasion, at the park or a birthday party or some such thing, but that would be it. That it became an enduring friendship was still something which could surprise me. That it became a friendship I valued was something that perplexed me at times. But I had always hoped it would last through the girls' childhoods and beyond. And if Isa hadn't died, who knows, perhaps it would have.

It was difficult, at first, to admit that dependence. Over the years I had always assumed Sarah needed me more than I needed her.

There was a frailty to Sarah, I knew. Something she was always so careful to mask with an outward show of confidence and moneyed self-assurance, but she would let it slip now and then and allow a glimpse of the real Sarah to show through. That had been the understanding which underpinned our whole friendship; we both reserved the right to only ever reveal what we wanted. We never pried and it was taken as understood that we had secrets we kept from one another. Private lives which we would never discuss.

It had been a mistake. I understood that now. My politeness, my unwillingness to ask questions for fear of appearing nosy, intrusive. I should have pushed past all that, past the manners and my own sense of, well, what was it exactly? Inferiority? The country girl not quite as good as the city slicker? Stupid, such an insecurity, I knew that. But it existed. I *was* intimidated at times by Sarah's well-heeled nonchalance and apparent confidence. But that veneer of self-assurance had always impressed me because it was the one thing I lacked.

If only I had scratched the surface, asked a few questions now and then, listened more closely, I'd have seen that it was all for show. That the confidence masked a far deeper frailty than I realized. I'd have asked the questions that could have made all the difference in the end. Uncovered some truths that could have prevented all of this pain.

Isa would still be alive if we'd both been more upfront with one another. I was sure of it. Without a shadow of a doubt.

So, I thought. Do something for once then, Louise. If Sarah won't pick up the phone, then go to her. Make her talk to you. Make her tell you what's going on.

CHAPTER SIXTEEN

Katie

Just carry on as normal. That was what I decided. Summer was over, Isa was dead, and it was time to fall back into a routine. I was surprised by how much I wanted it—that regularity, the boredom of it. Home, school, the brief relief of the weekend.

So, when Dad casually asked me how I was "holding up," I saw my chance.

"I want to go back to school," I told him. "I want everything to be the way it was before. Just, normal, you know?"

"Are you sure you're ready?" Mom asked me.

I thought it was a stupid question. The wrong question. Who could ever be ready? A week from now, a month, even a year. It would make no difference. I knew that. It wasn't a question of being ready. It was simply a question of taking a deep breath and then a step forward. Daring to do it because standing still was as good as going backwards, and as much as I longed for it, that direction of travel was impossible.

"I'm going in tomorrow, okay?" was all I told them. "I know you don't want me to, but I'm going. I don't want to sit here at home, thinking about Isa and the summer and what's going to happen now."

Dad at least had the sense to say nothing, not so much out of understanding, but more through weariness, as if the shock of all that had happened had wiped him clean of energy. He had no resistance to give. Much like James, he seemed defeated by the weight of it. Isa's death had sapped them both of vitality.

Only Mom persisted.

"Are you really sure?" she asked me, more than once. As if she'd forgotten she'd already asked the question. "Are you sure, Katie? Are you sure?" It was driving me nuts.

"Just leave her, Louise," Dad had finally said. "We're all going to have to find our own way through this. If she needs to go, then let her."

"But a few days more at home will do no harm," Mom insisted. "School's just started back and some of those kids will be hearing about all this for the first time. They need a chance to let it sink in. And on top of that, the school, I don't think they want this just yet. They'll have things to talk through with everyone."

I knew what Mom was leaving unsaid. That it didn't look right, going back to school as if nothing had happened. There was something too coolheaded about it.

The easiest thing would have been to admit the truth. Just tell everyone that I wished none of it had happened. That all I wanted was for the unimaginable events of the summer to unravel somehow. Impossible, I knew that. But it didn't stop me longing for it. Maybe that was how the shock and the grief worked for me. I needed to block it all. Try and carry on as if none of it had happened.

So, we'd agreed to a compromise.

"Just let me go and see what happens. If it's too much, I can always come home."

When the morning came around, I pulled on my backpack, zipped up my jacket, and headed to East 68th Street subway station to start the familiar journey. Just another autumn day in New York.

I settled into the subway car and let the thrum and rattle soothe me. The sway of the car on the rails rippled through my legs and my arms and lulled me just as it always had. At 59th

Street, the usual suspects boarded, ashen faced and dazed-looking, heading to work, or some of them even headed home after a nightshift and longing for sleep while the rest of the world was getting started. At Grand Central Station, the squeeze of bodies tightened, everyone lost in their own little worlds. Headphones on, mobile phones out, everyone a specialist in avoiding eye contact. I had hoped the familiar sights would feel comforting. Just knowing that the world hadn't changed, not really, that all these small things still happened, that New York was still its buzzing, busy self. I had wanted to experience that and feel comforted by it.

But the truth was, everything had changed. I rode the subway alone. I stared at the blank-eyed commuters and didn't laugh at them, because laughing wasn't something you did alone. Laughing was something you did with Isa.

And Isa wasn't there.

At Brooklyn Bridge station, I got off and walked the last few blocks to school in silence, aware that Isa wasn't there with me and that she never would be now.

When I arrived, I saw there was a group congregated on the sidewalk outside the school doors, as if they were waiting for me, and I felt my jaw clench and my mind begin to focus on what was ahead.

Don't look at them, I thought. Just walk.

It made me look steely, untouchable and I could feel them part as I walked through, no one catching my eye or uttering a word. All of them waiting for me to do something, say something. Show them my grief, I supposed.

They were not expecting to see me so soon, I understood that now, but it was too late to turn back, too late to admit that walking up those stairs was very different to how I had imagined it. Too late to realize that the school was buzzing with the news and my presence only heightened the tension.

I should have expected it. Tragedy brings its own peculiar sort of excitement, after all. But I hadn't counted on it being so incessant, the melodrama and the bullshit.

All morning there was a constant background whisper.

"Isa's dead, did you hear?"

"Katie was there. She saw it happen."

"Poor Isa. I can't believe it."

On and on. A barrage of gossip and whispers and excited voices. I had to remind myself that if this was happening to someone else, I would be one of those whisperers, one of those gossips.

All I could do was return sympathetic looks with an impassive gaze that caused them all to look away. I didn't need to say it out loud for them to understand what I thought of them. That they were ghoulish, eager spectators, relishing the aftermath of some tragedy.

It was worse even than the maudlin outpourings online. The sighs of grief, the #RIP tags, the teddy bears and roses and candles, the "heaven has another angel now" memes. The cheesiness of it all had become unbearable and I'd had to switch off and turn away from it.

The whole day, I could almost hear Isa laughing at me: *God, Katie. Did you honestly think it would be easier in real life?*

But I had, for some reason. I had hoped that everyone would look me in the eye and understand that too much had happened. That they'd see the smallness of me, the way I had shrunk in some way since the summer, and understand I needed to pretend that normality still existed, that life, all the boring stuff, was still happening, and that despite the tragic events of the summer, I could be a part of it again, this happier world.

But the whole morning, I had sat alone in the classroom, no one daring to sit beside me, in case… well, in case of what? I thought. Bad luck? It felt that way sometimes, when I caught them looking at me, that I posed some sort of danger. I'd been there when Isa died and there was something hanging over me now. Something ominous no one wanted to get close to. I had walked from lesson to lesson alone, surrounded by hushed, superstitious whispers. The only word I could decipher, a name: Isa.

And when they did get close, their sympathy annoyed me. Those gentle pats on my shoulder, from teachers keen to let me know they were "available to talk if I needed it." I wanted to shrug them off and tell them I was okay. They should just leave me alone. Treat me just as they would always treat me. Allow me to become invisible again. Just Katie Lindeman, no one special.

It was only when I walked along the school corridor between lessons that I realized the stares and the whispers were something I wanted. That it was all a punishment of sorts.

Go on, I thought. *You've every right to whisper. Every right to judge me. I wasn't there to help her and now she's dead, so blame me if you want to.*

And maybe I should have given them what they were waiting for. Maybe I should have stood there in the corridor and wailed. Lain there on the floor, broken down and crumpled, waiting for someone to come and lift me up.

God knows I'd felt it rising every day since Isa died, some sort of roiling in my veins, but every time it bubbled to the surface, I swallowed it down, I pushed away the grief, the shock, the horror of it all. Because wailing didn't feel like enough. Falling to the ground didn't feel like enough. Nothing felt enough.

Someday, when I wasn't expecting it, I knew it would happen. Something would push me over the edge. Something small and insignificant. All I could do was wait for it to happen.

And I wanted to turn to all those staring faces, all those whisperers and explain it to them, tell them that I couldn't cry yet, I couldn't break down because Isa was still too present. I wanted to tell them that I still imagined I could pick up the phone and chat to her, just have a stupid conversation. Ask her what she thought of those shoes I was thinking of getting, or what she thought of Amanda's new haircut, and had she seen Lara's tattoo?

It was still too easy to imagine Isa was alive. Go back a few weeks and it would even be true. Go back a few weeks and we'd all be sitting there on the beach, the sand sticking to our legs, the smell of coconut oil on our skin, coating our lips and tongues, the sun, shining in our eyes. Go back, just a little bit, and none of it had happened. And it felt so close still, it was so easy to believe it was possible. That with one step I could get there. Get myself back to that time and place. Back to a happiness I didn't even realize I had until it was gone.

And then the bell rang, its sound as harsh as laughter. As harsh as the here and now. Recess. And I knew what was coming. I could already hear the gaggle of voices, waiting to pounce. They'd bided their time all morning. Kept a respectful distance. But now they were ready to come and get me.

Stephanie. I could have guessed. She made a beeline for me as soon as the bell rang, followed by a swarm of hangers-on all buzzing behind her, whispering, giggling, stifling their nerves, all desperate to know something, anything.

"Oh Katie," Stephanie simpered. "I'm so sorry. What a terrible thing to have to go through."

I tried to say something. Remind her that I hadn't "gone through" anything. Isa was the one who had died. But Stephanie enveloped me before I had a chance to open my mouth, embracing me in a phony show of concern. All I could do was smile and say, "thanks."

"What happened, Katie?" Stephanie asked, and as she said it, the throng of girls around her leaned in closer.

"An accident. It was some sort of accident."

"Oh, poor Isa. Were you there? Did you see it happen?"

And I wished I had a snappy reply, wished I could think on my feet and find some way out, but Stephanie's question, the brutality of it, was too intense.

"No," was all I could muster, and even that was a whisper.

Stephanie leaning in as if she hadn't heard what I said, a new question on the tip of her tongue. But Principal Shapiro had spotted the crowd gathered around me and decided enough was enough.

"Come on then, people," he said as he barged through them and stood beside me. "Let's give Katie some space, okay?"

I was glad of the intervention, because I could feel something coming, something in Stephanie's tone. The thing I've asked myself a thousand times already but have never dared say out loud.

Why didn't you do anything? Why didn't you help Isa? That was what Stephanie wanted to know.

It was the same question that had tormented James ever since they found Isa washed ashore.

"We should have made her come home with us." He kept repeating it. As if he couldn't quite believe we had walked home and left Isa behind, alone, in the dark.

Mom had immediately intervened. "It was an accident, James. Just a horrible, terrible accident."

I understood the truth of it, the logic of it even, it *was* an accident. But I also understood how James felt, because the same question troubled me too. A question which will never leave, I was certain of it.

Why did you leave her alone on the beach? Why did you abandon her?

"Katie? Katie?"

Principal Shapiro pulled me from my thoughts, the crowd around me at a distance now, but staring at me with worried looks as if they didn't know what to make of me.

Where did she go just then? That's what they were thinking. Imagining some story there, some secret I was keeping to myself. The answer to Stephanie's question.

Why didn't you help her?

And I wanted to shout it at them, *I don't know what happened! It was an accident. Just a stupid accident. It wasn't meant to be like this.* But Mr. Shapiro squeezed my elbow and guided me away and I heard him talking again, his voice filtering through.

"… think again about taking a few days off… so shocking… time to recover…"

And I must have nodded in agreement, because suddenly I was back in the subway car and heading home.

Making the journey in reverse. Brooklyn Bridge, Grand Central, back up the line and then out, blinking and dazed, into the daylight again on East 68th Street.

Time to recover, I thought. If only it were that simple.

CHAPTER SEVENTEEN

Louise

My finger trembled as I pressed the doorbell and I stuffed my hands deep into my coat pockets to stop them shaking. When Sarah opened the door, I wanted to appear calm, and in control. I wanted to feel ready.

Though ready was far from how I felt. I had needed to walk the block three times in an attempt to steady myself.

With each circuit, I told myself that whatever happened, Sarah would not close the door on me or turn me away. But that was what I feared. A slammed door. A continuation of that long, unbearable silence.

"Louise," was all Sarah said when she opened the door.

And we stood there, face to face, for a moment, in silence, looking at one another, the way strangers would. As if we needed to make an appraisal. Weigh up the other and decide what to do.

"Hi, Sarah," I eventually replied, the stammer in my voice something I couldn't control.

Perhaps it was the vulnerability Sarah needed to see, because she opened the door a little wider and said, "Come in."

But there was no embrace. No kiss on the cheek. No smile. The old familiarity and warmth were gone, and as Sarah walked down the hallway ahead of me, I noticed the straightness of her shoulders, the slight stiffness to her gait, and recognized it for what it was. That show of collectedness, that outward veneer of calm and control. Sarah was as nervous as I was. She didn't want me in her house, that was obvious.

We sat in the living room and I tried not to look at the photos on the walls. Isa and Katie together in happier times. I wondered how Sarah could bear it, to walk into the room each day and be confronted by all that she had lost.

If it had been the other way around, if it had been Katie who had died, I would have ripped every photo from the wall, tried to rid myself of every painful memory. At least for a while.

And it was as if Sarah had read my mind.

"Willem thought I should take them down," she said. "He says it hurts too much to look at them. Looks like you feel the same."

I was too stunned at first to reply, and needed to catch my breath, and take a moment to think of a reply.

"I didn't think it would leave me feeling so sad," I explained. "I mean, to see them together, smiling like that. It should make me happy. But it doesn't."

"Just reminds you of what we've lost?"

And again, how to respond to that? I could feel the weight of it, the way the statement was loaded not just with grief and pain, but again with something accusatory, too. As if Sarah believed that we had all forgotten. That Isa's death was something in the past, something the world had moved on from.

"Yes, it does," was all I could say.

"You know," Sarah continued, as if she wasn't really listening to a word I said. "I've been looking at those photos a lot recently."

"Well," I began, "If it offers some comfort—"

Sarah didn't let me finish. "No, it's not comfort I'm looking for," and she paused as if she was checking that I was listening. Then, satisfied, she continued, "It's more, answers I'm after."

"Answers?"

"Yes. I look at Isa, remember how she was, and it doesn't make any sense to me."

"Sorry? What doesn't make sense?"

"The way she died. The way they say it was an accident. I mean, do you believe that?"

Believe. It wasn't something I thought I needed to believe. There was no question there, no doubt as to what had happened. A teenage girl, drunk and a little the worse for wear, made a mistake. She went for a swim and then found herself in difficulties. An error in judgment with tragic consequences. Surely Sarah understood that? Because if she didn't, then what was it exactly she thought had happened?

"Sarah," I said. "I don't think it was anything more than that. Isa, she made a mistake. A terrible mistake. But it was a mistake. You can't think it was anything else."

"No? Why not? I mean, you knew Isa. You knew how she was. Oh, a little wild sometimes, but no more than any other girl her age. She was sensible. She was responsible. I know she was. And so do you. So, tell me, Louise. The Isa you knew, would she have done a thing like that? Walked into the sea, at night? Really?"

And I'd wanted to protest, to explain that the sensible, responsible girl wasn't who Isa was. Not that night or, as it turned out, any other night. That alcohol, drugs, the freedom of a summer without her parents, all of it had combined to make her act irresponsibly that night. That it wasn't wholly out of character. The girl who walked into the sea was the real Isa, the one she didn't know. Surely Sarah wasn't going to force me to explain that again?

But when I looked Sarah in the eye, I saw it—the conviction that was there. The total belief she now had. She had gone over events, again and again, and had come to a conclusion from which she would not be dissuaded.

However Isa came to find herself in the water, Sarah was certain of one thing: she had not walked into the sea of her own accord.

CHAPTER EIGHTEEN

Katie

Their absence was conspicuous, though none of us spoke about it. No one dared admit that Sarah and Willem were keeping their distance.

But it upset me to think that they wanted to keep way from us, that their silence was a choice. That they couldn't bear to call or visit because there was something unfinished about it all, some apportioning of blame or responsibility; I wasn't quite sure what it was. All I knew was that it wasn't fair, it wasn't right, but there was nothing we could do. Sarah and Willem would have to come to us when they were ready. Perhaps they would never speak to us again. It was starting to feel that way.

I tried to call them a few times, just to say hello, ask them how they were doing. But my finger always hovered over the screen and I never managed to press the little icon, "Isa's Mom," because at the last moment, I couldn't bear the idea of having to start the conversation. To sit there and ask Sarah if she was okay. It seemed wrong, for some reason, as if the question was too glib. What was Sarah supposed to say in reply?

Oh, hey there, Katie, so nice of you to call. Yes, everything's fine, and you? How are you doing?

No conversation between us would begin that way now—relaxed, spontaneous, free from the past. And that thought alone had been enough for me to swipe away the contacts list and toss the phone on the bed.

But now I had no choice.

No one had warned me an announcement was coming, and so I had sat there in the school hall and waited for the assembly to begin, not quite sure, at first, if what I was hearing was correct.

They were planning a memorial service for Isa. A way for the school to "come together and remember one of their brightest and loveliest pupils."

Loveliest. That was the word they used, and it was this that did for me. Because it was the word Sarah always used when she spoke about Isa.

"You look lovely in that dress, Isa. Your hair's lovely up like that, Isa. How did I come to have such a lovely daughter?" That sort of thing.

Though it was never cheesy when she said it. It always seemed genuine and felt nice, because she meant it, and you could tell it made her happy to say it.

But hearing it said out loud like that, when Principle Shapiro announced it, hearing someone else say it, made me want to rush over to Isa's house and tell Sarah, let her know that other people had noticed it too and they had not forgotten. Isa, lovely Isa.

So, there I was, at home, trying to work up some courage. Trying to pick up the phone and call, because the school asked me if I wanted to say something at the memorial.

"Only if you feel able to, of course," Principle Shapiro had emphasized.

Some sort of eulogy was what he was thinking.

"I think, as her best friend, it's something you might like to do, as a way to help us say goodbye, together, as a school."

How many ways are we meant to say goodbye? I had wondered, even as I nodded to Principle Shapiro, even as I watched him walk away, happy that it was agreed and that the asking of it had been a simple thing after all, no need for him to have worried so much about it.

But I felt I had said goodbye so many times already. On the beach, at the graveside, over, and over again, into Isa's voicemail. Calling to say goodbye had become a compulsion. The sound of Isa's voice, something I needed to hear still.

And if Sarah or Willem were picking up Isa's messages, if they were listening to the voicemails I left, then I hoped they understood that I said goodbye each day, because each morning I woke up and forgot for a moment that Isa was gone. It was the best part of the day, because there was a lightness to things again, an easy sort of happiness that had disappeared since Isa's death. But it returned in those forgetful early mornings and, for a brief amnesiac moment, everything felt okay, until it crashed down again. Isa was dead. And all I could do was call and say goodbye. Again, and again and again. Goodbye, Isa, goodbye.

But a public goodbye? I felt I needed permission to stand in a hall full of schoolkids and say something. I needed Sarah to tell me that it was okay. So, I breathed deeply, closed my eyes and dialed the number.

"Katie?"

For a moment we were silent, and I could hear Sarah breathe on the other side of the line. Short, anxious breaths, as if she was panicked.

"Mrs. Egberts," I finally replied.

And then a sob. A quiet, muffled sort of sob. Not something she tried to hide, but still something she tried to contain.

"Sorry," I said. "I'll call back some other time. I just wanted to—"

"No, no it's okay, Katie, really, it's okay. I just wasn't expecting it. To speak to you, to hear your voice."

"Sorry," I told her again.

"Are you okay?" Sarah asked, as if she suddenly realized that there must be some reason for me to be calling.

"Yes, I'm fine. Everything's okay."

"Right."

And again, silence. A little awkward. *Okay, just talk*, I thought. *Just talk to her.*

"I was calling about the memorial. For Isa. The one they're planning at school."

"Oh, I see."

She sounded disappointed, as if she was hoping I was calling with some other news, something I'd remembered about Isa, about the night she died. It made me want to put the phone down and start over.

"Is it okay if I ask you something? I can call back again if you want, really, it's okay," I said.

"It's just so nice to hear from you, Katie," Sarah told me. And there was a trace again, a quivering trace of emotion. I could hear her holding back the tears.

"I should have called earlier," I replied. "It's just, I... I didn't know what to say. I didn't know what you would think."

"Oh Katie, you can always call me, do you understand? Always."

It surprised me to hear Sarah say this. I didn't know I could call her. I thought, if anything, that I was the last person she wanted to hear from.

And I didn't know how to react, so all I could say was, "Thank you. That means a lot to me," and hope I didn't sound too insincere.

"I mean it, Katie. You and Isa…"

She couldn't finish, but I knew what she meant. We were friends. Best friends. It still meant something.

"So," Sarah continued. "What about this memorial then?"

"They want me to say something. Something… well, I don't know what. Just about Isa. The way she was. Something like that."

"Oh. Are you sure you want to do that?"

"I don't know. Sometimes I do. Right now, I do. I guess that's why I called you. I thought, maybe if I could come over and talk to you about it? Because I don't know what to say, or what to do."

And I could hear Sarah sigh, feel her smile.

"If that's what you want, Katie. I'd like that. If you said something. Reminded people who she was."

"No one's forgotten, Mrs. Egberts. Really, no one's forgotten her."

And that was it. It was too much. She started to cry, uncontrollably this time. Then, she just said, "Okay, Katie, okay. I'll see you soon," and hung up.

I listened to the faint buzz of silence at the end of the line and tried to grapple with what it meant.

Say something, it seemed to suggest. You'll know yourself what to say. So, say something. But as I sat there on the edge of the bed, I could feel my whole body shake, as if every cell in my body was in disagreement.

Remind them who Isa was. Is that what Sarah wanted?

Isa Egberts, I found myself thinking. Remind me who she was again?

It was only as I walked over to Isa's house that I realized I had no idea what I should say to Sarah. Not just about the memorial but about everything. Since the funeral, they didn't want to talk to us or visit, and even though it was understandable, it felt like a punishment of sorts.

Everyone looks around for someone to blame when something terrible happens, I knew that. But it was more difficult to accept than I imagined it would be. The idea that Sarah and Willem could look at us and think, *If only you'd taken better care of Isa, she would still be here with us. We would still have her.* I wondered if they realized how it felt to be looked upon this way. If Sarah and Willem thought about how it felt to have something like that hanging over you. They didn't. I was sure of it. And now the prospect of seeing Sarah again, of sitting there in her living room and having a chat, filled me with dread.

A chat? No, they would probably never be able to just chat. Isa would always be there, somewhere in the background. And when I thought about that I felt a little sad, because I would have liked that, to have Sarah to talk to once in a while. An older female voice I could turn to that wasn't my mom's.

It had been like that a lot since Isa died. Moments like this, when things such as future conversations presented themselves, and I realized they would never happen. It was as if the future needed to be re-plotted somehow. Things that could never happen now needed to be set aside, then forgotten. I wondered if Sarah and Willem understood this. That a piece of my future had vanished too, when Isa died. But how to explain such a thing without appearing self-absorbed? Without diminishing their grief?

It wasn't that I wanted to be wistful about any of it, but it happened anyway. By the time I arrived at Isa's house, by the time I pressed the doorbell and Sarah opened it, I was deep in my thoughts, sad even. When Sarah saw me standing there at the top of the brownstone steps, a little lost, a little melancholy, she did what she always did. She reached forward and clutched me in a bearhug, and I could feel her need to comfort me, all that maternal energy inside her that was now in need of an outlet, and there I was, standing on her doorstep, able to provide it.

"So," she said at last when she finally let go. "Let's get inside, eh? You must be dying for a drink after walking all the way over here."

Inside, the house was horribly familiar and unchanged. It was as pristine as ever, in fact, and I had to stand there and take it in, because for some reason it didn't seem right.

Our house had descended into a shabby state of disarray since we got back from the beach house. The cleaning lady came twice a week, just as she always did, and Mom pottered about, much as she always had, picking up discarded bits and pieces, but for some reason the place seemed to have taken on an unruly air, as if nothing could be done to bring it back to the state of glossy magazine, interior design perfection my mom always aspired to. The events of the summer left everything seeming irrelevant. Cleaning, tidying, what difference did it make? That was what it felt like, as if small things had lost their meaning and importance.

Yet Sarah seemed to have attained it. At least in the living room. It still had the same whiter than white, neater than possible, unlived-in look it had when Isa was alive. I still didn't want to sit on the pale grey sofa when I was invited to, for fear I would stain it somehow.

It seemed odd that a mother would go to such lengths to keep a perfect house when her only child, her precious daughter, had died. And all I could think was, *How can she give a damn about any of this?*

Because if it was me, I would close the door forever and just let the place fall apart at the seams. I'd let it all run to ruin, let the mess of life just pile up around me in a squalid heap and I wouldn't care.

It was only when I watched Sarah move around the living room that I began to understand, and it suddenly made sense.

This was how she dealt with it. This was how she tried to block it out.

And I watched her as she flitted about the room, swiping away a stray feather which had come loose from one of the seat cushions, then pacing across the room to the coffee table to square up a pile of books that didn't need straightening.

It was a nervous sort of energy and I didn't quite know if it was because I was there, and Sarah simply didn't know what to do with company any more, or if she was always like this now, flitting around like a nervous bird, twitching at the sight of motes of dust and stray feathers and greasy fingerprints on glass tabletops.

I understood that I needed to tread carefully though. Be quiet and thoughtful. Listen more than talk.

"It's so lovely, Katie, that you want to say something about Isa at the memorial. It's so touching."

"Lovely." That word again. Only this time it was directed at me and I had to smile because I was not used to it. It wasn't a word that accompanied me that often.

"Thanks," I said. "I know it's not going to be an easy thing to do and a piece of me is scared I'll bottle it when I'm up there on the stage in front of everyone."

"You'll be fine, I'm sure. You and Isa, well…"

She didn't need to finish her sentence. I knew what she meant. You and Isa were so close, such good friends. I knew what it implied, that I had a thousand and one things I could say about Isa, a million ways to remember her. Memories both good and bad. It was the things I knew I couldn't say though, that worried me. The idea that I would stand there and sing Isa's praises while everyone watched me and saw that I was holding something back. That there were things I could never reveal. I wasn't a natural liar, and something about keeping Isa's secrets felt like that in a way, like a lie. Like something I would be caught out for.

What are you not telling us, Katie? That was the thing I imagined when I thought of standing in that hall. A sea of faces looking up at the podium and all of them with the same thought: *You're keeping something from us, Katie Lindeman, we can see it.*

It agitated me just to think about it, and something of my nerves must have shown because Sarah shifted in her seat, then got up, nervous again.

"Sorry," she said. "I forgot all about that drink. Hot chocolate okay?"

And she must have seen the surprise on my face and the way I had to stifle a laugh.

"Oh," she laughed, "sorry, that was stupid of me. It's just sometimes… you know?"

"You forget we're no longer little kids?"

"Yeah," she whispered. "That. Exactly that. How about tea then? Or coffee maybe?"

"Yeah, tea is good. Any sort, I don't mind."

"Right," she said. "Right. Good. Okay then." And off she went.

And it was a relief not to have her there in the room, even for just the few minutes it would take to make tea. Just so I could take a moment to get my bearings because it was obvious that Sarah wanted to talk about more than the memorial.

I had watched her as she'd fidgeted about the room. The way she had fussed around straightening the books on the coffee table. I wouldn't even have looked at them or paid them much attention at all if it wasn't for the way Sarah had turned away from me and tried to place herself between me and the books. She was trying to make sure I didn't see what was there on the table. Rearranging things so that when I turned back and walked away, all I would see would be some heavy, expensive art book that she'd stacked on the top.

So, when I could hear Sarah was busy in the kitchen, I got up and walked over to the table and lifted up the heavy book to find it there. The photograph album. And though I knew I shouldn't, I opened it anyway, because I knew Isa would be in there and I wanted to see her again, see her in photos that I didn't recognize. Intimate photos that I'd never seen before, from when Isa was just a kid, not the over-posed and over-polished Instagram pictures I'd seen a thousand times. Or the geeky, awkward school portraits that still sat in silver frames scattered across various tables throughout the room. Real pictures. Pictures of Isa as she really was.

And there she was on the first page. A scrawny kid in a white pinafore, hair in tight plaits, a scowl on her face as she looked at the camera. She must have been three or four and I could hear her. "I don't want my photo taken! Go away!" And I couldn't help it, I laughed when I heard her voice, when I saw her tiny, toddler face. The sweetness of it.

"She was cute, eh?" Sarah said.

I hadn't heard her come in and the shock of Sarah standing there behind me made me drop the photo album.

"Oh! I didn't know you were there."

"Sorry," she said. "I didn't mean to startle you."

"I don't remember seeing photos of Isa when she was really small," I told her as I picked up the album from the floor.

"No?" she replied. And she seemed genuinely surprised, as if there was a missing piece to my friendship with Isa that she had simply assumed existed, this trading of silly stories from when we were kids, the giggling at old photographs. But for some reason, it was only the high-school version of Isa I remembered. The almost perfect girl—gap teeth and pigtails gone, the skinned knees now tanned and gleaming. The version of Isa that was an illusion. The plastic Instagram girl. It was as if our childhood days had never happened. So long ago now, that it was impossible to remember. *Me and Isa as kids*, I thought. *No, all that had vanished years ago when she became this sleeker version of herself.*

And it made me wonder what kind of claim I really had on Isa. Best friend? Really? When it turned out I could easily forget so many things?

"It must be strange to see her again like this," Sarah said.

"It just seems so sad. More than anything, it just feels so sad."

Sarah sat down on the sofa then beckoned to me to come and sit down beside her. The tea was in a cup on a side table, a small plate of buttery biscuits accompanying them, the biscuits neatly arranged in a fan shape on the plate. A small thing that unsettled me. That unnecessary attention to detail again.

I sat down and took a sip of tea and waited for Sarah to say something.

"I've been thinking a lot about Isa this past week," Sarah began. And I nodded and hoped the pause wouldn't last too long.

"What I mean is, I've been thinking about the Isa I didn't know. The Isa that managed to put herself in that situation, out late at night swimming in the sea, in the dark. I don't know that girl, Katie. I really don't. My own daughter, but I don't recognize her. When did she get so reckless?"

It wasn't a question I wanted to answer. Even with Isa dead, to tell Sarah anything about Isa, not just the things she got up to over the summer, but all the stuff with Alex, it felt like a betrayal. And Sarah saw my hesitation, recognized the doubt.

"She was clearly no angel, Katie. I'm no fool. But she got herself into trouble that night and I need to know how that happened."

She was so calm when she said it, as if it was something she had been rehearsing. Getting that line ready, over and over, so that when I was finally sat there in front of her, she could ask it with a steady voice.

"There must be something you remember, Katie. No matter how small it is. Because I know she would never have gone into the water alone at night. She was always scared of the dark as a child, and it never really left her. I keep thinking about that. She wouldn't have walked onto the beach in the dark on her own. Someone must have been with her. And whoever it was, they left her there in the water, alone. They left her to drown."

"She was just hanging out with the usual crowd that night, Mrs. Egberts," I replied. "That was all, I swear. All summer, that's all we did."

"With some boy called Luka?"

"Yes, with Luka. But not that night. They had some kind of falling-out a few days before she died, so they didn't go to the party together. But I swear, Mrs. Egberts, Luka is a good guy. Kind, you know? He would never have hurt Isa, if that's what you're thinking."

"I don't know what I'm thinking at the moment, Katie. I have no idea who Luka is. And maybe what you say is true. Maybe he is a lovely boy. But how do I know that? And all those beach parties. No one's talking about that and I think it's about time someone did."

She paused then, as if she was waiting for me to say something. Hoping, it seemed, that I would just blurt it all out. A full report on what happened that summer.

Hold it together, Katie, I thought. *Just sit here and say nothing.*

"Sorry," Sarah continued. "I know I've put you on the spot just now. But I need to know. Willem and me, we need to know what happened to Isa. So, as her friend, as her best friend, I need you to think as hard as you can. Any small thing you can remember, promise me you'll tell me about it. Will you do that for me, Katie? Will you do it for Isa too?"

"Sure," I told her. "I promise I will. It's just—"

"No, let's leave it at that. You promised you will. So, let's leave it at that."

And that was it. We were done, and I was walking back home again, the bitter taste of black tea coating my mouth and making me feel nauseous.

On the way home, all I could think about was what Sarah was asking me to do.

"Tell me about Isa. Tell me about the daughter I didn't know."

It was an impossible request. How could I tell Sarah about Isa? She was still my best friend. Death didn't change a thing like that. All the things that happened over the summer, all the stuff before then, with Alex, I didn't want to think about any of it. It was done and best forgotten. Dragging it all up wasn't going to change anything. It wasn't going to bring Isa back and it wasn't going to help Sarah either. Better she kept a polished picture in her head of who she thought Isa was. That sweet little kid in the pinafore and pigtails. Why tarnish it?

Willem had apparently kept quiet about it all, and I liked that about him, that he had been discreet, known what was best left unsaid, even though telling Sarah about Alex would probably have helped him sort things out. It might have saved them even, from getting carried away with all that stupid honeymoon shit.

But now that Isa was gone, I wondered if he thought the same way. Maybe none of them needed protecting any more. The damage had been done. Maybe it would be better if the truth came out?

It was the sort of dilemma I would have gone to Isa with, and asked her for advice. *What do you think I should do, Isa? What would you do?*

And I had to smile at that. The irony of it. That I was still having to cover up for the mess Isa made. Some things never change.

*

Isa Egberts. She wasn't the girl everyone thought she was. How many times have I thought about this since the summer? A thousand times? It felt that way. There were things about Isa no one knew. Things they could never know. Sarah might want me to tell her about her daughter, but there was no way I could do that. She had an image of Isa that was closer to that pigtailed girl in the pinafore than the headstrong, fun-loving girl Isa became.

And it was my job to keep that illusion going. Why add to Sarah's grief by telling her the truth? The drugs, the sex, the lies. I'm sure, deep down, Sarah must have known all about it, but if she needed to pretend, then I wasn't going to be the one to shatter her illusions.

I would concoct a version of Isa for her. I would stand in that school hall and tell them all about the Isa Sarah wanted them to remember. Her lovely, lovely girl.

And they would listen and smile and nod their heads, but know it was a lie, a polished version of who Isa really was. But they would go along with it, for Sarah's sake. They'd sit there and listen to me present my perfect picture and they'd think, *What a load of bullshit*, and then later we would all offer Sarah our smiles and condolences and tell her how awful it was that Isa was gone. The lie was all that mattered. The illusion was all that was needed.

I would lie for Isa one last time. But once it was over, that was it. I'd forget about her. I had to. She'd ruined so much, and

I wasn't going to let her ruin the future. I wasn't going to let her take anything more from me.

Oh God, and sometimes I think I should never have hoped for that. Sometimes I think it was as if I sent that wish up into the air only for it to turn into a curse. There was plenty of damage to be done still. Even dead, that lovely, lovely girl could unleash chaos.

CHAPTER NINETEEN

Louise

They weren't that close. That was what I thought. So it confused me at first, when James' behavior became increasingly erratic. Isa was Katie's friend. Her best friend. And that was the direction I had looked once the initial shock had died down and I'd had time to absorb it all.

In the days after Isa's death, what with the chaos and the shock, things had fallen apart a little. We had all retreated to our own separate cocoons of grief, no one watching out for anyone else, because the horror of it all was too much. The daze of grief stops the world for a while, but at some point, you look up again and see what's been happening while you were lost in the fog of it all. And when I came to, there was Katie, looking so pale and skinny and far too quiet.

"You need to eat something, Katie," I had told her. "You need to take care of yourself."

And she had looked at me as if she didn't recognize me for an instant, as if my presence there in the room, my sudden attention, my revived mothering instinct, was something unwanted and unexpected.

"I'm fine," was all she said in reply.

I had stroked her hair and looked her in the eye, held her gaze for a moment and then shook my head.

"No, you're not fine, Katie. You look tired and sad."

"Well, I am. Aren't you?"

"Yes, of course I am. We all are. But I'm also your mother and I need to look out for you and make sure you're okay."

"Oh yeah? The way you looked out for Isa you mean?"

And it caused me to draw breath. The idea that Katie thought of me that way. As someone negligent. As somehow responsible for what happened. I thought all that had been settled. I thought the guilt had dissipated.

So, I'd asked her. "What more could we have done to prevent it then, Katie? Hey? Tell me, what more could we have done? None of this is our fault."

"I guess we're just going to have to keep telling ourselves that until we believe it, then, aren't we?" Katie said.

"Maybe," I replied. "If that's what it takes, then maybe."

"Well, maybe it will work for you, but I'm not sure I can do it."

"Damn it, Katie, what do you want me to say then? That it's true? That all of this is our fault? Isa wasn't a child, Katie. She was seventeen."

"I know, I know, it's just…"

And I understood it then. From now on, this would be the way these discussions would always end. With some indescribable feeling that we had done something wrong, but with no way to push past it and get to the heart of the matter, to where exactly we had failed.

My mistake was to assume that it was only Katie who felt the shame and guilt of not being there to help her friend. It made sense that Katie would dwell on everything that had happened that summer. So, I didn't look at James too closely. I didn't think about what this was doing to him. If I was honest, I would even say that it never occurred to me that James was anxious about it at all.

How could I have been so stupid? How could I have failed to see it? That he felt the guilt and the shame more than any of us. He was just a kid still. And things hit you harder when you're a kid.

And then, I heard a noise one night. Someone downstairs talking.

I had woken Peter when I heard it.

"Peter, do you hear that? There's someone downstairs."

And I had tiptoed down the stairs behind him as he went to investigate, the relief I felt when I saw James sitting on the sofa talking to his phone, almost made me laugh.

"Hey, James," Peter had called out to him. "What are you doing? It's three in the morning, for God's sake. Put that damn phone away and get to bed."

It was only when James turned to look at us, jumping with the shock of a sudden voice there in the room, that I saw something was wrong. That it wasn't just insomnia that had dragged him out of his bed, or some teenage addiction to whatever was happening online that he was scared to miss out on.

I saw it immediately as he turned to face us. The shadows under his eyes, deep, as if he had been punched. There was something almost ghoulish about him, as if he was only half there in the room with us. Some other part of him was gone. And I had squeezed Peter's arm and whispered in his ear.

"Hey, you go back to bed and let me deal with this. Let me find out what's up with him."

"You sure?"

"Yes, you've got a busy day tomorrow. Go on, go and get some sleep."

And Peter had smiled and kissed me on the cheek and said, "Thanks," and I watched him slump back upstairs and waited for the bedroom door to click shut before I walked over to the sofa and sat down beside James.

"Hey," I said. Softly, slowly, aware now that I needed to tread carefully. "You okay?"

"Yeah," was all he said. No eye contact. He just stared across the room and out the window at the glow of the streetlight.

"It's a bit late for you to be up checking your phone messages, don't you think?" I said. "Can't it wait until morning?"

"I was just awake, was all," James told me. "I like it at night when it's so quiet."

And he got up then and walked over to the window and sat in the window seat, letting his head fall against the glass. In the glow of the streetlight he looked lonely, the dark of the windows in the apartments across the street only adding to his isolation.

"What is it, James?" I asked him. "It's not like you to be up in the middle of the night. What is it? What's wrong?"

And there was a dreaminess to his voice when he replied, as if what he was telling me was not something real. It was a story. Something imagined. Or something wished for.

"Do you remember the Christmas carols?"

It had taken me a second or two to register. Carols? What did that have to do with anything?

And in the silence, while I tried to think, he kept on talking.

"When we were little kids. We'd always go out with Isa. Don't you remember? With our lanterns, knocking on the doors and singing. It was nice."

"Yes, I remember," I said. "But why are you thinking about that?"

"I don't know. The streetlight made me think of it, I guess. It's all such a long time ago, don't you think? Almost so long ago that it's hard to remember. The details, I mean."

And I tried to lighten the mood and misjudged it.

"Yeah, well, wait until you get to my age. Your whole life feels like a blur."

He spat his reply at me. Not loudly but there was a rage there all the same. "I'm talking about Isa. Not you."

I felt the force of it as if he wanted his words to feel like a slap in the face. And they did. I could feel the sting of them on my cheek and I wondered why he was so agitated, so upset. Christmas carols,

Isa, those days back then. Those were memories that should make him smile, was what I thought. Happy memories. Happy days.

"Sorry," I said. "I'm just… well, I don't know why you're thinking about that is all."

And he looked out the window at the street.

It was dark outside, despite the streetlights. The old, orange glow that defined this part of New York at night. The night-time dampness of the streets. Not quite autumn, but close to it. Soon, winter would be closing in, and the trees would be almost skeletal. On nights just like this, they had gone out to sing those Christmas carols. Homemade papier-mâché lanterns swaying on the end of sticks as they rushed about in a blur of excitement and then home afterwards to gorge on hot chocolate and cinnamon biscuits.

James was right, it was all such a long time ago. And again, I tried to think of a reason why it should make him sad. Why remembering this should wake him in the middle of the night and have him leave his bed and come down to the living room to sit alone in the dark, muttering to himself.

"I was just thinking about Isa," he said.

"You miss her?"

"Yeah. I do. I really do."

And I heard a trace of surprise in his voice when he said it. As if he had only just realized himself that this was what was going on.

"It's going to take us all a very long time to come to terms with what happened to Isa," I said.

"Come to terms?"

"Yes, to learn to live with it."

"I don't really think that's possible," he said. "Do you? Seriously, I mean. You think someday we'll just get used to it?"

"No, that's not what I meant, James. It's not something to get used to. But it is something we have to accept has happened. None of us can turn back the clock. We can't undo any of this."

"Don't you want to?"

"I don't know. Sitting here remembering things. Christmas carols, things like that. I'm sad more than anything else. Sad that it's over. Sad that there won't be any new memories to make. But I can't wish for the impossible, James, and neither should you. You can't zip us all back in time."

He didn't hear me. I could see it immediately, even in the dim light. He had decided I had nothing to tell him. I would never be able to help him make sense of any of it.

He was gone again. Somewhere else. Some place where he imagined he really could turn back the clock. Back to a time and a place when Isa was still there. When none of this had happened.

And I wanted to walk over to him and wrap my arms around him and tell him it would be okay. That time really did make a difference. You forgot things after a while. Even people you loved. They faded a little with every day that passed, with every day they weren't there beside you. It seemed unbelievable, impossible even, I knew that. God knows it shocked me too at times, when I suddenly couldn't recall the face of my own father. It was surprising how quickly the dead could disappear. How thoroughly.

But they had to disappear. It was the only way to stay sane, the only way to keep going. You had to forget. Not always. There were times to remember, moments to sit and dwell and feel nostalgic about it all. But there was also no turning back. No willing life to take a different direction.

That way lay madness. And when I looked at James sitting there in the window, surrounded by the orange glow of the streetlight, I saw it immediately. That this was where he was headed if I didn't watch out. He had taken a step in the wrong direction while I had been stumbling around in the fog of my own grief and worrying only about Katie.

And for one horrific second, I wondered if I could pull him back. Wondered if, again, I was too late.

CHAPTER TWENTY

Katie

The assembly hall was packed to the gills. Pupils, parents, friends. There weren't enough seats to go around and there wasn't enough space in the hall for everyone who wanted to attend. People spilled out of the room, and outside they set up a video screen so that people could watch what's going on in the hall.

It was a spectacle. A happening. A horror show. And I was at its center with no way of extricating myself. The star attraction whether I liked it or not. The girl everyone had come to see.

When I took to the lectern and looked down at all the faces, I wished I was one of them. Just a face in the crowd, watching, listening, waiting for an explanation.

What happened to Isa? Tell us what really happened to her.

I could feel it in the room, the expectation, the excitement, could see what it had done to Sarah and Willem. They looked exhausted and deflated by the energy in the assembly hall, lacerated even, by the lack of decorum.

Because the buzz had created the wrong atmosphere. There wasn't the calm, thoughtful sorrow you'd expect from such an event. The reflective, quiet contemplation of the dead.

I thought perhaps I should try and excuse myself in some way. Just give in and claim it was too much for me after all. But it was too late. The whole carnival had been set in motion now and there was only one thing for it.

Try and change the mood, I thought. *Just remind people why it is we're all here.*

And I repeated Isa's name like a mantra as I waited for the room to still.

Isa, Isa, Isa.

Waiting for a minute or so, and simply looking out at all the faces, seeing no one in particular. Looking out for no one in particular. I just stared at them all in silence until the discomfort reached such a level that the first tiny coughs of embarrassment and awkward shifts of chairs began to echo through the room.

Okay then, Katie, I thought. Breathe in and just start.

"The last time I saw Isa, she was laughing. No one who knew her will be surprised by this. Laughter was one of the things which defined her. I can still hear it, her laughter. I can still feel it. It's as if she's still here. Somewhere inside of me. Somewhere inside all of us. It's as if she lives on.

"Only that's not true. She doesn't. And no platitude, however well meant, is ever going to change this one brutal fact. Nor is it going to diminish the pain I feel, when I remember that Isa is gone—and I remember it every day, many, many times. And I can't ever imagine this will go away. Isa's absence is too big to be forgotten. The empty space she leaves behind can never be filled. No other laughter can ever sound as vibrant as hers.

"But I know I'm not the only one who feels this way. All of us are aware of this loss. All of us feel it. We all want just one thing—to have Isa back.

"And I wish I had something wise to say right now, some word or phrase that could help us and heal us. Something to say that could take the pain away. That could explain why it is such a terrible thing had to happen.

"Why Isa? That's what I've been asking myself. Why her?

"How can it be that someone so beautiful, so kind, so funny and smart, can be whisked away from us like that?

"It doesn't seem possible, it doesn't seem fair. And I know there are some people who wonder if maybe I could have done more. Found some way to keep Isa safe. And what can I say, other than that I wish the very same thing. I go over that night, the last time I saw her, every single day. And I obsess about all the what-if scenarios.

"What if we hadn't sneaked out that night? What if we'd stolen only one bottle of wine? What if we'd stuck together? What if we'd made her come home with us? What could I have done to have stopped this from happening?

"But I just don't know. I don't know. Because I did none of these things, and for this I am truly sorry.

"All I can do, all any of us can do, is remember her. Remember the laughing, shining Isa we loved and never forget her."

The hush took a long time to lift and was only broken by the sound of a soft sob: Sarah. I watched as she rose from her seat and mounted the steps on to the stage, her sobs growing louder, as she embraced me and whispered, "Thank you, Katie. Thank you so much."

And it felt like a release, to feel that embrace. As if Sarah had forgiven me for something. This wordless embrace, in front of everyone, felt like Sarah was giving me permission to breathe again. Permission to put it all behind me and carry on and let life begin again.

And I stood there, holding on to Sarah and I thought, *Okay then, okay. Let's start again.*

CHAPTER TWENTY-ONE

Louise

The season was turning, the beech trees in the park already russet and gold, and a smell of damp in the air, that wasn't too unpleasant. I felt the new autumn cold seep through my clothes and settle in my bones and gave a little shiver.

I preferred New York this way, when the chill in the air seemed to send all the people into cafés and shops. For a while, as everyone adjusted to the new season, Central Park emptied out a little and it felt like an oasis between the skyscrapers and the traffic and the constant background buzz. A quiet place you could escape to whenever you felt the need to pretend that the city wasn't surrounding you. Though it had also become a barrier, one that separated us, Sarah and I, the walk across the park from East 71st over to Sarah on the Upper West Side seemingly impassable.

I was glad Sarah had agreed to meet me. When I first suggested it, I wasn't sure if she would come, but the worry which filled me about James had forced me to pick up the phone and ask Sarah for help.

"I need your advice," I had told her. "It's James. There's something wrong and I don't know what to do."

Though when Sarah had suggested the park, I had hesitated. There were so many memories lying dormant there. I had felt it as I walked to the Boathouse café, the way the air held more than just an autumn fog, and I felt sure Sarah would feel it too. All those moments from our lives that seemed to have caught in the branches and which clung to the trees like leaves the wind couldn't shake.

When I got there, I heard Sarah call to me, "Over here," and looked up to see her sitting outside on the terrace, snug under an outdoor heater. She looked happier and more relaxed than I expected, as if the school memorial had comforted her in some way. Just knowing people loved Isa still, remembered her still, was something to cling to. Though how long such a comfort could last, was the question. But I had smiled and waved and hoped that, for today at least, we would allow ourselves a little respite from the grief. Hoped too that my reason for asking Sarah to meet me would not be the thing which ruptured this momentary happiness.

It had been Peter's suggestion. I would never have dared even imagine it.

"Why don't you talk to Sarah about it?"

"Sarah? Why Sarah?"

"I don't know. Just a feeling," he said. "She understands it, more than any of us. Grief. The things it can do to you."

"You think it's grief then?" I had asked him.

"Can it be anything else?"

And he was right, I realized. When I had told him about my conversation with James that night, his strange reminiscing about Isa, I had been unsure what it was I had been describing to him.

"He seemed so vacant, as if he wasn't there," I told Peter.

"He's only fifteen, Louise. You don't expect your friends to die when you're fifteen. Dying is for old folks, not your friends. He just needs to absorb it. Let the grief come. All we can do is wait. Let it happen and keep an eye on him."

When I admitted I didn't know how to do that he had suggested Sarah. And so, here I was, walking towards the Boathouse to meet her.

"I already ordered you a cappuccino," Sarah told me as I approached the table. "Is that okay? I figured in this cold you'd want a warm drink immediately."

"Thank you," I replied. Not so long ago, we would have leaned towards one another and kissed each other on both cheeks, but not today. And again, I felt a sudden sadness at this loss, as if circumstances had changed our lives not only in a big way but also in these small imperceptible ways.

"I'm glad they've put the heaters out already," I had commented as I settled down and shunted my chair a little closer to the table, so I could sit completely underneath the radiated heat.

For a while we sat and watched the comings and goings of the park. The kids on their way to the zoo, the dogs in their fancy quilted jackets, the runners braving the cold. The odd walker now and then sauntering along lost in thought. We talked about nothing in particular. Nothing personal. All of it a preparation of sorts, we knew, for the things we had really come there to talk about.

It was Sarah who eventually broke the lazy easiness of it all.

"So, is everything okay?" she asked.

And I wanted to let it pass, to just say, "yes, everything's fine," but I knew I had to swallow it down. Because things were not okay, and Peter was right, if there was anyone who could help, it was Sarah.

"I shouldn't be bothering you with it, Sarah," I began. "You've got enough to think about."

"I do," Sarah agreed. "But that doesn't mean I can't listen to a friend."

"Thank you," I said. "I've felt so nervous about it. Talking to you about my problems. It's just…"

"Who else would you turn to?"

"Yes, exactly."

"Is it Katie?" Sarah asked.

"That's just it," I explained. "I've been watching her so closely. I think I was expecting that she would be the one to snap at some point, that Isa's death would suddenly hit her, and she'd not know how to deal with it."

"She's pretty strong," Sarah said. "Sensible too. If she felt overwhelmed, she'd ask for help. She's not the sort of kid who's going to shut themselves away."

"No, you're right. It's just, well, sometimes I feel as if I'm waiting for all of us to implode."

"None of us can know what's going to happen, Louise. I've felt as if I was a different person every day. Something or other would happen and I'd react to it in a way I didn't recognize. It's as if too much of me, who I was before, before Isa, has disappeared… As if… I mean… Oh, it's so difficult to explain."

"Just give it time. That's what everyone keeps telling us, right?"

"Yes," Sarah said. And she smiled a little. "Sometimes I think if I ever hear someone tell me that again, I'll scream."

"But it's true though, isn't it? Day by day. Step by step."

"I know it is. It's just a day can feel so long sometimes, so impossible to navigate."

"No way back to shore, eh?"

"No, there's no way back."

The waitress came and asked if we wanted more coffees and I had nodded, relieved that the break in the conversation gave me time to compose myself. I could feel the burden of what Sarah had just said settle on my shoulders and I needed to take a breath and decide what to do. Talk to her about James or leave it be, focus on Sarah after all, and what, if anything, I could do to help her.

When the waitress returned with the drinks, Sarah took a sip then spoke. She knew me so well, knew that I would never start the conversation, that it was up to her.

"So, if it's not Katie…" she began.

"Then it's James," I said.

"It's a lot to deal with, when you're still so young."

"It is," I replied. "And I don't know why I didn't spot it. Why I thought it was Katie I needed to keep an eye on."

"Hey," Sarah said. "Don't beat yourself up too much about that. The girls were so close."

"It's not that she's not upset about it," I said. "She is. I can tell. Small things, you know? Less chatty, more withdrawn, no appetite. But she's coping, despite it all. Somehow, she's coping. And I should be grateful for that, I suppose. I mean, I am grateful for it."

"It takes so many forms, Louise."

"Yes, it does."

"And James?"

"That's the strange thing. All the things I worried about with Katie. The way I imagined she would react. It's James who's coming undone."

"But it's manageable?"

"Manageable? I don't know."

"All those years, growing up together. I've been thinking about that a lot recently. Isa had no siblings, and God knows, I wish she had, but Katie and James, they were as close as anyone could get to being Isa's brother and sister. A friendship like that, all those years, it's almost the same, in some ways. And it's bound to take its toll on them, losing Isa this way."

And I knew what she was withholding. Even as I agreed with her and nodded my head and held her hand and said, "Yes, I know. They lost more than just a friend, Sarah. Isa was always more than a friend, for both of them. For all of us."

Even as I said it, I could see them again, James and Isa, hanging out together over the summer. They had seemed closer than ever. Though at the time, I had thought nothing of it. Katie and Isa were obviously having one of their "moments," and I knew it was probably about Luka, and had chalked it up as just another silly teenage drama that would pass eventually. James had always been the mediator when it got this way between them. The one who always seemed to find a way to clear the air and get everyone smiling again and back on speaking terms.

But looking back, I thought I spotted something sometimes. Little flashes which had stuck in my memory at some subconscious level, as if my mind had been alert to things even as I tried to push it all away and simply enjoy the sea and the sun, and the freedom summer brought.

The smiles that passed between them, the laughter. The way they lounged around together on the porch, both of them squeezed into the same hammock and swiping through whatever it was on the internet that was amusing them, their heads together, limbs brushing against one another.

Yes, Isa was as close as a sister. But even at the time, when I looked at them together like that, I felt awkward. I thought that it should be Katie there, swinging in the hammock with her friend. I wondered why it was that Katie wasn't there. Why the tiff with Isa, or whatever it was that was happening between them, hadn't blown over by then, with the last days of fun still ahead of them.

But I didn't give my unease full rein and maybe I should have. Maybe I still should, because it was an explanation of sorts, a clearer reason as to why James seemed to be filling more and more with despair as the weeks passed and the full realization that Isa really was gone sank in.

Their closeness had that feel to it, I thought now. That sense that, given time, it would have developed into something more. Something illicit, was what I thought. Because it was, wasn't it? There was an inappropriateness to it—James and Isa as something more than good friends, the thought of that still made me shudder. It still made me flinch.

"If you want me to, I can talk to him?" Sarah said. "See if I can help him through it?"

I had almost not heard her. "Help," the only word that filtered through. My reply coming before I had time to think. "Would you? I think that would be good. I think he'd like that."

Then my instinct taking over at last, as if I sensed the danger there without fully understanding what it was. "Let me talk to him first though," I explained. "He needs to be ready."

"That's okay," Sarah said. "Whenever he's ready, I'll be here for him."

CHAPTER TWENTY-TWO

Katie

Isa Egberts was good at keeping secrets. Far better than I was. And there were times I admired her for it, the way she could carry on as if nothing was wrong. Always so relaxed about things, so sure of herself and of everything she did.

Maybe that was the way you needed to be, if you were going to be a successful liar. It was what Isa had become in my eyes, towards the end. What was the difference between secrets and deceit? Was there one? I had started to think there was none. You fooled someone, and in a way, you were lying to them. The things you didn't tell them, the omissions, they counted in the end, because their impact was the same. Someone always got hurt.

It was something Isa found funny.

"Why do you always overthink things, Katie?" she said. "And always, so black and white."

"What? Isa, what the hell does that even mean?"

"I mean, sometimes it's better to keep things to yourself. Sometimes that's how you protect people. What they don't know won't harm them. It's a cliché, but it's true."

"Yeah, well, that's your opinion."

"Listen, I know this thing with me and Alex freaks you out…"

"No, it doesn't."

"No? Really? Come on, Katie. Be honest with me at least."

"I am. It doesn't 'freak me out.' It's more, I don't want you to get hurt is all. I don't want him to hurt you."

"Why would he do that?"

"I don't know. Just a feeling."

"Because he's older than me?"

"Well, yeah, that's part of it, I suppose."

"Why? What's his age got to do with anything? You think someone our age would be more reliable? You think they couldn't hurt me? Look at what Jacob did to Lauren. You think that wasn't a shitty thing to do?"

"Yeah, I do. It was. But this is different."

"Why?"

"I don't know. I don't know."

I had never been able to answer that question in the end. Why was it different with Alex? Telling Isa, it "just was," was never going to work and I wished I could have explained it, wished I could have had an answer, something better than a gut instinct.

Though if I had had a good answer, if I had been able to explain it, would it have mattered? Isa always went her own way in the end. There was never any telling her. She was always too headstrong for her own good.

I knew how that sounded. Judgmental, a little prissy even. "Meddlesome," was how Isa sometimes described me.

"Quit worrying and interfering and let people get on with their lives, Katie. You need to chill out more, seriously, just give me a break."

Easier said than done though. Of all the stupid things Isa had gotten herself mixed up in, I knew Alex was the worst. And I couldn't be the only one who had misgivings about the age difference. Surely Alex's friends had said something about it?

But when I had asked her what they thought, the answer was shocking and revealing.

"I mean they must ask him how old you are, or look at you that way, as if they're trying to guess your age." I'd said.

"I haven't met his friends yet," Isa had told me.

"What? None of them?"

They'd been seeing one another for two months by then. Long enough for Alex to have introduced her.

Isa had just shrugged it off, as if it wasn't important.

"I guess I'm his little secret."

"His dirty little secret," I had wanted to add. But I had held my tongue. A snide remark was never the way to get Isa to listen. And there was no point in making her mad.

"But all those places he takes you. The cafés, the clubs. His friends must be there."

"New York is a big city, Katie." Isa had smiled. "Big enough to hide away in if you know the right places."

And I had wanted to scream at her, because the smug, knowing little smile was almost too much for me. The way Isa cocked her head as she said it, letting me know that she had raced ahead in life and left me standing there, just a kid still, just a girl who knew nothing and who worried too much. Katie Lindeman, so prim and meddlesome and annoying.

But it had made me so anxious. Alex was ashamed of Isa, that was the only explanation, surely? He was ashamed of what he was doing. Because he knew it was wrong.

And that was all I had needed to know. He was persuadable. And to hell with it. I was the one who was going to persuade him.

*

I had pretended to be in Williamsburg and just passing by.

"Hey," I'd called out as I opened the door, the little shop bell tinkling overhead as if this was some rarefied and pristine world I was entering. Alex's hipster credentials were certainly impeccable.

When Alex saw me, he was surprised.

"Katie, what brings you here?"

"I was looking for Isa, actually. Wondering if she fancied coming with me on a shopping spree."

"Oh, right, well, she's not here. Why don't you just give her a call?"

"I did, and she didn't pick up, so I figured, well, you know, that she must be with you. She never picks up when she's with you."

And the weird thing was, this made him blush as if I had caught him in the act or something.

"Sorry," I said. "I wasn't trying to embarrass you or anything."

A straightening of the shoulders then, when I mentioned it. He didn't like being caught off guard, I saw. Didn't like the awkwardness I'd caused.

"That's okay," he said, and he'd made sure to hold my gaze as he said it. Hold it long enough that I had to turn away and look down at my shoes, because stares like that always made me cringe, always tied a knot of panic in my gut.

"Listen, seeing as you've taken the trouble to come all the way across town, why don't I make us some coffee and we can have a little chat?"

He hadn't waited for an answer. Just walked over to the shop door and turned the sign to closed, then flicked the lock to shut the door.

"No, it's okay," I'd said. "I need to get going. Shopping spree, remember?"

"Just a quiet word, Katie. I think I need to explain a few things. About me and Isa."

And I could feel my hands getting clammy, feel the heat rising in my face and neck. The idea that I was locked in there with Alex. That no one knew I was there even. How stupid could I be?

He noticed it, of course, the slight panic that had come over me and he walked up to me, and put his hand on my elbow, walking me over to a little table in the corner where the espresso machine sat.

"Cappuccino okay?" he asked me.

And for some reason my head cleared then.

"I'd prefer an espresso if that's okay," I said. My sudden assertiveness taking him aback and giving me a second or two to compose myself.

Because when I looked at the situation, I realized it was what I had come for. I was here to talk to him. Looking for Isa was just a ruse. And if it had happened a little more abruptly than I had imagined it would, well, so much the better.

So, I took off my coat and draped it over the chair, took my seat and crossed my legs. Acted just like Isa. Self-assured and not in the mood for any bullshit.

And if he noticed it then he pretended not to. Just fiddled with the machine and set it to hissing and dripping while I watched him and waited.

When he placed the tiny cup of coffee in front of me and took the seat opposite, I was ready.

"Look," he began. "I know you feel awkward about me and Isa, and, honestly, I understand. She's your friend after all and you just want to look out for her."

"I do," I replied.

"Right. And that's cool. Honestly, it's great and I'm glad she has a friend looking out for her."

"Well, I think I need to look out for her. I really wish I didn't have to though."

"I'm not going to hurt her, Katie, if that's what you think."

"So, she told you that then? That I think you're going to hurt her."

And he didn't know what to say. If he should reveal the fact that Isa had spoken to him about our conversations, about my opinion that Alex should find someone his own age.

"We talk," was all he said. "The point is, Isa can decide things for herself. She's more than capable of figuring out what she wants to do, and who she wants to do it with, and I think you should respect that."

Respect. It made me blanche to hear him say that. As if he had a right to the word, as if he understood what it meant, and lived by it. Respect. *Jesus*, I wanted to say to him. *What the hell do you know about respect?* But I kept my cool. Swallowed it down. Took a second to think before opening my mouth. The espresso sharpening my senses and giving a nice clear edge to my thoughts.

"Is that why you've never introduced her to your friends then? Is that why you keep her a secret? I mean, would you go and meet her parents, if she invited you over to her house for dinner?"

He laughed at that, but I spotted it, the tiny nervous trill. He wasn't as calm as he was trying to make out.

"There's a time and place for things like that," he eventually replied. "After all, people aren't so understanding about things like this, are they, Katie?"

So smug, I thought. *How can anyone be so smug?*

And again, I bit my tongue. Kept my thoughts to myself.

"You know," I said. "If you'd just started seeing Isa, then maybe I could have agreed with you on that point. But after two months? Seriously, what's holding you back, Alex?"

"You think I'm ashamed, that's it, isn't it? You think I'm ashamed of her?"

"No, I think you're ashamed of yourself."

"And I should be, right?"

"You don't think it's a bit leachy then? A thirty-five-year-old guy with a seventeen-year-old girl?"

"Whoa!" he said. "Isa told me you were sanctimonious, but I never realized how much."

The sting was far greater than I anticipated. Sanctimonious. Is that what Isa thought about me? Is that what she told him?

"I don't believe you," I replied. "Isa would never say a thing like that about me."

"Oh no? I wouldn't be too sure about that if I were you."

He stood up then and gathered up the cups and nodded to someone who was standing outside the door and wondering why they couldn't get in.

"Just a minute," he called out to them.

Then he stood over me, leaned across the table, his face close to mine so I couldn't look away.

"Listen," he said. "I don't know what your problem is, Katie. And to be honest I don't really care what fucking issues you have or what's going on in that fucked up, *sanctimonious* head of yours. It's not my problem and it's not Isa's problem either. But I swear to God, you better butt out and learn to mind your own business. Is that clear? Otherwise, you might learn a few things you really are better off not knowing. Okay?"

And I nodded because the way he clenched his jaw, the way his words seemed to contain a seething sort of energy, it scared me. I could feel his anger. And all I wanted to do was get out of there.

I stood up and fumbled with my coat, heard the door click and the little bell tinkle, the customer greeting Alex with a bright hello.

"You sure are shut a lot these days. Business that good?"

And Alex had laughed and said, "Never better, never better."

When I squeezed past him and walked through the door, I felt his hand on my shoulder.

"See you around, Katie," he said.

But I didn't answer. I just walked out onto the street and headed away, my head spinning, my feet directionless. Away, was all I could think. Just get me away from him.

It was only when I reached the East River that I realized how far I had walked. How far my anger had taken me. Halfway across town without even noticing.

At the Brooklyn Bridge I stood for a while trying to catch my breath, trying to calm down. Matching my breath to the beat of the riverboats as they chugged by.

And as my breath slowed, an idea emerged. A way to end it. That smug son of a bitch. I wasn't finished with him. I'd show him what a real friend was like. Isa too.

"Sanctimonious? Right, okay then. If that's what you think, Isa, then so be it."

*

It was a gamble, I knew that, but I had to do it. So, I waited outside Willem's office one Monday evening and when I saw him appear, I walked up to him and said, "Hey Mr. Egberts. Can I talk to you for a minute?"

"Hey, Katie!" he said, surprised at first to see me standing there, then worried. "Is everything okay?"

"Yeah, yeah, everything's fine. No emergency or anything like that. I just wanted to talk to you about something was all."

"Okay, sure. You need a ride home? We could talk in the car?"

"How about a walk?" I said.

"Oh, sure, Battery Park is not too far."

"Fine," I said.

Battery Park, someplace I remembered from when I was a really small kid. My parents would take me and James there to get ice cream and watch the ferry shuttle tourists over to the Statue of Liberty. It felt funny, in a way, to be headed to a place like that, knowing I was going to tell Willem something about his daughter that was bound to shock and upset him.

When he spotted the ice cream stand by the park gates and offered to buy us both one, it was all I could do to stop from laughing.

But we'd walked in the sun and eaten our ice creams and chatted for a bit between creamy licks, about this and that, until Willem had wiped the specks of vanilla from the corners of his mouth and turned to me.

"So, what's all this about then, Katie? Is Isa in some kind of trouble?"

Parental instinct. I didn't know why it always shocked me to realize parents always had an inkling about things.

And there was no point in holding back, so I just decided to spill it all in one go. All about Alex and how Isa had met him, and the affair they'd been conducting the last couple of months and how worried I was, because there was something about Alex I didn't trust, the way he hid Isa away—"He does that, you know, he sneaks around town with her, ashamed to introduce her to his friends because he knows, of course, deep down he knows it's creepy what he's doing." I explained that this was why Isa was falling behind at school. She was out so late the nights with Alex that she'd been half asleep in the class some days, and hadn't he noticed that? That she was sneaking home at all hours of the night and was half dead all day?

And Willem had listened to my outpourings and shaken his head and stared at me as if he was trying to decide if I was telling him the truth. It wasn't an Isa he recognized. It wasn't the daughter he knew.

"I would never have told you about this if I wasn't worried about Isa," I explained, finally.

"No, it's the right thing to do, Katie. And I'm glad you did. Sarah and I had no idea."

And he'd looked away then, over my shoulder, as if he was embarrassed about it, that they'd been so lax, that they'd not thought to question Isa when she rolled through the door late at night and headed straight to her room without so much as a hello, never mind an explanation.

Because he had noticed it, I was sure he had. But he'd probably put it down to typical teenage behavior. Just Isa testing her boundaries. Still, I thought, he should have paid more attention, asked Isa now and then where she was going and who she was with, given her a time when she had to be home. Because Isa wasn't good at having too much freedom. She needed boundaries and they should have realized that.

But until then, Willem had apparently assumed Isa could handle it, that she'd be responsible and trustworthy. That she knew when to walk away and stay out of trouble.

But a thirty-five-year-old guy, that was trouble, even Willem understood that. And I could see him turn pale and swallow down his unease as I spoke to him. And I was relieved he felt the same queasiness that overcame me when I thought of Isa with Alex. It was sickening that a guy that age would even consider such a thing.

Yes. It was a vindication, I thought. I had been right to tell him about it, to let him know that Isa was out of her depth and needed help.

A week later Isa had called me, gasping with anger and tears.

"Alex doesn't want to see me again. Fuck, Katie. He says he doesn't want to see me."

And I had feigned sympathy and listened to Isa's whiny woe-is-me tirade and thought, *Good, thank God that's over.*

I should have realized that, with Isa, nothing was ever over until Isa decided it was.

*

When she turned up at my house one evening and threw herself down in the bed, she was shaking with rage and disbelief.

"I can't believe those two were ever allowed to be parents. I swear, Katie, they're hopeless."

"Why? What have they done?"

"My dad, he only went around to Alex and told him to stop seeing me. Can you fucking believe that? I mean, how the hell did he find out?"

"Shit," was all I said, "Oh, shit."

"The son of a bitch. How could he do that to me?"

"Well, maybe he was just worried."

But Isa wasn't listening. She wasn't there to listen. She was there to rant and rave.

"Stupid thing is he never figured two can play at that game."

"Huh?" I had asked. "What do you mean?"

"I told her," she explained.

"Told who?"

"My mom. I told her about Dad and that idiot girlfriend of his, Jessica."

"What? Why? Isa, for fuck's sake. How can you be so stupid, so cruel?"

"Cruel? Damn it, Katie, it wasn't me sneaking around and lying."

It had stunned me to hear Isa say that. The way she brushed aside the fact that she had also lied to her mother for months. She had known all about her father's affair for a long time, after all.

She had spotted him one day by accident downtown. He was with some woman she didn't know, and she had been about to walk up to them and say hello when she saw the woman kiss her father. And she had watched as he returned it.

But instead of demanding an explanation, she had decided to keep his secret. Worse, she had even turned it to her advantage as only Isa could. Her price for keeping quiet a shower of gifts and trinkets. A rose gold iPhone, a Marc Jacobs bag, a pair of gold hoop earrings.

She had taken it all and never even thought about suggesting to her father that maybe it was better if he told Sarah what was going on, if he examined his marriage and came to a decision. Jessica or Sarah, which one was it to be?

"You could have told her straight away if you wanted to. Or told your dad to quit what he was doing. But you didn't, Isa. You just took all the stuff and kept quiet. That's a lie too, Isa. You know it is. You must know it is."

"What? Oh, seriously, fuck this. I came here to get some help, not a lecture. Why'd you always have to be so sure of yourself about stuff like this, Katie? Always so high and mighty and better than everyone else. Thanks for being a friend when I needed you."

And that had been it, Isa had stormed out of the house, and the chaos had started. And I never got to hear the answer. Isa never told me.

Why did you tell her, Isa? Why did you do that to your own mother?

CHAPTER TWENTY-THREE

Louise

All that honeymoon business, the more I think about it, the angrier I get with myself for not getting to the heart of it. I should have probed a little deeper, asked Sarah why she thought this was the only way to save her marriage, because it was so out of character for her, so melodramatic. That should have been a warning signal, a sign that I needed to find out what was really going on. Because I knew there was more to it than just Willem's affair and I shouldn't have tiptoed around it. I should have asked her why she felt things were so bad she had to take off for a month and leave her daughter behind. I was stupid. So stupid.

But the shock of Willem's affair had wrong-footed me. I had always assumed Sarah's marriage was pretty solid. Something about their easy nature around one another, the way they gave each other space to do their own thing, I admired that, and wished I had the same sort of relationship with Peter. Sarah never seemed to have lost herself in family life and motherhood. She always pursued whatever she wanted, free apparently from the doubt I always felt when I did something for myself—that little voice that always questioned my right to do what I wanted. A stupid self-flagellation that ironically led to occasional bursts of irresponsibility when the good little wife routine became too much.

I'd told Sarah so often that I wished I could shake off that little voice.

"Well," Sarah had told me, "Willem's really supportive, that helps. I mean, he never complains if I make time for myself. I'd even say he encourages it."

And if it was a veiled criticism of Peter, then I chose to ignore it. Though I did wonder how much of Willem's generosity was ego driven. Those high-achieving, high-earning types had a way of using their wives as some perverse sort of status symbol, always wanting the world to see that they could afford to indulge a "high maintenance" woman.

I'm not going to lie though, when Sarah called me in tears to tell me what had happened, I couldn't stop myself from thinking: *So, he's not so perfect after all then.*

"Can you meet me somewhere?" Sarah had asked me.

"Of course, Sarah, what's wrong?"

"Not over the phone."

For some reason we had ended up on Madison Avenue. A spur of the moment suggestion on my part because it was close enough to home and I didn't feel like crossing town to meet her.

It was only when I arrived that I realized I had made a mistake. The place was too bright, too cheery, the space too small and intimate. A private, tear-stained conversation would be impossible. It was a place to come for a quick lunch on a shopping trip, not a discreet venue for a tête-à-tête. What was I thinking?

But the afternoon was early, lunchtime was nearly over, and the offices had still to empty out, so if we were lucky, we would be able to talk in peace, tucked away in the corner table I chose, away from the windows and the harsh unforgiving daylight.

When Sarah arrived and the waitress ushered her over, I could see from her red-rimmed eyes that I'd guessed right. Willem.

"Hey," I said, as Sarah took a seat opposite me and ordered a large glass of red wine for both of us, "everything okay?"

Sarah had blinked at me as if the question was too dumb to be worthy of a reply, then shook her head and took off her coat, loosened her scarf and thanked the waitress for the wine, when it came, before steadying herself with a long sip.

I thought she would build up to it slowly, have some rambled sort of story in place to explain what had happened. Not excusing him, more looking for an answer, a reason for it. But Sarah was not in the mood for explanations. She was in the mood for wine and venom and anger.

"She's younger than me, of course. Oh, and blond too, because why not go the whole hog, eh?"

I had reached for my own glass then, even though I didn't want the soothing effects of alcohol so early in the day. But it meant I didn't need to reply. I could just drink my wine and nod and let Sarah get it all out her system before saying anything.

"God," Sarah said. "You think you know someone, you think you can rely on them, depend on them. Stupid really, isn't it? I mean, why should I ever imagine I'd be saved all this, eh?"

"I guess... I..." I had stammered.

"Seriously, Louise, even the good guys, guys like Willem, they're no different from the rest of them. Given half the chance, they'll take it."

And I felt compelled to say something then, to come to Peter's defense even though I knew Sarah would sneer at me, call me naïve, challenge my certainty. But it felt disloyal somehow to not at least make an attempt to place Peter outside of Sarah's generalizations.

"That's not true, Sarah," I began. "Not all men..."

"No? You sure? You always know where Peter is then? I mean, because I thought I knew where Willem was all this time. Slogging away at his desk all hours of the day, working his butt off so he could get ahead, so we could have a good life. Not fucking some bimbo in a hotel room."

"Are you sure?"

"Yes."

"But how? Did you see him with her?"

"I didn't need to. He admitted it. When I asked him, when I confronted him with the evidence, he just admitted it. Honestly, just like that, as if it was a relief or something, as if he was happy he could finally tell me about it. God, what an asshole he is. And me too, for that matter. Idiot that I am. I'm an absolute idiot, Louise."

"I'm sorry, Sarah," was all I could think to say. "I thought you and Willem were good."

"Yeah, so did I. Shit, Louise, what am I going to do?"

"I don't know. I mean…"

"Oh, I'll try and make it work. I'm not stupid. I know what it would do to Isa if Willem and I were to split up. But how? How do you do that, Louise? Forgive, I mean?"

It seemed a strange thing to ask, I thought. As if I could possibly have an answer to a question like that. The answer only ever came when it happened to you, when you were forced, through circumstances to act. Nothing you could think of or imagine before then made sense. Only the shock of feeling it would reveal what you were prepared to do.

It was a reality I hoped I'd never have to confront. I had learned a thing or two over the years when it came to making a marriage work. Pick your battles. Figure out what to ignore, figure out what you can handle. Learn how to smile, even when you don't feel like it. Forgive and forget wherever necessary.

That was what I wanted to ask Sarah then. Why did you confront him about it? Why not just let it pass, and pretend you didn't know? If you say you'll do anything to stop Isa getting caught up in a marital rift, then why provoke it in the first place? It made no sense.

But it hadn't been the moment for such stark truths. This was simply lancing the boil, I knew that. Letting all the muck seep out. So, I let Sarah cry and drink and talk. Listened to the old familiar story. The late nights, the perfume, the furtive telephone calls. The whole clichéd tale. I'd found myself tuning it out after a while and letting the wine take hold as I watched the few customers that had started to come through the door.

After several hours, I had started to feel woozy from the wine and I could see Sarah was waning too.

"Maybe we should call it a day?" I'd suggested. And Sarah had looked around her then, as if she had forgotten where she was, stunned that the café was starting to fill up, and woozy too now from the wine and all the talk and the tears.

"Thanks for listening to me, Louise," she said. "I think I needed to get it off my chest more than I realized."

"Hey, that's what friends are for, eh?" I had smiled, wrapping my arms around her and squeezing her, hoping she hadn't caught the hint of relief there in my voice.

I was tired of listening to it all. Exhausted by the emotional outpouring. All I wanted was to get outside, get some air, clear my head. Get home.

We said goodbye and I had watched Sarah hail a cab and head home, then I walked in the direction of Central Park, happy to be on my own at last and moving in the fresh air. But after a few hundred meters, I'd needed to stop. It came over me suddenly, a rush of bile in my throat that I had to swallow down, and I'd needed to steady myself before I could continue. Sarah's emotional reaction had unnerved me and left me fighting to push away fears of my own. Things I never wished to confront. Because whether I wanted to admit it or not, Peter and I weren't immune to the same sort of marital troubles.

Okay, Louise, I thought. *Just calm down and walk it off.*

I carried on ahead on foot and reached East 60th Street without even noticing how far I'd come. When I saw the trees in Central Park I thought, *Why not?*

There was still enough daylight left to cut through the park on the way home. And the slight chill to the air would make a walk pleasant. So, I crossed 5th Avenue and headed into the park. The kids would have to fend for themselves. I texted Katie to let her know I was running late and there was a casserole in the fridge she could warm up for dinner.

In the park, under the trees, I could walk and get my head straight. But it was impossible. Something about Sarah's face, the despondency there, as if a part of her had given up, as if she had already decided her marriage was over. It had unsettled me more than I realized. I had sat there with Sarah in the wine bar and held it in. Nodded and consoled and soothed and smiled, as a friend was supposed to do. But inside something was brewing. An unease I had never acknowledged until then.

A sense that there was not really so much separating me from Sarah. For all my bravado, for all my insistence that it was better to turn a blind eye and allow things to pass, there was a part of me that feared it. A piece of me that worried that with every passing year, Peter and I would grow apart, that Peter would find out about my indiscretions, and would not take it well.

It took me a while before I started to get to grips with what it was that was niggling at me. Sarah and Willem. I'd assumed so much about them. Viewed their life as something close to perfect. Something steady and secure. Something unbreakable. But if it could happen to them… I shuddered and left the thought unfinished. Focused on my steps as I walked and forced myself to think about Sarah. What would she do now? Divorce? Would she dare go down that path?

My mind wandering and crowding out the very things I should have been paying attention to. Because I should have listened more closely in the café, rather than trying to tune Sarah out. If I had, then perhaps I'd have caught the inconsistencies in her story. The unexplained things.

Like, *How did you find out?*

I could have asked her that if I had listened more carefully. And an honest answer from Sarah might have changed everything. If I'd known the whole sordid business had been started by Isa, I would definitely have said no when she asked me if Isa could join us for the summer. I would have advised Sarah not to go rushing away on some fanciful honeymoon but to stay at home and sort things out properly. Not only with Willem, but also with her daughter.

And Sarah should have given me the chance. A true friend would have been honest. A true friend would never have put me in such a hopeless position.

CHAPTER TWENTY-FOUR

Katie

If I could, I would forget it all, just pretend it never happened—Alex, the summer, Isa's final days. But no matter how hard I tried to push it away, I couldn't stop that idea creeping up on me: Isa deserved it.

I knew it was wrong to think that, I knew it was awful and heartless and terrible, but a part of me believed it, a part of me insisted on it. Isa was always going to meet some messy fate and, sad as it was, I needed to accept that. Everything she did was taking her in that direction. The tragedy of her end was inevitable. That she should meet it so soon, while she was still so young, was heartbreaking. But sooner or later it was always going to happen. And maybe I was fooling myself, pretending there was nothing anyone could have done to stop it; maybe this was just my way of trying to make it easier to accept, a little lie I needed to tell myself in order to keep going. But I needed to keep going. We all did.

I needed to focus on moving on and keep my judgments to myself, because things were settling down at last, not back to normal exactly, but calmer at least. Well, save for James. He seemed to be plodding through the days as if Isa's death was a burden he alone had to bear. That was what he looked like too, hollow eyed, hunched over and grey skinned, as if he was carrying some invisible and unbearable load.

I just wanted things to turn around was all. I just wanted something good to happen again, something to distract us all from what had happened. Something to make us smile, make us laugh. A few carefree months to let us see that it was possible to carry on, that life hadn't stopped when Isa died.

Anything to push away the thoughts of those last summer days. I wondered if this was how people came to believe in ghosts, because it felt like that sometimes, as if the summer was haunting me. As if Isa had managed to push herself back, front and center, into our lives, just to make sure we were destined never to forget what happened to her.

Not that I could forget her. I had access to her on my phone any time I needed her, and I've clicked on that film so often now it's in danger of becoming an obsession. Some days I needed to stop myself.

Why go over it all again? Delete it and give yourself a break.

But I can't press the button. When the message comes up asking if I'm sure I want to delete the file, my finger always hovers over the screen and the doubt always creeps back in.

Because there is Isa, happy and carefree and alive. It's mesmerizing to watch her. As mesmerizing as it was when she was alive. It's not something I can erase. I need to see her for some reason. To have this little piece of her that isn't dead. I can watch it and pretend she's still with us. That's she's not dead at all. And it's something I hold on to when it all feels too much. I watch it and remember that Isa really was beautiful and amazing and funny and cruel and infuriating and vain. Isa, eternal Isa. Immortalized in pixels. She'd have liked that.

There was an irony to it, in a way, I thought. That this is what the film had come to mean for me: a way of holding onto the memory. Because that wasn't my intention when I made it.

I'm going to let you see who you really are, Isa Egberts, is what I thought when I decided to start filming.

It had started earlier that evening when we were getting ready to head out to the beach party.

I wasn't sure if I wanted to tag along. Not after that conversation with Luka, listening to him tell me about Isa and the cold-hearted way she had simply dismissed him, as if he was some plaything she had no use for now that Alex was back again. I couldn't believe Isa could be so cruel. Worse, that she didn't even seem to be aware of what she had done. It was as if she thought Luka was dispensable, that his feelings didn't matter.

And that thought was still gnawing at me later that evening, as we sat around the fire on the beach.

Why can't you see what you were doing? Why don't you take a good look at yourself, Isa Egberts?

And it was as if Isa had given me the perfect opportunity.

The last party of the summer, and there she was, determined to enjoy herself and have "one last blowout before school and all that crap starts back up again."

And if Alex wasn't there by her side, then she'd find someone else. I didn't know who he was. Not someone we'd seen over the summer. Just a boy down at the beach for a party. Cute in a rough sort of way.

I had seen Isa sit down beside him, had watched as the flirting began almost immediately. They passed a bottle of wine between them, danced around for a while to the music, then fell onto the sand, entwined and oblivious to everyone else.

And that's when I thought, *Okay then, Isa, let me show Alex who you really are*, pulling out my phone and filming as Isa lay on the sand with some guy she barely knew, not caring who saw her, not caring who was there. Just Isa in the moment, thinking only about herself. What felt good, what she wanted. All of it evidence. I would show it to Alex as soon as we got home. Let him see that Isa was out of control and unpredictable. And he would understand how dangerous that could be for him, and this time, he would ditch her for good.

The video was grainy, a little wobbly, the orange glow from the campfire flaring on the screen and at times obliterating everything, but anyone who watched it would be able to see what was going on. Two bodies in the sand, drawing closer and closer to one another, until they seem to realize where they are, a campfire with twenty or so people all around them. Too many people. Too many prying eyes. The guy whispers something in Isa's ear and she laughs and kisses him and says, "Yeah, come on, let's go."

And up they get, both of them a little unsteady on their feet, the wine hitting them, or perhaps it was just the urgency of the moment. The need to get out into the privacy of the dunes where they could be alone.

And I filmed them as they went, two shadows disappearing into the night, arm in arm and stumbling, Isa's shoulders shivering as she giggled. Then they were gone. And I panned back to the bonfire, scanned the people sitting there. James already tipsy and half asleep. He was looking in the direction Isa was headed, a small crease of confusion there on his forehead as he turned to Luka as if to say, *Hey, what's going on?* And Luka sitting there, rigid and stony-faced, swallowing down his anger and sadness.

"You know," he said to James, "I really don't give a fuck anymore."

And he pulled the bottle of wine from James' hand and glugged down a mouthful, then raised the bottle in Isa's direction and said, "Good riddance."

CHAPTER TWENTY-FIVE

Louise

It's astonishing how easily you can get used to unsettling and upsetting behavior, even when it's your own child who is acting strangely. Somehow, I became used to the muttering in the middle of the night. I would go downstairs and find James in the window seat, talking to himself, and whenever I asked him what he was doing he'd say: "Oh, just thinking out loud."

"What about?"

"Isa mostly."

But when I tried to dig a little deeper and have him tell me more, he'd clam shut, and wait for me to go back to bed. There was nothing I could say to pull him out of himself.

Some nights, I'd sit at the top of the stairs and try to listen, but even in the still of the night, his whispers were too low to make out, save for the odd word now and then.

How often had he said her name? I wondered. *How often had he apologized? Told her he was sorry.*

I wanted to scoop him up and tell him he had nothing to be sorry for. Sometimes life just threw these things at you for no apparent reason, and all you could do was take the blow and then slowly learn to pick yourself up. And if that sounded clichéd and trite, well, so be it. But it didn't make it any less true.

It was just one of those things, I thought. Grief. The first time you encounter it, you never know how it's going to affect you, how long it's going to take to get over it. But I hoped he would be over it soon. Once the shock had settled, I hoped he'd shrug himself awake and that our lives would begin again.

It was only when I came downstairs one night and saw the locket in his hands, that I realized his grief had taken on a form I didn't fully understand. This wasn't something he was going to simply shake off.

I'd caught a glint of it when I came down the stairs, after I'd been woken by him for the fifth night in a row. I'd had enough, I decided. We all needed a good night's sleep.

He hadn't heard me on the stairs; either that, or he was so deep in his own thoughts he didn't realize I was there beside him, watching as he turned the locket over in his fingers, rubbing the lock of Isa's hair between his thumb and forefinger while he gazed out of the window, muttering something, unintelligible at first, until I made out her name and understood he was talking to her. Talking to her as if she was sat there beside him. The silences, the pauses, I supposed must have been when he was listening to her reply to whatever he had said.

And I stood there, frozen to the spot, not daring to touch him for fear I would shock him. The way you are not supposed to wake a sleepwalker. He had that look about him, as if he wasn't really awake, wasn't really aware. If I pulled him back to reality too abruptly, he would have shattered.

"James," I whispered. "James… James."

It took a minute of whispering and repeating his name before he turned to face me, and I thought I saw his eyes focusing, then registering my presence.

"Oh," he said. "It's you."

"Yes. Who did you think it would be?"

And I saw it there, on his lips, Isa's name almost slipping out. I saw him lick his lips as if he was swallowing it down, realizing how it would look, if he was to say her name out loud like that, if he was to tell me it was Isa he had been talking to just then. This ghost of a girl sat beside him in the window seat.

"Is that Katie's locket?" I asked him. "The one Sarah gave her?"

And he looked at the locket, and at Isa's hair as it caught the light from the streetlamp outside, a gleam of gold that was horribly alive still. Then he snapped it shut and folded his fist around it.

"She gave it to both of us," he said.

"What are you doing with it, James? Sitting here in the dark, talking to Isa as if she was here. Alive still."

"How else am I supposed to talk to her then?" he asked. "Or should I just sit here and think quietly? If the dead can hear us at all, then they can hear our thoughts as clearly as our words, is that it? I'll remember that the next time then and be sure not to wake you."

"Oh, James, please…"

"What? Is it so strange that I want to talk to her?"

"She's dead, James. She's dead. She can't hear you."

He clutched the locket tight as I spoke, his knuckles whitening as if he was terrified to let it go.

"I know that," was all he said. "My God, do you think I don't know that? I miss her is all, but that doesn't make me crazy. It just means I care. Unlike anyone else around here, it seems."

"Oh, James, that's not true."

"Oh, just shut up. Just shut up, okay? Because it is true. None of you give a damn."

Then he got up and brushed past me and headed upstairs to his room, leaving me alone in the dark of the living room, shivering with the sense that I too had just spoken to a ghost.

*

Two nights later, I heard the door click shut and checked the clock. One thirty in the morning.

James, I thought.

When I got out of bed and looked out of the window, sure enough, there he was heading down the street. I thought about waking Peter to let him know I was going out after James, but why bother him when he slept so soundly.

Let him sleep, I thought. *He needs it. He's got another day of meetings ahead of him. There's more than enough on his plate.*

So, I pulled on my jeans and a sweater, tiptoed downstairs and headed out the door after James.

Up ahead I could see him heading towards 5th Avenue. Despite the time, there were a few people on the streets and it struck me that not one passerby stopped to ask if he was okay, or just put a hand on his shoulder and said, "Hey, are you okay?"

A young teen, alone at night, why did that not give them cause to stop? But he was just a part of the New York landscape, nothing unusual. And I needed to fight the urge not to rush over to him and bundle him home.

I was ready to walk over to him, reveal myself, when he turned and headed towards West 59th. His stride suddenly purposeful. It took me a while to understand where he was headed. The park was too dark to cut through at night, so he was heading around it. But it was clear to me now where he was headed: Sarah and Willem's.

Okay, I thought. *Then keep your distance and follow him, that's all you can do.*

The darkness created the sort of atmosphere you'd find in a movie in that moment when the suspense increased, and some sinister chain of events was set in motion. And again, I had to control a sudden urge to call out to James and tell him to turn around and come home.

In the silence, I worried he would hear my footsteps and turn around or, worse, make a run for it. But he had no idea I was here. He just kept shuffling along, the glow from a cigarette flaring now and then as he puffed at it.

But I was glad of the slow pace. It gave me time to think about what James was doing.

Why head to Isa's? I wondered. *Why go there, of all places, and why in the middle of the night?*

I hung back a little when he arrived at Sarah's house, taking cover behind one of the trees that lined the street. From there I had a pretty good view of him, illuminated by the glow of the streetlights.

He was standing on the sidewalk, staring at Isa's house, looking up at the window of her bedroom, as if he believed that if he stared at it long enough some epiphany would occur. Some explanation at last as to why Isa had to die. As to why fate could work in such a terrible way. He had that look about him, I thought. Like a pilgrim at a shrine staring hopelessly at the devotional candles and praying for a miracle.

If you didn't know better, if you didn't know Isa was dead, you would almost expect to see a face there any minute, waving behind the glass, opening the window a bit and whispering, "I'll be down in a minute." He had that look of expectation about him. Like he was waiting for her. Waiting for the dead. Or an answer to something.

Maybe he thinks if he stares long enough, she'll come back. All he has to do is stand there and will it to happen.

And it immediately gave me the shivers, because a part of it felt horribly true.

I watched him, for a minute or two, as he stood there looking up at Isa's bedroom window. Then, not finding what he was looking for, he turned around and sat down on the curbside, with his back to the house, his head drooping almost as if he was in prayer.

Seeing him sitting there like that, so sad and despondent and alone, was too much, and I moved out from my hiding place and walked across the road towards him.

"James," I said, as I approached him, and he looked up and didn't seem surprised to see me.

"Hey," he mumbled. "I was wondering when you were going to show your face."

"What are you doing, James?" I asked him.

"Just sitting," he replied. As if being out there in the middle of the night was nothing out of the ordinary.

"Just sitting?"

"Yeah. Why, is that so weird?"

"James, it's almost two thirty in the morning and you're sitting out here in the cold, staring at Isa's house. Don't you think that's weird then?"

I must have raised my voice without realizing it. The sound, in the empty night, ricocheting across the brickwork, because a door opened, and light flooded the street. I had woken someone up. And in the bright light of the open doorway it took me a moment to realize who was standing there. Whose door it was. Sarah standing in the doorway looking at us, not sure if what she was seeing was real.

"James?" she said. "Louise?"

I thought about getting up and walking over to her, apologizing for the disturbance, but I was nervous James would take off and I would lose my chance to get some sense out of him. So, I took his arm and coaxed him up and said to Sarah, "It's okay, Sarah. I'm taking him home."

And Sarah nodded and looked like she was trying to think of something to say but couldn't get the words out, so she just stood there in the doorway, shrouded in a halo of yellow light as I led James away and back down the street towards home.

"What are you doing out here actually?" James asked me as if he was only then aware of my presence.

"I heard you leave so I followed you."

"Oh, you didn't need to do that. Why did you do that?"

"Why? Don't you think I should worry that you're out wandering the streets late at night, sitting outside Isa's house for no apparent reason? Don't you think I should follow you and make sure you are all right? I'm your mother, for God's sake."

"I *am* all right. You can quit worrying."

"No, James, I can't, and I won't. I mean, look at you, you look like a zombie."

"Yeah? Maybe I am. It feels that way sometimes. All hazy and stuff. And then there it is again," he said.

"Sorry? There's what?"

"I dunno. A flash of something."

I had to take a second to absorb such a stray, out-of-the-blue statement, because it sounded meaningless at first, as if he had gone off on some strange tangent again, the meaning of which made sense only to him.

"What do you mean?" I asked him.

"That night, when Isa died. I've forgotten most of it. It's just a blur. A weird orange blur and everything is all mixed up in my head—what there is of it, that is."

"Apparently no one remembers much of that night," I said. "Save for the drinking and the smoking."

"I know," he said. "And if it was just that I'd let it pass."

"You really miss Isa, don't you?"

"Yeah," he muttered. "I do. Sometimes it feels like I'm the only one who does though."

"Oh, James. That's not true. We're all trying to come to terms with what happened."

He slumped against me then and let me put my arm around him as we walked home, as if the exhaustion had suddenly caught up with him.

"What did you mean just then though, James? When you said you got these flashes?"

"I guess I just imagine things, is all," he said.

"Like what?"

"I don't know. That things happened differently."

"We all wish that, James."

"I know but it's not a wish. It's more like I can rewind that night and make it all end differently."

"Don't do that to yourself, James. Nothing can be changed, you know that."

"I know, but it's weird though, how real it can feel. It's as if, sometimes, that night is really clear to me. It's as if the haze lifts, and the blurriness disappears, and I can see it all happening. And I have the power to stop it all, but, for some reason, I don't. I just let it all happen. Over and over again."

I knew the dangers of thoughts like that. The ever-decreasing circle of chaos that came from going over events and trying to imagine something different. Believing you could still change the outcome. I hadn't realized he had fallen so far into this delusion and it made me sick to think that I had failed to notice it. I felt negligent again. As if events were still conspiring against me and ensuring everything got broken or bent out of shape.

So, hear him out, I thought. *See how far he's gone.*

"What is it you see then, James?"

"We're on the beach together, me and Isa. In the water. Just floating, you know? And it's nice because the water is warm still and the sky is clear, and you can hear people on the beach singing and laughing. And we just float, and there are stars, and it's nice, it's really nice."

He paused as if he was struck by the image again. As if it was so beautiful, he needed to step back again for a moment and enjoy it, take it in. I could feel him relax, the tension release in his shoulders as he spoke, as if just talking about this dream provided physical comfort.

"And Isa, I can see her in the water," he continued. "She's lying back and floating, her eyes closed, arms at her side, gently bobbing, hardly moving at all. And she's like a mermaid. What I mean is, she looks like that, you know? Her hair fanned out behind her in the water. The moon or something shining on it, so it looks like real gold, I swear. And that's all we do. We float there for a while and then I hear her splash a little, and cough and when I look over, I can see she's trying to stand up. But we're drunk. The swimming, the floating, it turns your legs to jelly. So, I turn on my belly and swim over to her. Hold her arm and help her to her feet. The water's shallow. We're not so far out. You can stand up if you want to and if a wave catches you and you topple, it's no big deal. And we do stumble a little as we get out the water. We stumble and laugh then feel the beach underfoot and we gather up our towels and head back to the bonfire to get some heat. And the night passes, the next day comes and there we all are, together still, no one harmed. All of us just sleepy and wanting to go home. And that's how it ends. That's what we do. The sun comes up and we go home. Yeah, that's how it ends, all of us together, walking home."

His voice petered out at the end, as if he knew it was just a dream, just wishful thinking.

"Oh, James," I said. And I squeezed him tight. "I wish it had happened that way. I really do."

"Yeah, me too. But when I think about it, when I try to remember it, when it's not a dream or wishful thinking, there's nothing there. I keep trying to remember but all there is, is that orange blur again."

"An orange blur?"

"Yeah, it's the campfire, I think. And sometimes, sometimes there's something else."

"What?"

"A question. Something I wanted to ask her. Something important. But she keeps disappearing, so I never get to ask her…"

"Ask her what, James?"

"About Luka."

"Luka?"

"Yeah. Why she did that to Katie."

"Did what?"

"You know? Why she went off with him when she knew Katie liked him. I never thought she could do a thing like that. Did you?"

"No," I said. "No, I didn't."

And we had walked the rest of the way home in silence, leaving the question unanswered. It wasn't something I felt able to explain to him. I wasn't sure I really understood it myself, all I knew was that I didn't want to think about the awful ways friends can betray one another.

*

The next day Sarah called, her voice trembling, unsure if her call was welcome.

"Is everything okay?" she asked. "With James, I mean. When I saw you both outside the other night, well…"

"No, I don't think he's okay, Sarah. I really don't," I said.

"What was he doing here last night?"

And there was no point trying to pretend that his nocturnal visit was nothing to worry about. That it was something I could cope with and sort out.

So just tell her, I thought. *Just tell her the truth. Ask for help.*

"He was looking for Isa," I replied. And I heard the gasp at the other end of the line, and thought about apologizing, but I couldn't find the words. Because how do you apologize for such a strange thing? For someone who is looking for a ghost.

"I'm not sure I understand," was all Sarah could say.

"He misses her, is all," I told her. "And I don't think he knows how to cope with it. How to grieve for her. None of us do." And it was true. I didn't know how to do anything anymore. How to grieve, how to help my son, not even how to be angry with Sarah for creating this mess in the first place.

But when Sarah offered to talk to him, I didn't have the energy to say no. *Why not let someone else talk to him?* I thought. See if they can make any sense of it all.

"Would you?" I replied.

"If you think it might help," Sarah said. "And if you want me to, that is. I know we have things to talk about. Isa and all those things I never told you about."

"Perhaps that's a conversation for another day, eh?"

"Yes, I guess it is. So, shall I try and talk to him? I don't know if I can help, but you know…"

"It's worth a try?"

"Yes, I think it is."

A decision made, while I struggled to get a grip on my thoughts. Sarah would talk to him and see what she could do.

And it's the way fate unfolds. I understand that now. It happens in those moments when your guard is down, when you're not capable of thinking things through, of pausing for breath just long enough to sense the danger. You just nod and smile and say, "Yes, yes," then walk away with a feeling that something has just happened. Something wrong. Something you should set about undoing, and quickly. Before it's too late.

When Sarah arrived, James was still asleep. The nocturnal excursion had taken its toll again. Another day at home. Another day of missing school and falling behind. Falling into something. Some despair he couldn't pull himself out of.

"Is James not going to school again?" Peter had asked me in the morning.

"Not today, no."

And he had been about to ask me why, but I stopped him.

"I'll tell you when you get home, okay?"

"Listen, I can take the day off if you need me?"

"No, it's okay, Peter. Go to work. Sarah is coming over later for a talk."

"You spoke to Sarah?"

"She called, after last night. Seeing James there outside her house, it spooked her a little."

"Are you sure you're up for this?"

"I asked her to talk to James."

"To James? Why? How can she possible help him?"

"I don't know. I just think maybe that was why James was over there at her house. Maybe he needs to talk to her."

"Are you sure about this?"

"Listen, trust me, it's all okay. Go to work and I'll tell you about it later."

But facing Sarah in the living room, I wished I had thought it through. Just taken a moment to figure out what it was I wanted Sarah to talk to James about. I needed more time to figure out if it really was such a good idea after all. Because seeing Sarah sitting there, waiting for James to get up, it suddenly seemed foolish.

But it was too late to worry about the reasons. Sarah was there now, so I went upstairs and roused James and explained that Sarah was there to see him.

It had taken him a couple of minutes before the name filtered through and he could make sense of it.

"Sarah? What, Isa's Sarah?"

"She just wants to talk to you about last night is all, James."

And he had turned over in his bed then and pulled the duvet over his head.

"Tell her to forget it," he said. "I didn't mean anything by it and I'm sorry if I freaked her out."

And I had peeled back the duvet and stroked his head and said, "No, James. I think you should talk to her. I think it might do you some good."

"It won't," he protested. "Nothing will."

The sound of Sarah's voice took us both by surprise.

"Why don't we give it a try?" Sarah said. "Hey? Let's try at least.'

When Sarah appeared downstairs half an hour later, she seemed paler, as if the conversation with James had weakened her in some way.

"Are you okay?" I asked her.

She nodded and took a seat on the sofa next to me, then leaned back into the cushions as if she needed all the weight to be taken off her.

"He's not taking it well at all, is he?" she began.

"No," I replied. "But I don't know what to tell him. I can't make it better. Whatever I say is no good."

"He just wants Isa back is all," Sarah told me.

"Is that what he told you?"

"More or less," she replied.

"Oh God, if I could work miracles, I would do it."

"You and me both," Sarah agreed. And she turned to face me, her lips pursed the way she always got when she was unsure if she should say what was on her mind.

"Just tell me, Sarah," I said.

"I think he needs the kind of help we can't give him."

"A doctor, you mean?"

"Maybe."

And I could see it there, the apprehension again.

"I think there's more worrying him than we realize," Sarah said. And she paused again, trying to figure out the best way to put it.

"What did he tell you Sarah? Whatever it is, I can handle it."

"Can you?"

"He's my son, I need to know what's worrying him."

"He thinks it's his fault."

"Well, we could all have done more, I think we've all come to realize and accept that these past months, don't you?"

"No, you don't understand. He thinks he left Isa in the water that night. That he was there with her in the sea."

"But that's impossible. Katie was with him that night. Everyone saw them at the bonfire. Isa went off and that was the last anyone saw of her."

"I know. And I told him that. But he just kept repeating it. He just kept insisting it was true. He says he remembers seeing her floating in the water. And I didn't know what to say to him, Louise. How do I respond to that? I mean, how can he tell me a thing like that and not realize how upset it's going to make me?"

"Oh, Sarah, please, don't. He doesn't know what he's saying anymore. He's exhausted and confused and that night, they had so much to drink, and God knows what else they took and—"

"He really believes it though, Louise. He just kept saying the same thing. That he saw her, in the water, and I tried to explain he was probably mixing things up. Some other night perhaps. Like you say, they'd all had too much to drink and no one's memory of that night was reliable. But he got so mad when I suggested it, just kept repeating that he knew what he saw. That he was with Isa in the water, and he could have saved her."

"He took something that night, he admitted as much. Some pill. He didn't know left from right, so why change his story now, why would he say he remembers something now?"

"I don't know, but he swears it wasn't a hallucination. Isa was in the water and he was there with her."

And a voice on the stairs then. James.

"Like a mermaid," he said. "She looked like a mermaid."

And Sarah had looked at me, unsure if what she had heard was correct.

"A mermaid?" Sarah asked him.

And I had needed to fight back the tears, had found myself clutching the arm of the sofa, because I felt it then, the light-headedness as if I were about to fall. It pushed me deeper into the chair, pinning me down.

Then Sarah stood up and turned to me.

"I tried," was all she said. "But none of it makes sense. And I can't hear him say that, Louise. I can't have him stand there and tell me that he was there. That there was a chance he could have helped Isa, no matter how delusional it is. I've got my own battles to fight when it comes to imagining how things could have turned out differently that night, if only this had happened or that had happened. And I can't do any of this. I'm sorry."

"I'm sorry, Sarah... I..."

"No, it's okay. But he needs help, Louise."

"Yes," I nodded. "You're right. You're right."

And Sarah had kissed me on the cheek and whispered in my ear to be sure James could not hear her, "He believes what he saw, Louise. He believes it."

And something in her voice made me think Sarah believed him.

Then she squeezed my arm and walked away and left me there standing in the living room looking towards the stairs where James stood looking down at me.

"James..." I began.

"It's true," he said. "Every word of it. I saw her. I remember. And don't tell me I didn't. Don't tell me I'm imagining it."

"A mermaid? James, please, come on..."

"Yes, that's what she looked like. Just like a mermaid."

"But James, Katie..."

"Katie?"

"Yes, she was with you that night. All night. You weren't anywhere near the water, James."

"It's strange," he said. "It never occurs to you, does it?"

"What?"

"That she could be lying."

"Oh James, come on, that's—"

"Ridiculous? Yeah, well, believe what you like. But it's one possibility and maybe you need to start considering it."

And he turned and headed back up the stairs. The click of his door like the sound of a key turning in the lock. Decisive and clear. *Leave me alone.*

I sat back down in the sofa and let my head fall back on the cushions, the weight of it all suddenly upon me now, just as it had been upon Sarah moments ago, a heaviness brought on by one simple question.

He can't believe Katie would lie about any of this, surely? His own sister?

And I would have looked for answers, if I'd been given the chance. But events, once again, pushed everything aside.

CHAPTER TWENTY-SIX

Katie

Piece by piece. That's how the truth is always revealed, though it had taken a while for me to understand that sometimes the people you care about most are the ones most capable of hurting you.

It was a form of willful blindness, I suppose. Or maybe it was just hope. The hope that all the trouble Alex had caused, the way he had come between us, was finally over. All I had wanted was for me and Isa to be friends again, close again, and I had thought, with Alex out of the way, we would be able to patch things up.

Turns out, a hope like that stops you seeing what's right in front of you. It colors everything, and makes it all seem rosy when, in fact, it's tarnished beyond repair.

Oh, but Isa had been so convincing. I really believed it when she had said it was all over with her and Alex. I thought she'd finally realized that I was right when it came to him, he was trouble and she was better off without him.

"I mean," she said whenever I asked about him, "I miss him…"

"Honestly? Why?"

"Is that so surprising? I really liked him, Katie. I know you don't like me saying that, but it's true. I just… I just wish I could understand why he split up with me. What did I do wrong, you reckon?"

I had simply shrugged. Alex wasn't someone I wanted to think about. Ever.

"If he'd just tell me why," Isa continued. "If he'd just explain it to me, then maybe I wouldn't feel so bad."

"He didn't tell you why?"

"No. He just called me up and said he'd been thinking about us and had started to think it wasn't such a good idea."

"The age thing?"

"Oh God, Katie, please stop going on about that, will you? If it was just that, then maybe I'd be okay about it. I mean, it would be a reason at least. But he never gave a damn about that. He told me all the time. He got sick of me mentioning it, in fact, sick of me asking him if he thought it was okay."

"You asked him that?"

"Yeah. Why?"

"I don't know. It's just every time I mentioned it…"

"I'd go off on one?"

"Yeah."

"Yeah, well, I just wanted to ignore it, that's why. But… I don't know… you put that thought in my head and I started to think that maybe it really was important. I started to think that maybe there was something wrong about it. Something dirty and scandalous. I mean, that's what you thought, let's be honest."

"That wasn't what I meant, Isa. You know that."

"No? That was what it felt like. That's why I kept asking him. I wanted him to tell me that it was okay. And he did. And I believed him. Which was stupid I guess, because it must have mattered in the end, don't you think? I mean, why else would he dump me like that? With a fucking phone call?"

"Because he's an asshole?"

"You really think that, don't you?"

"Well, if he's not, then he's definitely a wimp for not telling you to your face."

"Maybe I should be happy about it then? I mean, who wants to have an asshole for a boyfriend, right?"

"Yeah, good riddance."

"I guess I should have listened to you after all, eh?"

And I had smiled and said, "You should always listen to me, Isa. Always."

And she laughed at that.

"I never will though, you do realize that, don't you?"

But I didn't care. It was enough that we were talking about stuff and making plans, just as we had always done before Alex came on the scene.

"Friends again?" I'd asked Isa.

And I had noticed the look of surprise on Isa's face, as if the idea that we had stopped being friends for a while had never occurred to her until then.

"I didn't realize we'd fallen out," she told me.

"Well, let's just say you were a bit preoccupied."

I thought she would laugh, but instead she changed the subject.

"My parents, you mean, I don't want to think about them."

"You think you need to worry about them then? I mean, this honeymoon thing, that'll make it all okay, won't it? Things aren't really that bad between them, are they?"

"Ah, my dad had an affair, remember?"

"Yeah, I know, but your mom forgave him, didn't she?"

"I know, I just wonder if she'll ever forgive me."

"Huh?"

"Oh, nothing. Just ignore me. I'm being stupid is all."

And maybe I should have paid more attention then. Pushed it a bit further, not worried so much about saying anything that would come between us again. Then maybe I would have understood that Isa had always had plans for the summer. Plans that involved more than just swimming and partying. Plans I could never have imagined. Plans for what she was going to do to me.

*

It took that final argument for the truth to be revealed. Heat of the moment revelations which left me reeling and angry with myself, as much as Isa.

Because it was obvious, when I looked back later. Isa's enthusiasm for joining us for the summer, the way she had insisted that she was okay with watching her parents waltz off to Sardinia for a month without her. I should have known that it was never that simple, that Isa was never that easygoing and devil-may-care.

No, she cared alright.

She cared about what had happened to her. Not so much about her parents throwing everything into chaos with their arguments and seething resentments. She could let that go far more easily than she could let Alex go, it turned out.

All those weeks when I thought we were good again, it was just Isa biding her time, waiting for an opportunity to arise, so she could wreak havoc.

And I had set her up perfectly. I had put Luka there in front of her, almost as a gift. How stupid could I be?

I'd watched Luka mope and sulk after Isa had told him he was just a summer fling, and it was all I could do to stop myself from screaming at him and telling him that he should have stuck with me, stuck with the friend he knew would never hurt him.

Instead I took my anger out on Isa, not realizing that she had been waiting for this moment all along.

"Why did you have to hurt him like that, Isa? He's a good guy, and he doesn't deserve this."

"God, there you go again. Just give it a break, will you? I told you, it was a summer fling, and he should have realized. If he's too naïve to understand that, then there's nothing I can do about it."

"Why? I mean why should he have realized that from the start? Just because you knew that's what it was, it doesn't mean he did. I certainly didn't."

"No? I'd have thought you'd be glad. I mean now he's free again, you can try and get him for yourself."

And it stung, the way Isa said it, the way she smiled, as if she wanted to taunt me and hurt me. Luka, the guy I could never have. The guy she was now done with. Soiled goods.

"Shit, Isa, what's up with you? When did you start not giving a shit about other people?"

"Oh, I don't know, Katie. Maybe it was when they stopped giving a shit about me."

"Huh? What the hell does that mean?"

"It means, Katie, that I was happy. How many times do I have to tell you that? I was happy and I was doing nothing wrong and neither was Alex. And we should have been left alone. Because it was no one else's business. Especially not yours. But no. You couldn't let it lie, could you? You had to interfere."

"Sorry, what?"

And a flush of anger glowed in Isa's face then, a rush of blood she couldn't contain. I could feel it seethe and burn.

"Oh, come on, don't act all coy and innocent. Did you think my dad wouldn't tell me? About your little visit to see him? Oh, and now you go all quiet. Shit, Katie. I don't even know what I'm doing here. I don't even know why I'm still your friend after what you did."

But I couldn't reply. My throat was clenched shut, no air could escape, far less words. Words to explain myself, words to defend myself. All I could do was stand there and wait for it. My head growing woozy as Isa's words flew around my head. I tried not to listen, tried to block it out until Isa was done. Isa knew I'd been the one to tell Willem about Alex. All this time, she knew.

"I was only trying to look out for you," I finally managed to say.

"No! Stop saying that. Because it isn't true and even if it was, it doesn't matter. Don't you get that? It had nothing to do with you. Me and Alex. That was my life, my business, my decision. What part of that don't you understand?"

"I just—"

"Why? Katie? Why did you tell him?"

How to explain it without pissing her off again? I tried to find the words, but my silence only seemed to infuriate her.

"No, don't clam up. Don't you dare clam up. Tell me. Why did you tell my dad about Alex?"

"Why do you think?"

"Ha, why do I think? Why do I think? Katie, I haven't got a fucking clue! I still can't believe you did it. Have you any idea how mortified Alex was when my dad turned up in his shop like that and started lecturing him about 'inappropriate relationships with young girls'? I mean, there were customers there and they were all staring at Alex as if he was some kind of criminal. Some kind of freak. Why the fuck would you do that to us, Katie?"

"So, you knew? All this time, you knew, and didn't say anything?"

"What did you want me to say?"

"What? Isa, why would you keep quiet about it?"

"No, no, no, wait a minute. I'm not having you turn this around to make it about me. Answer the question first, Katie. Why did you tell my dad?"

"I keep telling you! I was just looking out for you is all. You know that. You know I thought Alex was going to hurt you. Shit, Isa, the state of you those last weeks. You were half dead most of the time. Flunking just about everything at school and messing everything up. And what for? For him? For Alex? Some guy who doesn't give a shit about you? What kind of guy starts seeing someone eighteen years younger than them?"

"I dunno. My dad maybe?"

"I'm being serious, Isa. You think a guy like that gives a damn about other people? He just takes what he wants, and to hell with what people think."

"Whoa, you're worse than I thought, Katie. You know that?"

"Huh? For trying to look out for you? For worrying about my best friend?"

"You just make up your mind about people, don't you? You just see what you want to see and then make a judgment. And based on what, exactly? What do you know about Alex and me? The things we talk about, the places we go, the things we do? You know all about that then?"

"No, but I saw you roll into school looking like a zombie often enough to hazard a guess."

"Okay, stop. Just stop. No one will ever convince you, little miss high and mighty. You're just never going to see it, are you? Fuck, and you still don't get it, do you? I thought you would by now. I thought after you'd had a taste of it, you'd finally understand how it feels."

"A taste of what? What do you mean?"

"Oh, just fuck off, Katie, will you? Just fuck off."

It was only when my breath had slowed, and my head had cleared, and I was sitting alone in the dunes that it hit me, what it was Isa had meant. What it was she had done.

Now you know how it feels to have someone take away the guy you want. Now you know how it feels when someone interferes.

And the spitefulness of it was more than I could bear.

You bitch, Isa, I thought. *You mean, selfish bitch.*

CHAPTER TWENTY-SEVEN

Louise

When I lifted the envelope out of the mailbox, I knew instinctively it was something ominous. The weight of it, the thick cardboard backing and the neatly typed label with the name and address all suggested something official and I had wanted to put it back in the mailbox immediately. To flip shut the door and turn the key with a decisive click.

I sat in the kitchen and opened it with a shaking hand. But the words made no sense, no matter how many times I read them, and I had difficulty absorbing it. Four times I read it, before I understood, and then I called Peter straight away, my voice quivering with fear and anger and confusion.

"Wrongful death," I told him. "They're suing us for wrongful death."

"What? Who? Louise, calm down."

"Willem and Sarah," I told him. "They say we were negligent. They're suing us for damages."

"Wait, what? That makes no sense. What sort of damages?"

"I don't know. What does it matter?" I told him. "Why would they do this to us?"

"Listen, don't worry, okay? We'll sort it out. I promise you, we'll sort it out."

But all I could do was worry, because I knew this wasn't about money. This was about blame. This was about pointing a finger and saying: "You. You did this. You are to blame. And you're going to pay."

This was Sarah and Willem telling us that they would never forgive us. They were saying to the world: our daughter is dead, and it is their fault.

*

Wrongful death. I had no idea what that meant, what it entailed, the systems, the procedures, all the mind-boggling paraphernalia which accompany litigation. For a few weeks, it came to take over our lives. Reports were filed, statements verified, questions answered. I hadn't realized the aftermath was something we would need to examine again so closely, that Isa's death was something we would be required to explain and revisit. And the understanding that we were now going to have to go over the events of that summer in minute detail in court left me anxious and uncertain.

What more could we say? I thought.

Isa had drowned. The medical examiner had already declared it an accident. There was no case to answer, so why pursue us like this? It felt so vindictive. It would do no good to try and piece together Isa's last moments. It wouldn't bring her back. It wouldn't change the facts. It would only prolong the pain and prevent us from healing.

It was only when I was sat in the attorney's office that I got a sense of how the whole saga was going to pan out. The whole case would turn on one simple question: Who was negligent?

Blame was to be apportioned, but it turned out that could work both ways. Our statements could not only form our defense, they could also form a counter accusation.

"The way it works is like this," he explained to me. "The Egberts must prove Isa's death was the result of some action or oversight on your part."

I sat there, incredulous and shaking with anger, unsure what to say, because it seemed so simplistic when he explained it this way. There was no cause and effect. And I told him so.

"I don't see how they can do that. Isa was alone when she died. No one is to blame. It's just a terrible accident. That's all it is. Why can't they see that?"

"This is not like a criminal case. I need you to understand that. The burden of proof is much lower."

"What do you mean?"

"All they need to show is that there is a reasonable degree of probability, a preponderance of evidence, that as a result of your negligence—and that can be anything, letting Isa go to the beach party that night, letting her drink and take drugs—you placed Isa in danger. They just need to show that you didn't watch over her. She was still a juvenile, so you had a responsibility towards her."

"Oh, and what about her parents—what about Sarah and Willem? Don't they have a responsibility too? Because they knew what Isa was like. They knew she wasn't happy. They should have warned me."

And he nodded and said that this was the line he wanted to take. We needed to show that Isa was already in trouble before she came with us to Montauk. That she was a child we needed to watch closely. But with no warning from Sarah or Willem, we had let our guard down.

"Because we trusted them," I told him. "We let our guard down because we trusted them. They gave us no reason to think that Isa was in any kind of trouble. That we needed to keep a close eye on her."

"So, let's get our statements clear then," he said. "I need you to tell me everything you know about Isa. Your daughter has already provided me with a very compelling statement, and I think we can provide the court with a very clear psychological profile of Isa before she left with you for Montauk."

"Really? What did Katie say to you?"

"I'd like you to tell me what you know first. It will help if I understand what parts of the story you were unaware of."

"Oh God," I said. "They're going to win this, aren't they? I mean, what is it you said? Preponderance of evidence? That's nothing, is it? They can easily convince a court we didn't do enough."

"Let's just go over your statement. I think there is a case we can make. We can counter their arguments. Please, trust me on this."

Trust me. I wasn't sure I could. I could feel the panic rising. They were going to win this. They were going to have us labelled and condemned and there was nothing we could do about it.

"Okay." I nodded. And I could tell he could see I didn't really mean it.

"First things first," he said. "Did you know about the trouble she was having at home?" the attorney asked.

"You mean all that honeymoon business? Willem's affair?"

"That, yes. But I'm more interested in the trouble she was having at school. She was falling behind and failing pretty much every subject, did you know about that?"

"No," I replied. "She was always one of the smarter kids. She always did well."

"So, you wouldn't say, before the summer, that you had noticed anything different about her behavior?"

"No, not particularly. I knew she was upset, of course. All that business with her parents, but that was why we all thought it would be a good idea if she came with us. Willem and Sarah would have time and space and Isa could relax and have some fun over the summer."

"So you knew nothing about the extent of her problems?"

"No. But maybe I'm the wrong person to be asking about this, you talked to Katie already. She can tell you more about all of this."

He leafed through a file on his desk and read something there, before continuing.

"She did mention something, actually. A man, named Alexander Smit. He was quite a bit older than Isa, but apparently they were in some sort of relationship. Your daughter told us he had been taking her out to parties and nightclubs. She blamed Alexander for most of Isa's problems. Did she ever mention him at the time?"

"She didn't, no, not at the time. But then again, she never would have told me something like that. It's the way teenage girls are, isn't it? They protect one another, they keep each other's secrets."

"But if you had known, would it have made a difference?"

"I'm not sure I understand. In what way?"

"Would you have considered taking Isa with you to Montauk if you'd known about the sort of problems she was having, the trouble she was in?"

"Well, of course it would have made a difference. I would never have let Isa come with us if I'd known any of this."

"Right. And that's what we need to get across. That Sarah and Willem withheld all of this from you. So you never knew what you were getting into. And if you had, you would not have taken Isa with you to Montauk."

And I knew what he was saying made sense. I understood that this was the logical approach to take. How could we be negligent if we weren't in possession of all the facts? But I couldn't contain the dread I felt as I listened to him. Because what he was talking about was a confrontation. What he was talking about was our word against theirs. And I wanted, more than anything, for there to be another way to deal with the whole sorry situation. Some way for us all to accept what had happened and leave it at that. No blame, no animosity, just sadness and grief.

"Mrs. Lindeman," he asked me. "Are you alright?"

"Yes, I…"

"Do you have a problem with my suggestion?"

"Do you think it will make a difference? I mean, it doesn't really change very much, does it? We still let Isa do what she liked while she was with us. We still failed to notice what was going on."

"I think, at the very least, it will show that the negligence is shared."

And a flicker of hope filled me then.

"Do you think they might drop the case?" I asked him. "If we can show them it wasn't our fault."

"We can suggest it, if you like?"

"But do you think they would do it?"

"Honestly? No. The mother seems quite determined."

"They want us to shoulder the blame for this, don't they? They really want to punish us."

And he had looked at me and shuffled the papers and then pursed his lips as if he wanted to show me the level of determination and resolve which would be required to come through it all successfully, then he told me, "Which is why I suggest you follow my advice."

*

The whole process at the lawyer's had felt like an interrogation and it sapped me of energy and left me feeling disoriented and uncertain as to what I should do. It felt wrong, somehow. All of it—the litigation, the accusations, the very fact that Sarah and Willem seemed set on going through with it. But I felt hopeless in the face of it all.

When I got home, I was emptied out and I slumped on the sofa, pulled a blanket around me and slept even though it was mid-afternoon. When Peter came home and found me there, he woke me with a gentle shake and asked me, "Hey, how did it go? I thought I'd come home early just to see if you were okay."

"Oh, hi. I wasn't expecting you back so soon."

He'd sat beside me and tucked the blanket back around my shoulders and stroked my hair.

"Was it so bad you needed to sleep it off?"

"I guess it was," I said.

And he kissed my forehead and said, "I'm sorry you have to go through this."

"It's not you that should be apologizing. It's them. Sarah and Willem, they shouldn't be doing this to us."

"I know," he agreed.

"I keep trying to understand it. I keep telling myself it's the grief that's making them do things they would never do. Because if they knew what this was doing to us, they'd stop, wouldn't they? If they knew how much this hurts, they'd stop."

"Maybe," he conceded. But I could tell from the little sigh that he didn't believe it. And, deep down, I knew I didn't believe it either. That was why it hurt so much. To know they were prepared to push ahead, despite everything, was unbearable.

"If it was the other way around," he asked me. "If Katie had drowned while she was with Sarah and Willem, what would we have done?"

And I looked at him and felt my throat clench as I swallowed. Too shocked to be able to reply immediately, because the question was too vast. And the answer, the honest answer, was too painful.

"We'd have done the same, I guess," I eventually conceded.

"I think we would," he agreed.

"Then why does it feel so vengeful? Why can't they just talk to us? We could sort it out amongst ourselves. Why do they have to make us feel like criminals? What good does that do?"

"I don't know, Louise. I really don't know."

"I do," I said. And he closed his eyes as if he needed to brace himself for what I was about to say. "I think they need to accuse us because they can't stand the idea that this is also their fault. I think they simply can't bear the truth."

"And what is the truth then?"

"Isa," I said.

"What about her?"

"She was pretty messed up. I just didn't know how much, until today."

"What do you mean?"

And I told him all about the conversation I'd had with the lawyer, and he listened, stunned into silence and shaking his head the more he understood the implications of what I was telling him.

"Do you really think this is what Sarah and Willem are after?" he asked me. "Deep down, I mean. Do you think they know what they've started with all of this?"

"I honestly don't know. I think they're just looking for some sort of closure or justice or… Oh God, I don't understand any of it. It's like they're accusing us. It's as though they're saying we shouldn't have let Isa go to the party that night. That she drowned because we didn't pay attention. What's going to happen to us, Peter? Are they going to take this further? I mean, what if…?"

"No, don't worry, Louise. Nothing's going to happen, okay? Isa drowned. It was an accident. That's all. I mean, there's no grounds even for litigation, as far as I can see. The kids were at that party on their own, but they were old enough to be there unsupervised."

"Yeah, I know, it's just, when it comes down to it, Isa was with us, and we have to take some responsibility for that, don't we?"

"I think we all need to accept some level of responsibility. But I don't think this is the right way to go about it. To lay all the blame at our feet, I really don't think they can do that. And, for what it's worth, I don't think any court is going to see it that way either."

"You think so?"

"I do, yes."

"Then we just have to trust our attorney, don't we?" I said. "And he's right, isn't he? I mean, if we'd been told everything then we would have paid closer attention. Hell, if we'd known how messed up Isa was, she'd never have been with us in the first place. He's right to pursue that angle, don't you think? Because it's the truth."

"It seems like a pretty strong argument to me," Peter agreed.

And he leaned over me and brushed my forehead.

"Listen, why don't you rest up some more? We can talk about all this again later." He pulled the blanket tighter around me and left me to curl up on the sofa.

But it wasn't Peter I needed to talk to. It was Sarah.

I needed to ask her why she had kept so many secrets from us. And I had to know why. Why she had breached my trust.

Talk to me, I wanted to say to her. *Talk to me and let's settle this the right way. Together and in private.*

As the days wore on, I found myself reaching for the phone more often, dialing Sarah's number, then hanging up because I didn't want to find myself blurting it out: "What was up with Isa? She wasn't happy, was she? And you knew she wasn't happy."

It sounded too accusatory. And yet, it was what I was thinking. That was my accusation: Sarah had packed Isa off knowing she was vulnerable and volatile. She had sent her away, without telling us things we needed to know. Things that might have meant I would have kept a closer watch, that would have stopped me from letting Isa run a little wild over the summer. Things that would have made me less willing to let my guard down and give the girls such a free rein.

Things that would have let me off the hook. That was also the truth. That was also what I wanted from Sarah. Some indication that there had been something wrong after all, something I didn't know about. I wanted Sarah to admit it, because it would soften the blow, would stop that thought from creeping in every day, the terrible idea that everyone thought we were to blame. That it was my decision to relax and let the kids do as they pleased which had brought about this whole mess.

I wanted Sarah to admit that she hadn't been completely honest with me and I didn't need to discuss it in court, I didn't need a formal proceeding. All I needed was the opportunity to look her in the eye and say: "You should have told me about this. Hell, for half the summer you didn't even call her. Your own daughter. You know you can't lay it all on us."

That was all I wanted. Something, anything, to absolve me of any blame.

Because, despite everything, every time I thought of Isa, that terrible familiar feeling returned. That dull aching pain of guilt.

*

I was stood at the kitchen sink washing out coffee cups when it hit me. The soapy cup slipping from my hands and crashing into the bowl, pieces shattering and scattering off the worktops and on to the floor. Katie. They could try and blame Katie for all of this mess. After all, she knew what was going on.

"Mom, are you okay?"

Katie looked at the broken ceramic, then fetched a dustpan and brush while I stood there, unable to move. As she swept it all away, she asked me again: "Are you okay?"

"Oh, I'm fine, yes. It's been a tense couple of days is all."

"You mean with the attorney? Yeah, it's pretty full on, isn't it?"

"Listen, can I talk to you about that?"

"Sure."

And I walked to the kitchen table and asked her to come and sit beside me.

"I need to ask you something," I said. And Katie had shuffled awkwardly in her seat and waited for me to continue.

"Isa was in a lot of trouble before the summer, wasn't she?"

"No, not really."

"Katie, please. No messing around. Just tell me the truth."

"Listen, it was just stupid shit, that was all it was."

"The attorney said she was in some kind of trouble, and that we should have looked after her more, kept a better eye on her, because maybe then—"

"Mom, it was an accident, okay? A sad, stupid accident. She drowned. We didn't do anything wrong. That's not what he was saying."

"You think so?"

"Yes."

"So, was there nothing else going on? I mean, she wasn't in any trouble because of this Alex guy, was she? She wasn't, you know?"

"Oh God, Mom, no. It was nothing like that, I swear. She was careful. She was sensible. It was just all that mess with her parents, that was all. But who can blame her for that? And anyway, you saw her. All summer, she was fine. Everything was fine."

And what was it I saw there? A small quiver of the eyelids, a turning away when I stared too long. A little nervous glance that told me all I needed to know.

She wasn't telling me everything. There was more to this. There was a lot more to this.

And it's ironic, I suppose, that the only one who ever really told me the truth about it all was him, of all people.

*

When I checked my phone, there were six messages and three missed calls. All of them from him.

Goddamn it, I thought, when I saw them. *What was wrong with him? Did he not understand I couldn't talk to him?*

I'd already told him that I couldn't see him or talk to him. And now he was forcing me to call him and explain it more clearly. I had enough on my plate without worrying about him.

But when the fourth call came, I was standing in line at the bakery and I answered without thinking. Heard his voice, "Louise—" and cut him off immediately.

"Listen, I can't talk right now, can you call me back?"

"No. Please, Louise, listen. I need to talk to you right now."

"I just told you, I—"

His turn then to cut me off. "I got a call today. Some lawyer for Sarah Egberts. They want to talk to me. About Isa."

I insisted we meet out of town and he agreed to meet me in High Rock Park over on Staten Island. He complained about being dragged out of town, of course, but I needed to be sure we were someplace isolated where we could walk and talk in peace without the risk of bumping into anyone we knew. And I hoped the woodland of High Rock would calm me down and help me focus on what I needed to tell him.

When I approached him, he leaned towards me for a kiss, and I needed to turn away and place my hand on his arm, to remind him that our days of easy intimacy were over.

We sat on a bench overlooking a small lake and watched the ducks swim towards us. Aside from the occasional birdsong I couldn't identify, the place was quiet and secluded, and the idyllic atmosphere of the moment seemed to make him wary of talking, as if nature unsettled him. Any other time and I would have enjoyed the silence, but today it made me irritable and anxious and keen to get the conversation out of the way.

"Listen, one of us is going to have to begin," I told him. "And I think, under the circumstances, it really should be you."

"Don't, Louise. Please, don't."

"Fine, just tell me what this is all about then. Sarah's lawyers called you?"

"Yeah, yesterday. They wanted to know about me and Isa. How close we were."

"Close. Oh, come on, don't come over all coy with me. Though maybe I should be glad that you're being honest about it at least. *Close* though, Jesus! You were fucking a seventeen-year-old girl, what the hell were you thinking?"

"Last time I looked, seventeen was an adult. Capable of consent. Don't get sanctimonious with me, Louise, we both know how hypocritical of you that would be."

His raised voice echoed over the lake, startling the ducks, and they skittered across the water and squawked a complaint.

"Okay, let's just start again. I didn't come here to start an argument. I came because you called me."

"But you knew already, didn't you? About me and Isa? And you knew I was sitting around trying to make sense of it all. Why didn't you call me?"

"And say what? Were you honestly looking to me to console you?"

"Actually, that would have been the decent thing to do."

"Oh, fuck you."

I got up to leave, there was no point in this. The animosity between us was too great. And, despite myself, my jealousy was too fierce. But he pulled at my arm and made me sit back down on the bench.

"No, let's finish this. Talk to me, Louise. How long did you know about us?"

I took a few deep breaths and stared straight ahead at the lake, gathering my thoughts before I spoke, because he was right, we did need to talk. Then I sat back down beside him.

"Since summer," I said. "And if you're wondering why I didn't call you about it, well, imagine how I felt, knowing you and Isa were... God, I can't even say it."

"But how did you find out?"

"I saw you with her. At the lighthouse in Montauk."

He didn't reply. He couldn't even look me in the eye. Though I saw him turn pale as the realization hit.

"Fuck, I'm sorry, I shouldn't have gone up there to see her, especially after I told you I didn't want to come up there to visit you, I—"

"No, stop it, Alexander. I don't want your sympathy okay?"

"I wasn't trying to be sympathetic, I just—"

"Listen, all I need to know is what you told the lawyer."

"Huh? What do you mean?"

"You were with Isa the day she died. Did you tell them that?"

"No, not yet."

"Are you planning to tell them?"

"What? I mean I have to, I can't—"

"No, you don't have to. No one knows you were there, do they?"

"Oh, come on, Louise, they'll find out easily, all they need to do is check the phone records and they'll see we spoke to each other. And anyway, why would I lie to them?"

"Why didn't you just offer it up freely then?"

"I don't know, I…"

"Oh, come on. You know why. Her secret lover, sneaking up to Montauk for a rendezvous on the day she died? You know how that will look to some people."

"Fuck, why didn't I just stay away? Why didn't I just do what I promised Willem…"

"Wait a minute. Willem? What's he got to do with anything?"

"Oh, he found out about me and Isa and made it perfectly clear I was to keep away from her. And I did. I didn't want that hassle. He came into the shop and started screaming at me."

"But how did he find out?"

"What? Well, Katie, of course. She told him."

I froze then. Why had it not occurred to me before?

"Why would she do that?" I asked him.

"Maybe you should talk to her about that. She was set against our relationship from the start. She hated it. That was why she put a stop to it as soon as she got the chance. Oh fuck, if she knew about the two of us. She'd never forgive you, Louise. You know that, right?"

"Is there any reason she needs to find out?"

"No, but, all this legal business. They said they want me to make a statement, in court. I can't lie to them, Louise. Whatever they ask me, I have to tell the truth. I mean, it's bound to come out."

"The only way it will come out is if you say something. And I'm going to assume that you will keep it quiet. No one needs to know about us."

"Did you hear what I just said? If anyone asks me about us, then I have to tell them the truth. I can't—"

"Listen, you need to be prepared for what they're going to ask you in court. I don't think you understand the trouble you're in."

"Me? Why would I be in trouble?"

"Sarah needs someone to blame, Alexander, I don't think you understand that. My lawyers think that Isa's behavior over the last few months showed she was going off the rails, that she was reckless."

"Oh, that's absurd."

"Is it? They seem to think they can make a case for it. And they definitely seem to think that your relationship with her was at the heart of all her problems."

"No way! That's not true at all. We were just having a bit of fun."

"I'm just telling you how they're going to pursue this, Alexander. That's all. I'm actually trying to help you out here, though God knows why."

He looked at me then as if he wasn't quite sure whether he should believe me. I needed to keep going. I had to convince him.

"You weren't to know how messed up things were for Isa at home. All that business between Willem and Sarah, I think it hurt her more than anyone realized. But she was so good at covering it up, at pretending that everything was okay. It's why she needed you. I think she just wanted to escape from all of that for a minute, and, to be honest, I can hardly blame her for that. But I swear to you, if I had known how messed-up she was, I would never have let her come with us to Montauk. And I think the same goes for you. If you'd known what you were getting yourself in to, you'd have resisted her."

"Would I?"

"Come on. Knowing what you know now, all the pain it's caused? You really don't think you would have gone out of your way to avoid it?"

"Maybe, yeah. Oh, I don't know. It wasn't like that."

And I had to make him understand now. He had to see things from my point of view.

"I just don't see why we should be blamed for any of this, is all I'm saying. I don't understand why Sarah and Willem think they can bring this suit and point the finger at everyone else when, at heart, they're the ones to blame. Isa was their daughter and whatever she did, whatever trouble she got into, it was all an emotional reaction to what was going on at home. I think all along Isa was trying to show us how she was hurting, but none of us noticed or understood. And if I'm guilty of anything then it's that—not realizing this until it was too late. But that doesn't make me responsible for her death. And it doesn't make you responsible either. And Sarah and Willem have to understand that."

He slumped forward then and let his head drop and I knew then that I'd gotten through to him.

"Fuck," he said. And there was a quiver in his voice as if he was close to tears. "What am I supposed to do?"

And I put my arm around him and drew him close to me and felt the weight of his head on my shoulder as he leaned into me for support.

"Just tell the truth about Isa," I told him. "That's all we can do. We didn't know her at all, really. But if we had, then I think she would still be here. If Sarah and Willem had been honest with us, then their daughter would still be alive."

"Do you really believe that?" he asked me.

"I do," I said. And I pulled away from him, laid my hands on his shoulders and turned him to face me. "And, I think, deep down, you also know it's true. So just tell the truth. We're not to blame for any of this."

And he nodded and held my gaze and I could see him thinking it through, the clear logic of what I was telling him, fixing itself in his mind, the idea taking hold. Yes, he was thinking, she's right. Louise is right.

I headed home, my hands shaking all the way, my legs like jelly as I tried to drive back into town. The idea that he would say something. That they would ask him a question and leave him no choice but to reveal the truth… it made me sick just thinking about it. And in court. Oh my God. One wrong glance in my direction would be all it took. If Alexander were to look at me, acknowledge me when we were all gathered there, Peter would notice it, I was sure of it. And all my discretion, all that effort to keep it secret, would have been for nothing.

But I was sure I could trust him now. He was Alexander, after all, and there was no way he was ever going to take the blame for anything.

*

I knew the court proceedings were going to be arduous and all morning I had tried to prepare myself. I needed to be calm and clear headed and make sure that my emotions didn't overcome me.

When I took the stand, my responses were forensic, almost clinical. The back and forth with their attorney, a game of wits I found strangely exciting.

"Would you say you were relaxed about your children and Isa attending all these parties over the summer?"

"Perhaps. But they were responsible kids. All three of them. They went to a lot of parties, but they never came home drunk or the worse for wear. I trusted them. Because they earned my trust. We had set the boundaries and they never crossed them. So yes, that made me relaxed, I suppose."

"Did you know that they were drinking? That there were drugs in circulation?"

"The last night, the last party, turned out to be wilder than I expected. But before that, I didn't notice anything, no."

"Really? You didn't expect teenagers to drink and smoke and get stoned at a party?"

"I did. But, like I said, all summer that was not what had happened. They'd surprised me with their sense of responsibility. So why would that last night be any different?"

And I looked across at Sarah and Willem, my face emptied of emotion. I wanted them to see that I was right. I trusted my children, I trusted their daughter, to do the right thing. I was almost defending Isa, in a way. Letting the court see that she was a responsible and sensible kid. One you could trust. But neither of them looked at me. They sat there with their heads down as if the sight of me was unbearable.

"So you thought they were capable of behaving. A fifteen-year-old boy and two seventeen-year-old girls."

"I knew they were capable of it. They gave me no reason to doubt them."

On and on he went. But I was prepared for it. And Katie was too. On the stand she was as precise and as calm as I was. We had gone over it together at home, what we would say, what their lawyers would ask us. She knew what she needed to do and what she needed to get across in court. We both did. This was as much Sarah and Willem's fault as it was anyone else's. That was what we were going to tell the court.

But James… He had seemed to bristle at the idea. It was almost as if he refused to believe it. As far as he was concerned, we were to blame. Only us. We were the ones who had let Isa down, and he didn't see why we should deny it.

No matter how many times I tried to explain to him that we weren't denying it, that all we were saying was we were not the only ones at fault, he refused to accept it.

And now he was going to be put on the stand and questioned and I felt as if my anger with Sarah and Willem would never subside. Because it was too much for him, and they knew it. Yet they still insisted he be subjected to the scrutiny of a court.

When he took to the stand all I could think was: *They shouldn't be putting him through this. It's cruel and unnecessary.* And I stared at Sarah, hoping she would look me in the eye, because I wanted her to see how much she was hurting my family. But she didn't even glance in my direction.

The formality of the process left James wide-eyed and stuttering at first. But I could see something more than nerves was bothering him.

The attorney asked him what he remembered of Isa's last night and he sat there and repeated his story. His version of events. And all I could think was, *just stick to the facts, James. Please, just stick to the facts.*

Instinct again. A strong sense of doubt that there were too many things being left unsaid and soon, someone in that courtroom would start to prize it all open.

I watched James and I could see it. He was struggling to get to the truth. He knew it was in the bits he couldn't remember; that it was in those black moments where he needed to search.

I saw it on his face as he answered their questions—a desperate realization that some vital clue was sitting there, deep in his memory, and all he needed to do was find it, but he couldn't. There was only a blank where his memory should be.

There were moments, as he spoke, when he seemed so lucid, when it seemed as if he was almost within touching distance of the truth. But in the end, the only story he had to tell was the one he had repeated time and time again.

He had gone to the beach party around midnight and had sat around the campfire listening to music and drinking wine for a while—he couldn't remember how long. It was dark, the mood was relaxed, and the alcohol was plentiful. The hash too.

And the implication was clear. With every word of his statement he seemed to be confirming everything Sarah and Willem claimed—that we were irresponsible parents, that we had allowed the kids to run wild over the summer. That we were negligent.

It was all I could do to keep myself from getting up from my seat and walking over to the stand to hug him because I could see the torment in his eyes.

When they pressed him as to what he could remember, all he could say was that it was a bit of a blur. He'd had a lot to drink. It was the last night of summer after all, so everyone was in the mood for one final party. Soon it would be back to school, back to rules, back to weekend jobs and limited opportunities for fun. So, all he wanted to do was chill on the beach and say goodbye to summer.

I could see that everyone had started to stare into the distance as he recalled all this. It was a story that had been repeated by pretty much everyone who had taken the stand. And no one's statement differed from the rest.

Then the attorney started to question him about the time he'd spent away from the bonfire and everyone leaned in.

"You were missing for a while, according to some witnesses, is that correct?"

And he nodded and said that yes, he had left the bonfire and headed to the beach.

"And you saw, or you think you remember seeing, Isa and another boy, Mark Adams, is that right?"

"Yes."

"And did Isa know him well?"

"No, she only met him that night."

And a murmur went through the court. Disapproval. I could hear it. They would turn against her a little because of this. A one-night stand. It made her look bad. It made her look reckless. And as awkward as it made me feel to listen to the whispers, I knew it would strengthen our claim. This was who she was. What were we supposed to do with such a girl?

"I see," the attorney continued. "And you watched them head into the dunes together?"

"Yes," he replied.

"And do you remember what they were doing?"

And he glowed red with the embarrassment of it and murmured, "Yes, you know…"

"Did Isa leave the party to have intercourse?"

"Yes," he said. "I mean, I didn't watch them, but it was obvious what they were doing."

What more was there to say than that?

"And do you remember what happened next?"

And again, people leaned in. This was the moment they had been waiting for. The cinematic denouement.

"They came back to the party."

"Isa and Mark?"

"Yes. I mean, I think so."

And I felt my stomach tighten then. *No, James*, I thought. *Leave it at that. Just leave it at that.*

"You think so? So you're not sure if Isa came back from the dunes?"

And he looked over at me then and I held his gaze and nodded slightly, encouraging him to keep going.

"No, I'm sure. Both of them came back."

"And do you remember anything more? At some point Isa must have headed to the beach, did you see her?"

And poor James. I could see him grasping at something, some faint memory that was just out of reach, but there was nothing. All he could do was explain to the court that he remembered falling asleep on the beach and then, somehow, having made it back home come morning, because when he woke up, he was in his bed and his head was pounding like a hammer on an anvil.

"So, you don't remember if Isa was at the bonfire when you left the beach?"

"No," he replied.

It took a mother to see that he wasn't as certain about that as he appeared to be.

And I knew then, as I watched him finish his testimony. He was so close to remembering, but it wasn't quite there yet, so the only honest answer he could give at that moment was that he remembered nothing. The jumbled-up mess of that night hadn't quite come into focus yet.

But when it did, I wondered, when the memories sharpened and he finally got there, to whatever truth he was hiding from himself... What then?

James left the stand and came back to sit beside me. I tried to hold his hand, but he shook me off and wouldn't look at me. As if he was ashamed of something. Ashamed of me. Ashamed of us.

The rest of the proceedings happened in a blur. I sat there feeling myself grow sleepy with it all, drowsy with boredom and the stuffiness of the process. I had never imagined that the repetitiveness of all the statements could be so uninteresting. Isa had died, here they were explaining what had happened that night, and all I could think was, *Oh, please get on with it.*

Perhaps it was simply because no one seemed to offer anything insightful or different. Just the same story told by different people, and all amounting to the same thing. Isa floating in the water waiting to be found.

By the time Sarah took the stand, my mind had been wandering, mundane thoughts filling my head. Household things. Day-to-day chores. Normality reasserting itself. The juxtaposition of such ordinary thoughts set against the tragic story of Isa's last night, amusing me somewhat.

But when I heard her name called, I snapped to attention and watched as she composed herself and got ready to testify. And again, I tried to catch her eye, but again, she refused to look in my direction.

I squeezed Peter's hand to steady myself and was surprised to feel how nervous he was. His hand was moist and when I turned to look at him, he was chewing his lip, the nerves overcoming him. But as Sarah started to answer the questions, he leaned forward to listen and let go of my hand as he became engrossed in the proceedings. I sat there beside him, felt the small anxious trickle of sweat form at the back of my neck, and wished to God I could be someplace else.

"There were tensions at home, is that correct?" her attorney was asking.

"Yes," she said. "Things had been a little disorderly."

Such a Sarah way to put it, I thought. Disorderly. As if it was simply a question of rearranging things, shuffling a few papers on a table back into neat little piles, but all the while, trying to hide something beneath them.

"Could you elaborate on that? Did the situation, for example, result in Isa behaving differently?"

"My husband and I were having some marital problems and yes, Isa was upset about it. Worried that perhaps we would divorce. But I wouldn't say she behaved differently, no."

"And she'd been doing less well at school during this time, is that correct?"

"Yes."

"And did that not worry you? It's a prestigious school, is it not? The entry requirements are quite high."

"At the time, we weren't fully aware of the extent of her problems at school. We didn't know she had fallen so far behind. But her behavior hadn't given us reason to worry. At home, she seemed her usual self."

"And it was around this time that your daughter started a relationship with Alexander Smit, is that correct?"

"It was, yes. Though Isa kept this from us."

"Because he's an older man, is that correct?"

"Yes."

"Thirty-five, I believe?"

"Yes."

And I felt the little ripple and murmur of disapproval fill the room as everyone absorbed this fact. Everyone making the calculations in their head and coming to the same conclusion, that an eighteen-year age gap was unacceptable and simply wrong. And I wondered then just what they were thinking. What picture were they forming of Isa? Not a pretty one, that was for sure. And it surprised me, how sad it made me feel that she wasn't there to defend herself. To stand up and let them see who she really was.

"And what happened when you discovered your daughter had a relationship with Alexander Smit?"

"My husband went around to visit him and told him to end it. He thought it was inappropriate. Isa was only seventeen."

"And did this upset her?"

"Yes. She was very upset."

"And how did she react?"

"After Willem visited Alex, Isa told me about Willem's affair."

"So, you learned about your husband's affair from your daughter?"

"Yes."

"And why did she tell you about it?"

"To get back at her father, I suppose. Because he had stopped her from seeing Alex."

"And how would you say all this tension had affected her in the run-up to the summer?"

"I don't know. I suppose she was angry still. A little upset. But nothing unusual for a teenager. After a while, she seemed okay."

"And did Isa's behavior make you angry? Did it upset you?"

"Well, yes, but I could understand why she was upset."

"And how would you describe Isa's state of mind before the vacation? Would you say she was her usual self?"

And Sarah hesitated, because there was an implication in that statement that was almost too much. Isa's state of mind, something which could be questioned and qualified. It was a strange question for her attorney to ask, I thought. I watched as Sarah turned to Willem as if to ask him why she was the one there on the stand bearing the brunt of the questioning. It was his actions, after all, that had started it all, the tension at home, the whole sorry drama.

And again, I found myself feeling unexpectedly sorry and wished I could stand up then and make some sort of intervention on Sarah's behalf. Remind everyone that none of this was wholly Sarah's fault. But I knew how it went. The responsibility of mothers for their daughters, especially wayward girls such as Isa, was always greater than the father's. Unfair, perhaps, but the reality, nonetheless. And I saw it then, on Sarah's face as she stared at Willem quietly seeking his help, the dawning realization that she would always be judged for this, that the failing would always be hers and hers alone. That all this needless litigation was never going to absolve her of any of that. She would always be blamed.

And the pain of that thought focused her attention.

"Isa was happy, despite how it may appear, she was happy. Happy that Willem and I had managed to resolve our problems. And she was sorry too, she told me that. She was sorry for telling me about Willem's affair, and she wished she hadn't done it, because she hadn't really thought about the way it would hurt me. She saw our Sardinia trip as a way to make everything better again."

"So, you didn't worry that she would be at risk over the summer when she was allowed to stay with her friend?"

"At risk? Of what exactly? She's known the Lindemans since she was a child. It was more like a family vacation. She was looking forward to it."

"And did they know that all these things had been happening at home?"

"Yes, Louise knew all about the affair and why it was we needed to go away together."

"And she knew that Isa had been in trouble at school? She knew about Alexander Smit?"

And again, I saw her hesitate as if she knew that what she was about to say would reveal something about her that she preferred to keep hidden.

"No," she said, her voice barely more than a whisper. "She didn't know about that."

"You didn't think it was something you should tell her?"

"No. I didn't. Perhaps I should have, but some things are private and not the kind of thing you choose to discuss outside your own family. We just wanted to move on. Isa was happy again and it was all over."

"And do you think perhaps the Lindemans would have kept a closer eye on Isa if they had known about the problems you had been having? Would they have agreed to have Isa stay with them for a month over the summer if they had known all this?"

"You would have to ask Louise that. But I think Louise could see that Isa was her usual self. She had as little reason to be concerned as I did. She knew Isa well enough. She knew who my daughter was."

"Before all this, Isa was a responsible child, would you say that's correct?"

"Yes."

"Never in any trouble? Got good grades?"

"Yes."

"But that changed once your husband's affair came to light?"

"I suppose so, yes."

"And would you say she needed a little more guidance than usual?"

"Maybe."

"Maybe?"

"Like I say, once that whole business with Alexander was over, she calmed down again. She was herself again."

"Could you describe that?"

"Just Isa. She was just Isa. Happy. Easygoing. No trouble. Everyone else has already confirmed that today. They've all said the same thing. She was happy. She was okay."

"So, before she left on vacation, this was her frame of mind?"

"Yes, absolutely. If she had been even remotely unhappy, I would never have let her go. Never."

"Okay. Let's talk a little about her behavior over the summer. She attended a lot of parties, drank a lot of alcohol. The medical examiner confirmed that there was MDMA and hashish in her bloodstream at the time of death. Would you say this was consistent behavior on Isa's part? Recognizable behavior? Drinking? Taking drugs?"

"No. I was shocked about all that. I didn't believe it at first, because it wasn't the Isa I knew. But teenagers do that sort of thing, don't they? It's part of growing up. I guess I'm going to have to accept that, as a parent, you can't really stop them from experimenting with all this stuff, not if they're really curious about it. And I guess, when she was presented with the opportunity to go a bit wild over the summer, she took it."

"So, it wasn't a manifestation of anything more than that? It was just curiosity?"

"I think so. I mean, she could be rebellious, but she was never reckless. There's a difference."

I had wondered at that. I could see no discernible difference. All I could think about was that Sarah had sent Isa off with us, knowing she was hurting, knowing she was angry and upset. And Sarah had never told us. And now she had admitted it in court. Now the whole world understood what had happened. Now the whole world would have to agree that the negligence was not ours, it was theirs.

Willem's affair. Isa's betrayal—that mean, stupid revelation. Isa's misguided affair with Alex. All of this was a mess of their own making. Isa, Sarah and Willem's. And I could feel the release.

This was not our fault. I could say that now, at last. I could let the whole world know that this wasn't our fault, and they would believe us. Because Sarah had just admitted as much.

There was a break in the proceedings and Alexander was due to be questioned when they resumed. In the lobby, I looked around for him and was relieved not to see him there. It was enough that I needed to avoid Sarah and Willem. The thought of speaking to them was too much at that moment and I had insisted we all go outside for some air and a quick lunch. Though none of us were hungry or enthusiastic about returning.

"We've made our statements," James had complained. "Why can't we just go home? I just want to get out of this place."

"Because we should be there when they conclude," Peter had explained. "We need to know we've been cleared."

And James had looked at his father and laughed.

"What makes you so sure we'll be cleared?"

"Trust me," was all Peter said in return.

But it was a chance to avoid it, and I took it.

"Listen, Peter," I said, "we can wait here, wander around town for a while then come back for the conclusion. We don't all need to be there, to listen to more statements and questions, do we? It doesn't seem fair to force James to sit there for another few hours."

Peter had looked at me, surprised. I would need to explain it to him later, that the whole process had left me reeling and I needed a moment away from the drama to let it all sink in.

And it would mean you avoid Alexander, I thought. Which was true. Any opportunity to stay away from him was one I was going to take. The risk that I would sit there and listen to his story about how he and Isa had met, the details of their affair, his defiant insistence that it was all okay, that there was nothing seedy about it. I was in no mood to hear any of that, to feel humiliated by such details. And I was worried too that it would show in my face, that the anger would spill out and be there for everyone to see. Peter, Katie, James. They would wonder why it upset me so much, why the overreaction. No there was no point in risking it.

And besides, I knew he wouldn't let me down. He would tell the truth—the parts of it, just as I had asked him to. He would talk of his regret, tell them that he wished he had never started the affair with Isa. He would describe her to them in ways Sarah and Willem would not recognize—Isa, in his telling, a vulnerable and disturbed girl who needed parental guidance but had been cast adrift by parents too caught up in their own problems to see the suffering of their child. He would turn the screw, and Sarah and Willem would feel the pressure.

So, I wandered around town with James and tried my best to seem relaxed as we waited for it all to be over. The two of us returning to the court only when it was time to hear the summing up.

The conclusion, when it came, provided us with little comfort or satisfaction.

Accidental death by drowning was confirmed. A sad, teenage misadventure. But no one's fault. The blame could not be laid on us, nothing we had done had contributed directly to Isa's death. There would be no follow-up. Sarah and Willem had lost. We all shuffled from the courtroom in silence, no one knowing what to say.

It was over. Though it didn't feel like it. I had a thousand questions for Sarah and Willem but could feel the numbed, quiet anger growing within me. To confront them now would help no one, and besides, when I looked at James, I knew I had more pressing problems to deal with.

I had never seen him so pale. He looked like he had a thousand questions in his head and yet no answers. And again, when I tried to talk to him, or comfort him, he drew away from me.

I could see he was thinking about that night. Something was bothering him, and he was desperate to figure out what it was. But the day had been exhausting, and his head was buzzing with it all.

And I just wanted to get home. To close the door behind me and head to bed. Pull the duvet over me and have the world disappear for a few hours.

But when we walked into the lobby Sarah and Willem were waiting for us. A small group of people surrounded them, offering condolences, and when I saw Sarah standing there, clinging to Willem, my instinct was to head towards the exit.

Sarah's statement earlier had drawn the last ounce of sympathy from me, and I worried anything I said to Sarah now would be filled with anger and remorse.

I felt Peter take my hand and squeeze it, and it was only then I became aware of the fact that I had been standing still all this time, watching Sarah and trembling slightly.

"You don't have to say anything to them if you prefer not to," Peter told me. And I looked up at him and wrapped my arm around his waist and let him pull me close, his protective embrace something I needed.

"All those things she knew were going on with Isa. All those things she never told us about. She should never have done that. She could have warned us. It would have made a difference. It could have meant none of this had to happen."

And Peter could only shush me and hold me tight and whisper, "I know, I know." But it was enough to know he thought the same, that he had sat there in the courtroom and listened to Sarah reveal the full story and had understood that what he was listening to was a confession of sorts. An admission, if not of guilt, then of responsibility. The failure, Sarah's and Willem's, not ours.

My thoughts were interrupted by a tap on the shoulder, a small, quiet, "Louise."

Sarah had decided to approach me, and I turned to face her and nodded, saying nothing. Hoping the strength of my gaze would be enough to let her know how I felt. I wasn't feeling in the mood for understanding or forgiveness. And perhaps sensing my anger, she looked to Peter for assurance.

"Can we talk?" Sarah asked me.

And the silence in the lobby then, the realization that every ear in the room was leaning in towards us, breath held, to catch the moment. I felt the force of the intrusion shudder through me, saw the dawning of it in Sarah's eyes too, as we both gazed around the room and met a host of prying eyes.

"Not here," I heard Peter say. "Call us, okay?"

And then we were moving. Walking down the corridor and out into the drizzly New York afternoon. Then into the waiting car. The drive across town not something I remember because all I could think was: *It's over, it's finally over.*

*

They didn't call. A few days later the doorbell rang late in the afternoon and there they were, their faces sad and apologetic. Sarah looking pale and defeated, leaning on Willem for support.

I couldn't speak when I saw them. I just held the door open and ushered them in then went to get Peter.

We sat in the living room, Sarah and Willem facing us, coffee and biscuits laid out on the table, candles lit and flickering in their glass holders, the whole scene strangely comical because it was so cozy and warm and familiar. As if we were about to sit and chat about how our week had been and our plans for Christmas.

"Where are Katie and James?" I asked. "Should they not be here?"

Peter looked at me, confused, not understanding that I assumed Sarah and Willem were here to apologize.

"I don't see why they need to be," he said.

I shrugged, too tired to argue the point. Though I wondered why they should not be there. They had experienced the trauma of the summer too. They had sat in that courtroom and been made to suffer that pointless ordeal. And they had a right to hear Sarah's explanation, her apology, but I was too exhausted to insist on it.

And maybe Peter was right, maybe it would make things easier if they were kept out of it for now, James especially.

The thought of James filled me with an unexpected resolve, the clarity of my realization emboldening me. The need I now had to protect what was left. To protect James and Katie, my family, from further heartache.

I had relegated their protection to second place without realizing it. Had put Sarah first, because her loss was so great, her trauma so impossible to accept. But now the focus of my attention had shifted. I felt no need to tread softly now, to hover around Sarah and talk in whispers lest I upset her. After the decision from the court, I had received what felt like permission to finally speak for myself again.

So, I lifted a china coffee cup to my lips, sipped a few bitter mouthfuls, and looked Sarah in the eye, taking my time to place the cup back on the table and wipe the corners of my mouth with a napkin. My every gesture slow and deliberate, designed to make Sarah feel uncomfortable and uncertain, though why I felt the need to prolong the silence, to stretch out this moment of discreet intimidation, I could not say. Later, I would admit to having enjoyed it, to have watched Sarah sit there and feel uncomfortable, to have seen the palms of her hands moisten with sweat, so her coffee cup slipped from her grasp when she tried to place it down, and clattered on the tabletop like an accusation.

"You should have told us what had been going on," I began. "Perhaps then, we could have avoided all of these unnecessary proceedings."

And Peter had tried to soften the blow, my words too blunt, too forceful.

"What she means—" he began.

And I had stopped him. "I meant what I said. Every word."

"It's okay," Sarah said. "You're right to be angry."

"We have a right to an explanation too. Because you have no idea, do you? You have no idea what this has done to us?"

And Sarah moved to stand up, but Willem held on to her, as if he thought she needed to hear whatever it was that was coming. Though he couldn't stop Sarah from speaking.

"I lost my daughter, Louise. I lost my only child."

"You say that as if none of us understand. As if none of us feel the pain of it. But we do, Sarah. We do."

"How can you? How can you ever know how it feels? You can't, Louise. You can't."

And I could no longer hold it in then. It was not how I had wanted to explain it. It wasn't even something I wanted to say, but the words welled up inside me alongside the anger and then they spilled.

"She would still be here, Sarah, if it wasn't for you."

"What?"

"I would never have let her come with us if I'd know she had so many issues. With you and Willem, with this man, this Alex. I would have said no. But you didn't say a word. You let her come with us while you waltzed off to Sardinia and then you hit us with the god-awful, vindictive litigation. You accused us, Sarah. You said Isa's death was our fault. And now you're telling me I don't know how it feels? How can you say that? How? Look at what you've done to us, for God's sake."

I had raised my voice, and Sarah was crying, and on her feet then. Willem too. Both of them putting on their coats and heading to the door.

Willem muttered, "It wasn't like that, Louise. There was more to it than that."

But he didn't get the chance to explain.

"I want to go home, Willem," Sarah pleaded with him. "Please, let's just go home."

When the door closed behind them, I stood there staring at it and wondering what Willem meant. What more there could be to this whole sorry saga.

A voice behind me, so quiet at first, I almost didn't hear.

James.

"Why did you do that to her? How can you be so cruel? What's wrong with everyone in this family?"

But I had no answer. All I could do was turn to face him and shake my head, then walk upstairs to my bedroom and close the door. I had had enough for the day.

It's a moment I look back on again and again. A moment I relive and reinvent. In the retelling of it, I have an answer for him, an explanation. I tell him what he needs to know: *A secret can be as bad as a lie, James.*

I tell him this, and he listens and understands. He accepts this as the truth and lets that be the end of it.

And I am not unaware of the irony of it. That I should fall prey to the same hopeless delusion as my son. That sad, hopeless longing to turn back time and change the course of events.

CHAPTER TWENTY-EIGHT

Katie

My phone went in the middle of the night and rang out as I scrambled to answer it. I was still half asleep when I swiped, not quite sure what was up and what was down. But when James' name appeared on the screen, I sharpened up immediately.

It was one thirty in the morning.

Why the hell is he calling me? I thought. It took me a moment to realize what it meant. That he wasn't at home, asleep in the room next to mine.

And I felt the panic then. The cold of it creep across my skin. It could only be bad news. It made me hesitate before calling him back. I needed to steady myself, because my heart was still thumping wildly in my chest from the shock awakening, and my head was spinning with the thought that something was wrong. That something had happened to James and I didn't want to think about the thousand and one ways he could be in trouble.

Just call him back, Katie. For God's sake, just call him.

It took three attempts before he picked up. Three rounds of listening to the ring tone and biting my lip. Three rounds of hearing his voicemail kick in. Three rounds of waiting and feeling the acrid burn of dread rise in my throat.

Finally, on the third attempt, he picked up, though it was difficult to make him out at first.

I could hear traffic in the background, and some other noise too that I couldn't quite make out, voices perhaps, or laughter.

"Katie?" he said. His voice slurred and barely audible.

"James, where are you? Are you okay?"

"Yeah… yeah… no… I don't know."

"What the hell are you doing?"

"I dunno," he said. "Just walking."

And that's when I placed the sounds. Downtown some place. The music, the laughter, the chatter. The sounds of the city late at night and all the dangers and excitement that entailed.

"Shit, James," I said. "Are you drunk?"

"Not really," he said.

"And you're out there alone at night, wandering around in the cold?" I asked him.

"Huh?"

I repeated it as loud as I dared. Whatever was going on I didn't want my parents knowing about it. "James, stop walking for a minute and pay attention."

"What?"

"Just tell me where you are."

"Hmm… I don't know exactly. 5th Avenue someplace maybe?"

All I could hear was a scrambling, rustling sort of sound as he fumbled with his phone. And I imagined him, walking about in the middle of the night, with no idea of how to get home. All I could do was lie there and listen and wait and hope he managed to stay safe.

"Shit," I said. "James? James?"

It felt like a long time before he finally managed to get the phone back to his ear and talk to me.

"Hey," he said.

"Listen, James," I told him. "I need you to come home, okay? Hail a cab if you can. I can pay when you get here."

"What?"

"I said hail a cab."

"Why?"

"James, you're drunk and alone and it's almost two in the morning. Isn't that enough?"

"Right," he said. But he kept on walking.

"James, what are you doing?"

"I told you, just walking."

"Okay, then just tell me where you're headed," I told him. "Can you see a street sign? Tell me where you are, and I'll come and get you."

"I dunno where I am. I told you. I'm just walking. Just trying to get away from here," he said. "Away from everyone."

"James, what are you talking about?"

"You hated her, didn't you?"

"What? James, for fuck's sake, come on."

"No, it's true. You hated her for what she did to Luka."

"No, James…"

"I have to tell Sarah, you know. I have to tell her what we did to Isa."

"What? James, we didn't do anything. What are you talking about?"

"Oh, quit lying! I know you didn't tell the truth in court. We left Isa in the sea. We left her to drown, and I need to tell Sarah the truth, Katie. I have to."

"What? James, please, stop walking and talk to me. I don't understand."

"I remembered, Katie. I remember what happened that night. And I have to tell Sarah the truth. She deserves to know what happened."

"Listen, James, we didn't leave Isa in the water. I was there, remember? James? James? Did you hear me?"

"Why did you do that, Katie? Why did you lie about it?"

But I couldn't explain it to him over the phone. In his current state, he would never understand that sometimes a lie is the best thing. I needed to get to him and look him in the eye and convince him he had got it wrong. He was confused, his memories all jumbled up in a haze of alcohol.

And besides, I had to remind myself that it wasn't a lie. Not really. It was simply an omission. There were things I didn't need to say. Truths I didn't need to reveal, because to do so would be to put him at risk, and all I wanted to do was protect him. But he could never know that. All he needed to know was that he was misremembering things.

"Listen, James—" I said. But he cut me off again.

"Have you forgotten how upset she was in court? No, I need to help her. I need to tell her about the video, and then—"

"The video? No, James, wait—"

"Huh? What? I can't hear—"

The sound of a car braking. A thud. And then the line went dead. Like he'd dropped the phone. That was what I hoped. That he'd dropped the phone. Nothing more.

I called him again. Over and over. No connection. And I could feel it. The dread that tells you something really bad has happened again.

CHAPTER TWENTY-NINE
Louise

The morning was a bright one. The winter sky pale blue and when I looked out the window, I could almost feel the crispness in the air. I had lain in bed and felt unusually light. A night of sleep, I realized. It worked wonders, and I lay there for a while and let it all flow out of me, the tension, the worry, the tightness in my neck. It felt good.

Until the quiet of the morning was disturbed by the ring of the doorbell. When I turned the clock to face me, I saw it was eight thirty. Too early for a visit, I reckoned.

These were the small details you remembered, it turned out. The moments before everything changed. It was as if your brain had already figured things out and knew it needed to prepare you for the shock which was to come. The separation already beginning as you struggled into a dressing gown and headed down the hallway. The before and the after.

The before consisting only of minutes. The few seconds of normality you had left before it all came crashing down.

I remember the feel of the carpet between my toes, that I thought about going back to get my slippers. I remember the windows fogged up on the landing, the view beyond shrouded and ghostly, like a premonition. I remember the sound of a small dog barking, its high-pitched yapping piercing the air and bounding off the buildings.

I remember Peter's face, ashen and confused when he turned to me. I remember him saying my name, "Louise, Louise," as if all other words were lost to him. He had been rendered speechless save for my name. "Louise, Louise."

The before tumbling over into the after, in an instant. A rush of movement and voices and explanations I didn't understand. There was only the urgency, only the sudden recognition that the figure behind Peter was dressed in navy blue. A uniform. The police. Eight thirty on a Sunday morning. Katie there suddenly beside me, squeezing her hand.

And James? Where was James?

Something about a hospital.

"Grave injuries."

I will never, ever forget that. Not serious. Grave. As if it was a hint. An official way of letting you know there was no cause for hope. The double meaning of the word needing no translation. And I felt it. The hole in the ground, smothering me as I fell.

Then a gap. The only vague memory, sitting in the back of the police car on the long slow drive across town. Though I remembered nothing of the drive itself. The shift from home to hospital, New York whizzing by, everyone in their houses, oblivious to the drama inside the car that drove past, its occupants frozen with fear. They simply woke to another lazy Sunday morning, while James...

And then, all of a sudden, we were there, in the hospital. Left sat in a hallway, the three of us perched on a bench, waiting for yet another official to appear and confirm our fears.

James on the operating table. Surgery. His brain. Trauma. Critical forty-eight hours. If he pulls through.

If he pulls through. I thought about that. Couldn't make any sense of it. That tiny word. If.

"When," I wanted to say. "You mean, when." But nothing came. I was speechless and numb and incapable of even nodding my head.

If. If. That was all I heard. The word I kept repeating.

How many hours did we sit there like that? I have no idea. When the surgeon came to talk to us, it was dark outside. He looked exhausted, beaten. That was what I thought when I saw him. There was defeat there in the way he walked towards us. A slouch in his shoulders that indicated more than tiredness.

And I had clutched Peter's hand and felt him brace for the news too. Katie rigid there beside me, sitting on her hands the way she did when she was a kid in trouble. I had wanted to reach over to her and pull her close, but I couldn't move, couldn't take my eyes off the figure that walked towards us.

The news, not so revealing in the end. The operation done, but the danger not over. Forty-eight hours again.

And Peter asking, "Can we see him?"

A nod followed by a clarification. The accident. The swelling. Blood and skull. Tubes. Machines. I couldn't focus on more than a few words. Felt the shock of them as they penetrated. Heard the surgeon say the same thing, that we should prepare for a shock. "It isn't a pretty sight."

But I didn't care. That was what I thought. I just wanted to see my son. He was there behind the blood and the tubes and the machinery. James. My boy. I didn't need to know any more than that.

But the sight of him, when we walked into the room—"Sorry but, just a few minutes" I heard someone saying—it made us gasp. I felt it escape, the sound amplified by Peter and Katie as they too drew breath. No one crying. The shock of it seemed to muffle us. So, the room was silent. Just the beep, beep, beep of a machine. The rise and fall of a concertina pump. The suck of something in the tubes. James' closed, swollen eyes as he lay there.

"Can he hear us?" I asked.

But no reply. It took me a moment before I understood. That the silence was an answer, and the answer was, "no."

I spoke to him anyway, some hopeful part of my brain ignoring everything else, the words, the sounds, the facts.

"It's okay, James," I whispered. "We're here. We're right here. Everything's going to be okay."

CHAPTER THIRTY

Katie

There was a terrible symmetry to it all. First Isa and now James. As if the suffering needed to balance itself out.

We knew he was struggling and had tried to help him. Mom and Dad had agreed with Sarah that James needed professional help if he was to come to terms with what had happened.

But when we had spoken to James about it, he was scathing.

"A psychologist?" he had asked them. "You think I need to talk to a shrink?"

I had sat beside at the kitchen table one afternoon, the supportive sister who tried to bring him round to what my parents were suggesting.

"Not a shrink, James," Dad had said. "Just a professional."

James had looked at him, waiting for him to explain the difference, but Dad couldn't. So, I had tried to explain it as best I could.

"Like a grief counsellor, you mean?" I had asked them. And Mom had nodded.

"It can take a while for something like this to sink it. When someone dies, someone we love, especially when they're so young. It's easier to pretend, at first, that it hasn't happened. To just not accept it. There can be a delayed shock."

"God," James had said. "Did you read that in a brochure? It sounds like it. Mom, she's dead. Isa is dead. I know she is. I know what it means. I know she's not coming back. I'm not fucking insane."

And Mom had scraped her chair back from the table then and walked over to the sink to pour a glass of water, hoping James hadn't spotted the gleam in her eyes as the tears welled up as she began to understand that he needed even more help than she had realized.

"It's more about accepting it," Dad had tried to explain.

"What? Accept it? What the hell does that even mean?"

"Because we have to," I said. "Because we have no choice."

"God, it's that easy, is it? Just accept it? For you maybe, Katie. It might be easy for you."

"James," Dad said. "She means it's the only way forward."

And James had pushed back his chair then and thrown his arms in the air. He was finished with us.

"Just stop!" he said. The slam of the front door the end of the conversation.

"You want me to go after him, try to talk to him?" I had offered.

"No," Mom said. "Just leave him be. He'll come around, once he's had time to think about it."

It was a strange sort of optimism, I thought now. The way Mom assumed it was always so easy. That the world made sense, mostly, and eventually everyone came to see it that way.

Not James though, as it turned out.

I had knocked on his door later that evening and waited for the barely audible, "Yeah?" before opening it.

"You okay?" I had asked him when I peeked my head round.

"Sure, why?"

"Just, you know, all that stuff this afternoon. About the psychologist."

And I could see from the tilt of his head, and the way he fell back on his bed, that I was allowed to come in then, and I closed the door behind me and walked over to the edge of his bed, sat down on it and said, "They could be right though, James."

"Uh-huh," he mumbled. Then he eased himself up a little and propped himself on a pillow. "I suppose you know I went over to Sarah's house," he said.

"I heard something about it, yeah. Why?"

"I just wanted to talk to her. I mean, that's the deal, isn't it? That I talk about all the shit in my head. That's what everybody wants, no?"

"Oh, come on, James, it's not like that. No one thinks you're losing it or anything."

"I do," he said. "I think that sometimes."

"Fuck, why? That's not true."

"You ever think back to that night? The night Isa died?" he asked me.

"I try not to, to be honest. Not that there's much to remember."

"Yeah, that's what I thought. That there was nothing to remember. It's all just a blur, right?"

"Pretty much," I agreed.

"Only sometimes it's not."

"Huh?"

"Sometimes I get a little glimpse of it, that night. Isa, the sea."

"Yeah, that whole summer with Isa, it's hard to remember it now, knowing she's gone."

"No, I don't mean that. It's what I was trying to tell Sarah. I told her I could have helped her. I should have helped her."

"Sorry, what?"

"And she agreed."

"Who agreed? James, what are you talking about?"

"Sarah," he said. "She thinks the same thing. That I should have helped Isa. If I was with her in the sea that night, then I could have helped her. I should have helped her. But I didn't, and now she wants to know why. Why I didn't. Why I let Isa die."

"James, stop it. Please. I'm begging you. You're getting mixed up. You were with me the whole night. You weren't anywhere near Isa."

"Why do you keep saying that? Why do you keep telling me that? I know what I remember, Katie."

And I had pulled out my phone then and swiped the screen until I found what I was looking for. Photos from that night. The night Isa died.

"Look," I said, showing him the screen, swiping through a whole series of photos, showing him the date, the time.

"These are all from that night. See? There you are. And Luka, and Isa, and me. Midnight. Two in the morning. James, you're wrong. I swear it. You're wrong."

And he stared at the photos and shook his head as if they proved nothing, as if they couldn't counter the images in his head.

"But that can't be right," he said.

"Look!" I said again. "Look then."

"I know, it's just…"

"Will you think about it at least, James?" I asked him.

"About what?"

"What Mom and Dad said this morning. The psychologist."

"I'm not mad, Katie."

"Hey, I never said you were. You know that, right?"

"I suppose. I just can't get it out of my head, that I could have helped her."

"James, we all want that. We all want to go back and change everything. Do something differently so that it didn't happen."

"Yeah? You think about that too?"

"All the time. But then I stop. Because I can't, can I? There's nothing I can do. I just have to accept it. It happened."

"Sarah said—"

"She knows what you meant, James. She must think the same thing too, all the time. Every day, she must wonder what she could have done to stop it from happening. You think she doesn't beat herself up about that all the time? That she went away with Willem and left Isa behind? How is she supposed to cope with that?"

"I guess. I never thought about it like that."

"Yeah, well, that's all Mom and Dad mean. Sometimes talking about it helps you to see things differently."

"So, you think I should go?"

"To a psychologist? Yeah, I think so. I mean, what harm can it do?"

And he shrugged, gave a little nod, and said, "Maybe."

And it was a start, I thought. A small step in the right direction. And who knows, if he hadn't taken my phone, gone searching for Isa again, kept thinking about what he thought Sarah had said, that it was his fault, maybe it would have all worked out differently.

Maybe. I hate that word now.

*

James had been sat at the kitchen table when I had walked in and I caught him out.

"What have you got there?" I had asked him while he scrambled to hide something on his lap, nerves and shaking hands betraying him as my phone clattered to the floor.

"Is that my phone?"

And he had pushed his chair away from the table and tried to get underneath to grab the phone, but I was quicker than him.

"Were you looking through my phone?"

And he made no attempt to deny it. Just nodded and shoved his chair back to the table, picked up the mug of tea in front of him and took a sip. Kept his head bowed and didn't look at me.

"You've got no business snooping around in my phone, James. How the fuck do you even know the password?"

And he laughed a little and shook his head as if he thought I was beyond stupid.

"Zero, zero, zero, zero," he said. "You should change the default settings on these things you know, Katie? I didn't even need to guess."

There had been something flat about his voice, something strange. It stopped me getting angry, even though I felt it well up inside me. I wanted to walk over to him and whack him round the head, demand he explain himself. But I couldn't. I could feel it for some reason, that if I were to shout at him, he would just push back the chair again and walk out the room. Brush past me without as much as a glance. He wasn't there to explain himself. What he wanted, I realized, was an explanation.

And I had to think and think fast. What was it on my phone that would have drawn him to it? When he saw it there on the table, discarded and momentarily forgotten, what was it that tempted him to punch in the code and start sifting through it? What was he expecting to find?

I didn't even need to ask him.

"I was looking for pictures of Isa," he said. "That's what you want to know, I suppose? What I was doing?"

"Isa?" I asked him. "You must have plenty of pictures of her on your own phone. What do you want mine for?"

"I just wanted to see something new, that was all."

"Why?"

"I don't know. Maybe I thought it would make her seem alive again. A photo I'd never seen."

In that moment, those words gave me goose bumps. I felt the tiny prickles rise on my skin. Felt the shiver ripple through me. *How could he want that?* I wondered. *How could he even look at it that way?*

Alive again. I should have been alert at that point, I understood that now. I should have picked up the inflections in his voice. He had sounded down, robotic even, as if he wasn't in control of what he was saying. The words just coming out as if he didn't even hear them.

"And, did you find anything?" I had asked him as I pulled up a chair beside him and flicked open my phone.

It was frozen at the last thing James had been viewing. Not a photo as it turned out, but a video. Paused at a moment I knew only too well. I had watched that video a hundred times since Isa died. Knew every frame, every sound.

The orange glow to everything, the shadows around the bonfire coming in and out of focus as I steadied the camera and tried to zoom in on Isa and some boy, the two of them entwined and laughing and oblivious. Then a pan to the right, sweeping past the crowd of faces around the fire until I found them, Luka and James next to each other, chatting and drinking and trying not to look. But they can't help it. They look. They watch. They watch Isa as she sits there smiling and laughing and kissing, as she leans in to catch the whisper in her ear then throws her head back and laughs, kisses him, says, "Yeah, come on, let's go." They stagger as they stand up, Isa giggling, the guy catching her as she falls forward, almost into the flames. Then, arm and arm they head away to the dunes, to privacy and away from watchful eyes.

The camera stayed with them as they walk away, shadows glowing, until they were gone. Swallowed up by the darkness. Then slowly, back to those two faces, watching and drinking and shaking their heads. "Bitch," someone says. But who it was, it's impossible to tell.

"Did you watch this?" I asked James.

"Yeah," he admitted.

And in the pause, I didn't know what to say next, how to pose the question. But James wasn't waiting for me to say anything.

"Is that the last night?" he had asked me.

"Yeah," I replied.

"Why?"

"What do you mean?"

"Why did you record it? Isa and that guy?"

"I don't know," I had said. Though it wasn't true. But how to explain that to James without going over the whole story. Over every stupid thing Isa had done.

"I was just recording. Just for the hell of it."

"Isa and some guy?"

"No. The party. A memento sort of thing, you know? But I saw them together and just kept the camera on them."

"Spying?"

"No! James, come on."

"That's what it feels like. Like you were watching them."

"Well you were too. You and Luka."

"Yeah, I know. I'd forgotten. That night, it's so vague."

"The one night we should have been paying attention. Looking out for her."

"But we did though, didn't we? They came back to the party, don't you remember? Isa and that guy, they came back, and then she left again, said she was feeling sick or something and wanted to clear her head because she'd had way too much to drink. Remember? And she was on her own. And it didn't feel right, so I followed her. I know I did. I remember. I watched your film and I remembered."

And I sat there and listened and shook my head. "James, you're mixing everything up. This video. That night. I swear."

But he wouldn't listen to me. And he would never believe anything I told him then, I could see that.

"Fuck, Katie. You were there, you were right beside me. You know what happened."

And I didn't reply. All I could do was stare at the image that was frozen on the screen, Isa stumbling forward as the guy caught her. The moment before she walked away. The last moment anyone remembered seeing her.

"No," I said. "I don't remember any of it, James. And whatever it is you think you remember, you've got it wrong. You were with me the whole night. Right beside me. Trust me, James. I'm telling you the truth. You were with me."

But he wasn't going to listen to my lies. I'd lost him and I knew it.

CHAPTER THIRTY-ONE

Louise

"What happened?"

Sarah's call came that evening.

"I called a few times earlier, but it went to voicemail."

"Yes, I know," I told her. "I just wasn't ready to pick up, sorry."

"No, it's okay. I know how that feels."

And I felt a pang there, a wrench in my gut that twisted alongside the realization that we shared this too now. This loss. All day in the hospital, it was a thought I had forced down. I wouldn't let it rise, wouldn't let it consume me, wouldn't let it become some sort of truth, that we could lose him, that there was a chance he was gone already.

All day, I found myself looking upwards and saying, "No." In a whisper, at first, then out loud. Not caring who heard me. As long as God did, as long as fate did, as long as whoever was responsible for these things heard me and put a stop to it, saved him. I would shout it from the rooftops if necessary. *No! No! No!*

"Will he be okay?" Sarah continued.

"They don't know," I told her. "The next forty-eight hours will be critical. That's what they kept telling us."

"Oh God, I'm so sorry, Louise. I'm so sorry."

And I remembered saying the same thing to Sarah, not so long ago. The two of us there on the beach, looking out at the sea. So sorry. So sorry. Meaningless words, I understood, now that it was my own child in danger. I didn't want pity. I didn't want comfort. All I wanted was a way to make it undone. For James to be home, safe and whole. For none of it to be true. For "so sorry" to be unnecessary.

"I don't understand what he was doing there," I told Sarah.

"Where?"

"He was hit by a car, all the way over in Greenwich Village, on Hudson Street."

Sarah pausing while she configured the map in her head, drawing a line from the Upper East Side to Greenwich. A line over at least three miles long.

"Are you sure?" she said.

"Yes, the car that hit him, the driver said he came out of nowhere. Just walked across the crossroad without looking. He couldn't brake in time, couldn't stop."

"He'll be okay, Louise. He'll be okay."

But I had stopped believing it.

"No," I told Sarah. "He won't."

When the doctor had explained it to us, the speed, the impact, James being hit from the side, then thrust into the air, over the bonnet and onto the ground. That the driver had had to run over to him—"He was five meters away." I knew then, Peter too, that this was the end they were talking about. James hit the ground, so high, so fast, there was no surviving it.

We had to prepare ourselves.

*

Knowing something was coming, feeling the inevitability of it, I thought would cushion us. Just a little. But when the confirmation came, when the consultant stood there in the room and explained the harsh realities in a voice so smooth and calm, I had tried to block him out. The truth hit hard, and I had squeezed Peter's hand and hoped, if I gripped hard enough, it would do something. That the pressure which was turning my knuckles white would somehow change things, might wake me up from a dream.

But the room didn't shift. Nothing changed.

James still lay there in the bed, attached to machines I would never understand. Their purpose was the only relevant thing about them. This is what he needed to stay alive.

Though I knew it wasn't life. Not in any meaningful sense. Not in any way a mother would look at a child and see the future.

The doctor had explained it in simple terms. The swelling on the brain, the bleeding, the damage that had been done.

"He'll never wake up?" I had asked him. The simplicity of the question making me wince, because there was a truth within it that I could understand. Something basic that required the simplest of answers. Yes or no.

But perhaps he had seen it in my face, that I was prepared for it—for an answer so simple it would seem abrupt, or even callous to some.

"No," the doctor had said.

His honesty a balm of sorts. The soothing certainty of that one word, something I appreciated, and I found myself saying, "Thank you," to him. "Thank you for being so honest."

He had left us to discuss it. Suggested the decision be made soon—"Within a few days." The implication of it causing Peter to wobble. I had sat down with him on the chairs by the bed and we had tried to absorb it. A no is never as simple as it sounds. There were many layers to this one.

"Does he mean he's in pain?" I had asked Peter.

He shook his head. "No, I don't think so." He stared at the machines and tubes and drips that seemed to feed into every piece of James. "All this… it must be to keep him comfortable."

"He meant there's no point to this though, didn't he? No point in keeping him alive like this. In letting him suffer."

Peter leaned forward on the bed and placed his hand on James' arm then began to stroke it. Slowly, gently.

"Do you think he feels this?" he asked.

"No," I replied. "He doesn't."

"How can you be so sure? I mean, they don't really know, do they? What it is that's in there, what it is that makes us aware of things."

"His brain, Peter. You heard what he said. That car was doing forty miles an hour when it struck him. He never stood a chance."

"Then he's not here at all, is he?"

"No."

That word again. Weighty and small and more horrifying than it seemed.

And I looked at James, at the wreck of him which lay there in that bed, and realized that this was what it was going to take.

"It's not him," I said to Peter. "This is just what's left, but it's not him."

"I know," Peter replied. "But sitting here like this, touching him, having him here, even like this. It's…"

"A chance to say goodbye, at least."

And I thought of Sarah then. How did she manage to keep going, having never had this chance? She'd come home to find her daughter already dead and their final moments together something she could barely remember. What had she said to Isa? When had she last seen her?

It was not something I had understood until then, the emptiness of trying to look back and remember something so precious, only to find nothing there.

"We should tell Katie," Peter had said. "Have her come and say goodbye."

This was how he made decisions. He pointed to some other thing. A consequence. Though I couldn't blame him for wanting to keep the words at bay, for being incapable of saying it out loud, there in the room where James lay helpless and waiting.

And then, the formality of it all. The forms to be filled, permissions given, explanations laid out and the same question asked not once but multiple times.

"Do you understand?"

Understand that when these machines are shut down, the process will begin. A process which started the moment the car struck, the moment James hit the ground. All they had done was to postpone what was already underway. But once the switch was clicked, it would begin again. The end.

Two days we waited, in the end. Waited for Katie to prepare for it. When we told her what was planned, explained we would need to decide how to say goodbye, she had not been able to accept it.

"No, he's going to be okay. They just need to wait a little longer is all."

And no amount of persuading her could bring her to say yes and agree to it. We had taken the decision without her in the end. Told her that she could come with us to the hospital if she wanted to.

"To watch him die?" she'd asked.

"No, Katie. No. To say goodbye," I had explained. "When they turn it off, we don't need to be there if we don't want to."

She hadn't wanted to, and I couldn't blame her. No one should have to go through a thing like that. So, Katie had said her goodbyes the day before and stayed home while Peter and I made that final trip to the hospital.

Though it was peaceful in the end. No shudders or gasps, no beeping machines or alarms. That was what I had prepared myself for, the thing I had explained to Peter I might not be able to bear, because the doctor had told us, "It may not be pleasant."

"If he struggles, I can't watch that," I had told him.

"No, I know," he said.

And we had agreed to leave if we needed to.

When the doctors came to withdraw the tubing, we had been ushered out of the room and I had panicked. What if he died then, while they were standing there in the corridor? No hand holding his, no stroking the hair from his face and kissing his cheek. Alone after all.

But in the end, it had all gone to plan. We had been called back to the room and when I asked if James was still with us, the nurse had nodded a yes and led us to the bedside.

And how long we sat there, I don't know. Nor when, exactly, it happened. The moment James slipped from life to death. It took a doctor to come and measure and ascertain the facts. To tell us he was gone.

It had left me feeling disoriented and thinking, *Is that it?* As if death was an anticlimax. Something that happened so imperceptibly that even from close by, even when you held its hand, and stroked its hair, kissed its cheek, even when you sat beside it and breathed it in and tried to soothe it with soft words and gentle whispers. Even after all this, it still brushed past you invisibly and stole the most precious thing you had.

I had seen it in Peter's face too, his confusion, as if he couldn't quite figure out what had happened. He just looked at James and saw his son there. No apparent change. Still his boy lying there on the bed. Still James. Still warm to the touch and in need of care and attention.

But gone all the same.

We had left the hospital in some sort of state of disbelief. Aware of what had happened, knowing it was an irreversible truth, but not quite believing it.

Even when Katie opened the door and asked us if it was over—"Is he gone?"—I had found the weight of my head too much to bear. I couldn't nod to say yes. And my tongue felt thick and suffocating in my mouth, so the words couldn't come either.

All I could do was walk inside and pull the door shut behind me and wish the world would disappear.

CHAPTER THIRTY-TWO

Katie

Something had triggered him. Something in that video. The light of the campfire, glowing and guiding him towards a memory that faded in and out of focus.

"Don't you remember? You must remember," James had asked me.

And I had shaken my head and said, "No," and insisted there was nothing to remember. Just a party. Just a dull haze of alcohol and music and laughter.

I kept repeating it, hoping I could make the story of that night stick. All I needed to do was repeat and repeat it until it became its own truth.

Forget everything else, I had wanted to tell him. *Forget the video, forget the sea, forget Isa. If you forget it all, you'll never have to share the guilt. Let me remember. Let that be enough.*

I wanted to protect him from that night. I wanted to be sure that he would never feel the doubt and the guilt that troubled me. That gnawing sense that I could have done more to help her.

And as time had passed, I thought he had forgotten. We'd never spoken of it again—the video, erased in a way, as if it showed nothing more than a bunch of kids round a campfire, singing and drinking and making the most of the last days of summer.

But I couldn't control the images in his head. The dull haze of alcohol had not been enough, in the end, to completely obliterate the memories. Events had been laid down and stored, waiting to be recovered. And once the shock and the grief had subsided, things had started to come into focus again and slowly, the details of that night returned. The truth I wanted him to forget. The truth I wanted to protect him from. The truth I wanted to bear alone. There was nothing I could do to stop it.

I caught him staring at me sometimes, and I could see it there, the slow dawning realization that the dreams which troubled him, hallucinatory and nonsensical, were not as strange as he imagined. Mermaids and waves and stars and sea. A jumbled mess, but there was a truth there among all the drug-addled chaos. He could feel it.

And with every day that passed, that night became clearer and clearer. The mermaid, real. Those final moments, suppressed for so long, and all of it laid down so vaguely, all mixed up and jumbled by drugs and wine, but there somewhere, tucked away in the folds of his brain, grainy and out of focus at first, but becoming clearer.

I had watched him closely that night as if I had known at some intuitive level that there was trouble ahead. When I had seen him get up and leave the party and go after Isa, I thought at first to leave him be. Whatever it was he wanted to say to her, whatever argument it was he thought he had with her, I wanted no part of it. I was done with all of that. But when I saw him stumble across the sand and almost fall, I realized how far gone he was, the drugs and the alcohol kicking in. I had no idea how much he'd taken but watching him it was obvious he couldn't handle this sort of partying. I would have to go after him and make sure he was okay, because the sea was so close, and the sound of the waves lapping the shore was steady and strong and hinted of danger.

When I got to the water's edge, I hadn't seen him at first. The beach had been empty and dark, and I panicked, and called out to him, but got no reply. Just the incessant shush of the sea again.

Then, above the sounds of the waves, I had heard them. Laughing at first and chatting and I had realized I was too late. He was in the sea already and he was with Isa.

In the dark, I struggled to catch sight of them, the sky an indigo black. The sea sparkled in the moonlight, but the light only emphasized how black the water was and how cold, and it terrified me to know he was out there somewhere in the ocean where I couldn't see him.

"Hey, James!" I called out. And I walked to the shoreline and listened, following the laughter until I saw them, at last, in the water.

They were giggling, floating on their backs and staring at the night sky. Every now and then James would let out a "Whoa," as the drugs took hold, as if the star-filled sky was a wonder too great for him to contemplate. He was relaxed, and stoned, and it was funny for a while to watch him drift there in the water.

But I knew he had no idea where he was, and neither did Isa. She was drunk, and a little stoned, floating and smiling and humming one of her silly songs. James humming along with her, out of tune and off the beat.

When he again failed to reply after I called out to him, I waded into the water and slipped my arm around his waist, to keep him afloat.

"What the hell," he cried when I touched him. Then he smiled and said, "Oh, it's you," and I felt him relax as he laid back in the water and continued to float.

But the cold of the water had sharpened my senses and sobered me up and I knew we couldn't stay in too long. I could feel the current pulling us along and had to dig my feet into the seabed to steady us, and make sure we were safe. He was so high and so full of psychedelic wonder I worried he would drag us too far out, to where the water was deeper and colder and where the rip currents could catch you unawares.

"Shh, Katie," he giggled. "Do you hear that?"

"What?" I asked him.

"Singing. Shh, listen."

And I stood there in the water, with my arm in the small of his back and listened. First just to the waves, and then, faintly, singing. Isa in the water, humming and happy.

"Whoa," James said. "Whoa. Is that a mermaid?"

And I went along with it, because it was weird and funny and made a crazy sort of sense, as we drifted there under the night sky.

"Shush, you'll scare her away," I told him.

And when the singing quietened, he suggested a game.

"Hey," he said. "Maybe she'll let us swim with her. What do you reckon?"

He was so stoned I went with it. It was just a silly game.

"You reckon?" I asked him.

The hallucination as real as anything else to him, by then.

"Oh, look, there she is."

And there was Isa, illuminated by the moonlight, her blond hair glowing, floating out behind her in the indigo black of the sea. And in a certain state of mind, she did look magical, alien, a creature from a different world.

"Beautiful," he kept saying. "Beautiful, so, so beautiful."

Isa laughing then. "Holy shit, he's a goner, eh?"

When he saw her, he jumped up with an unexpected force and slipped from my grasp.

"I'm going to swim with her, Katie. I'm going to swim with the mermaid."

And he reached out for Isa then and grabbed onto her, and as I felt him slip from my grasp, I was caught by a wave and toppled. I had swallowed water and sand as the wave pushed me around and when I finally resurfaced, I caught sight of James flailing and grabbing hold of Isa's hair. He was singing and trying to dance with her in the water, and three times I heard Isa call out to him.

"Stop it. Let go of me, James. Let go."

But he didn't listen. He kept twirling her around and singing and then a wave came, and they fell. The weight of him pulling

Isa under. I waded towards them and felt James clutch at my leg and try to pull himself up.

And as he struggled to the surface, I saw his hand there, clutching Isa's hair, the other on Isa's shoulder. His knee at Isa's belly. James grabbing at Isa, pulling and pulling. The strength of him too much for Isa to counter. And I tried to pull them both up, to reach out and lift them both free but the weight of James was all I could bear.

When I felt a tug at my arm a moment later, I wasn't sure at first, who it was. Isa? Or James? James.

Isa there in the water, coughing and spluttering, as she drifted beneath the waves and struggled to get to her feet. I thought to help her, but again James pulled at me and mumbled something incoherent as he grabbed at me and threatened to drag me under too.

When I turned to face Isa, there she was, floating on the surface again and bobbing in the waves. Staring up at the stars, ethereal and beautiful.

"Night, night, mermaid," James called out to her. "Night, night."

And I heard her, calling back to him. I'm sure I did.

"Night, night, James," she laughed. "Night, night."

"Hey, help me get him out of here, will you?" I asked her.

But she didn't hear me. Her head in the water, the waves tossing her around. She was oblivious and happy and lost in her own little world again.

"Damn it, Isa, come on," I called out. "Help me, will you?"

And again, no reply.

"Fine," I yelled. "I'll do it myself."

And I left her there, to float under the stars. I left her in the sea to grow cold and woozy. The chill seeping into her body, numbing, disorienting. I left her there, alone, because, I figured, she didn't deserve any help.

How many times had I tried to help her, tried to make her see sense and understand that a friend, a good friend, sometimes does things you think are "meddlesome" and "sanctimonious"? But they do these things because they want to help you, because they care. Isa had never believed me when I told her that. She had never wanted to believe me. And now, when she needed me, I had stopped caring. I had no desire to help her. I was fed up with it all, fed up of trying to help her out, trying to save her. Whatever happened now, was no one's fault but her own.

No, now it's time to face the consequences, Isa. That was what I had thought.

When I finally pulled James ashore, I turned and took one last look at her floating on the surface and called out to her one last time.

"Isa, come on, you need to get out of the water."

And I had wondered, but only for the briefest of moments, whether I should wade back in and haul her out. But I felt the weight of James on my shoulder, felt him shivering as the chill started to take hold, and knew I had to get him back to the warmth of the bonfire. So, I turned and walked back to the party, James in a daze, half asleep from the exertion and still dreaming of his mermaid. Back to the bonfire and people. I tucked him up and told him to get some sleep. And when he woke the next morning, cold and hungover, he remembered nothing.

And then, that video brought it all flooding back and sent him hurtling down the road towards his own oblivion.

Even dead, Isa knew how to settle a score.

CHAPTER THIRTY-THREE

Louise

That afternoon had started out so well. Relaxed and easy and with no hint of the shock that was to come. Summer was coming to an end and for the first time since we'd bought the summer house, I welcomed it. I had decided to take a trip to the Montauk Lighthouse to buy some silly souvenirs for Sarah, and perhaps a little keepsake for Isa to remember the vacation.

The leisurely drive along the coast to the clifftop had left me happy and relaxed, a little drowsy, even. So when I saw them together on the terrace of the lighthouse café, I thought I was imagining it, that the sharp glare of the sun was distorting things, and I blinked into the light and looked again. And there he was, Alexander, with Isa. There was no mistaking it.

I stood on the path looking at them and felt my heart sink, the light-headedness making me so dizzy I thought even a slight breeze would topple me. He was here, in Montauk. He'd left Brooklyn and come here after all. And our conversation started to play over in my mind. He'd said he wouldn't come here, didn't he? That's what he said. But there he was. Though not with me. With her. And I couldn't move as I watched them together. It seemed so impossible, so unimaginable. It seemed so mean and cruel. So very Alexander.

I watched as they sat at a small table on the café terrace, arm in arm. Saw Isa lean on Alexander as he brushed a kiss on the top of her head, as his hand caressed her arm. And the intimacy of it all, the tenderness, was too much for me to bear. I had stifled a scream, swallowed down the burn of something acidic that filled my throat, a mix of rage and pain. Then, I had composed myself and walked a little further along the path so I could get close enough to watch them, but distant enough to remain out of sight.

The sight of them together left me incapable of thinking straight, my thoughts overwhelming me as I stood there. How did they know one another? How long had they been together? What was Alexander thinking? A man of his age with a teenager? Was he mad?

Though their happiness was an answer to that last question. Anyone looking at them as they sat there would see only that—two people together who were happy in each other's company. Relaxed. In love.

In love, I thought. And again, I wanted to scream. To rush over and demand he explain what was going on.

When he got up from the table and went inside the café, I had needed to fight the urge to run after him, to try and grab a hold of him. If Isa hadn't been there, I would have done so. But she couldn't find out about us, I knew that. My anger and confusion had not overwhelmed me enough to make me careless.

I closed my eyes and breathed deeply, in an effort to compose myself. The voice at my side, sudden and unexpected.

"Hey, Mrs. L, are you all right?"

Isa. I had looked at her and stuttered a non-reply.

"What? I... I..."

"Wondering if you should get yourself a bite of lunch too, huh?"

And I had looked over at Alexander again, seen him pay up and take a tray with drinks and crab cakes over to their table. If he caught sight of me, that would be the end of it. Isa would know immediately, and the chaos she would unleash would be unbearable.

I had rushed away, my face pale, my legs wobbly.

"Later, perhaps, later," I said. Not bothering to say goodbye or hang around. I had turned and walked away as fast as I could, praying that Alexander hadn't seen me. Isa's voice going fainter as she called out to me.

"Hey, Mrs. L. Everything okay?"

*

That afternoon I watched Isa saunter home and noted the satisfied weight of sex there. I could see it in the way she walked, the looseness of her limbs, the easiness of her smile, and I felt every muscle in my stomach tense, the reaction uncontrollable, because I wanted to feel the same thing. I wanted that looseness, that dreamy satisfaction. But all I had was a tightness in my throat that made me want to throw back my head and howl. Just let it all out. But I couldn't. I had to control myself. I had to stay quiet and appear calm on the surface. I had to breathe deeply and then swallow down my shame. And it was shame. I was jealous of a teenage girl and I had no way of controlling it.

When she saw me on the porch, she tossed her beach bag down and took a seat in one of the loungers, not knowing how much I wanted to scream at her. I wanted her gone. As far away from me as possible. But all I could do was watch her flop into the chair with a satisfied sigh.

"So, did you get your lunch?" she asked.

"Oh, not yet," I told her. "How was yours?"

"Yeah, really good. Fresh crab cakes by the sea, it doesn't get better than that, does it?"

Then a pause, a smile, as she pulled her legs up around her and laid her head on her knees.

"I guess you're wondering who I was with?" Isa asked me.

Okay, think, Louise, think carefully.

"It was a bit of a shock, to see you with a stranger," I said. "And, well, if you don't mind me saying so, he seemed a little old to be buying you lunch."

And she smiled at me and tilted her head in that faux naïve way she had when she was happy to have been caught in some delinquent act.

"I thought Luka would be treating you," I carried on.

"Ah, poor Luka. But you know how it goes? I mean, he's lovely, don't get me wrong, but Alex comes first."

Alex, I thought. The way she said it made him sound younger, hipper and so unfamiliar. And it struck me then that he had this other life. A life that seemed to belong to some other man. To this man called *Alex*, this man who preferred the company of younger women. Of girls like Isa. And it was enough to fill me with rage again.

"You okay?" Isa asked me again. "Shit, you're crying. Mrs. L, is everything okay?"

"Oh, it's nothing, it's nothing. Alexander should just…"

"What?"

"Sorry?"

"Alexander, you said something about Alexander."

"Oh, did I?"

"Yes, you did. I called him Alex. Not Alexander."

"Oh, right. I'm just confused, I guess."

And I turned away from her and stared out over the porch, at the dunes for a moment, watching the grass bend in the breeze and letting the movement calm me and keep me focused. Then I turned to face her and smiled.

"I have a friend called Alexander, is all," I told her. "I must have been thinking of him. He never lets me call him Alex, he says it sounds too harsh. I suppose my brain just automatically changes Alex to Alexander."

It sounded ridiculous, of course. So contrived, like I was struggling to explain myself. And the fact that I felt the need to offer up an explanation made her eye me warily, because she knew something wasn't quite right. She knew my explanation didn't quite stack up, though she couldn't think why, she just knew I was lying, she knew I was stalling.

"Anyway," I said, sniffing away my tears and trying to compose myself. "Who's this friend of yours then, this Alex?"

"Just someone I know from Brooklyn," she said.

"Brooklyn? What on earth are you doing over in Brooklyn?"

And she laughed. "It's only across the city. You should go sometime, there's a lot happening there. I think you'd like it."

And had that been a little sneer I caught there in her voice? A sly way of saying that she knew I didn't belong over in Brooklyn. That I wasn't the type of person who'd fit in there. And I so wanted to tell her how wrong she was. How well I knew the place. Far better than she could ever imagine. But instead I managed to shrug it off and appear casual, as if I was considering it.

"Maybe," I had said. "Anyway, it's such a coincidence that he's also up here in Montauk." And I hoped she couldn't hear the neediness in my voice, the hapless attempt to find out what was going on.

And then she smiled that satisfied smile again and said, "Well, you know how it is. He missed me."

And I should have taken a breath, I should have waited. I should not have reacted. But it was impossible. *He missed me*. Just hearing that felt like a punch in the gut, and the little gasp of pain was out before I could stop it.

And again, she had to ask me, "Are you okay, Mrs. L?"

"Yes, I'm fine," I told her. But my voice betrayed me. The quiver of emotion not something I could hide. My breath, close to a sob now.

"You seem upset is all," she continued. "Is it Alex? Are you upset that I asked him to come up here? I swear I wasn't looking to cause any trouble."

"Sorry, you asked him to come here? You asked him?"

And I could see the confusion rising. Because it made no sense for me to seem upset about it, to seem so uptight and emotional.

"Yes," she said, and she cocked her head slightly as if she was trying to figure me out, and I could see her thinking: *What the hell is wrong with her?* Then she continued, "I missed him too, I guess. And it's okay, isn't it? I mean it's not a problem, is it?"

"I don't know… I… No, it's not a problem, I just…"

But how could I tell her, that it was a problem, that it hurt to know that he had come up here because she had asked him to, that he would come running when she called him, but for me…

"Mrs. L? Are you okay?"

And I heard her. I registered that she was there, but for an instant I was alone, separated from the world by anger and confusion, and then suddenly releasing it without realizing I had even spoken.

"That son of a bitch," I said.

And she had looked at me then and all I could do was look back at her and see the realization flash across her face, as she took in my hurt and my anger, as she thought about what I had said—*I have this friend, Alexander*—and made an improbable connection.

"Shit, you know him, don't you? Alex. You know him?"

*

The sounds of the party filtered through the wash and flow of the waves. At the far end of the beach, I could see the glow of the bonfire and hear singing and laughter.

All along the beach I had spotted groups of kids at the water's edge, sitting in the sand and drinking, smoking. A few of them in the water, swimming, despite the chill which was now becoming apparent as summer drew to an end.

I had stayed close to the dunes, in the darkness, the light from a waning moon just enough to illuminate things.

I was looking for Isa and hoping to God she wasn't with James and Katie. Hoped it wasn't too late. If she told them about Alexander, if she told them I knew him, they would understand immediately what she was implying, and they would never forgive me.

But what was I supposed to say to her when I found her? Beg her to say nothing? Convince her my affair with Alexander was over. That there was no harm done. That she was welcome to him.

Would any of that count? I wondered. A petulant teen, upset and angry; it was impossible to say the right thing, to offer up an explanation that would satisfy her. But I had to try. Too much was at stake, surely even Isa would understand that?

Oh God, and Peter, he would never forgive me for putting Katie through such a thing. Her own mother with her best friend's lover. It was a humiliation too far. It would tear us all apart.

And then I saw them. Katie and James in the water together. Katie seemed to be holding James up and trying to get him out of the sea. I was about to call out to her, to let her know I was there, that I would help her, when I saw Isa floating in the water beside them and my heart skipped a beat.

She's told them, hasn't she? I thought. *The little bitch has told them.*

That would explain the state James was in. And Katie's frantic attempts to pull him free from the water and get him away from Isa. And I wanted to charge into the sea then and beg them for forgiveness.

But again, adrenalin-filled clarity prevailed and I held back and watched as Katie finally managed to lift James free. I watched as they stumbled along the sand, James the worse for wear and Katie holding him up. James was mumbling and singing, incoherent from the alcohol and God knew what else. And beside them, in the water, there she was. Isa. Alone and swimming in the moonlight.

Katie took one look over her shoulder and I thought at first that she was going to set James down on the beach and then head back to the sea to pull Isa free. Alone there in the dark, in the cold water, she was vulnerable and no doubt unaware that the sea here was deceptively calm. That the rip currents in shallow water were more dangerous than she understood.

But for whatever reason, Katie hesitated, and I heard her say something I couldn't make out and wait for a reply. When none came, she watched Isa float there for a few seconds, before she turned and walked away.

Good, I thought. Now I could talk to Isa alone.

I checked to make sure James and Katie were out of sight, then I walked to the shoreline and called out to Isa.

"Isa. It's me. We need to talk."

No reply. Isa as insolent as ever, floating there illuminated by the moonlight, ignoring the world and doing as she pleased. Her head was half-submerged, the sound of my voice diminished in the shush of the waves as they buffeted her about, so I called to her again. But again, no response.

"Damn it, Isa," I had shouted. "Will you listen to me, for God's sake."

And I pulled off my shoes and waded in, getting closer, calling out to her. Because she needed to listen to me this time. I had to make her understand what was at risk if she told anyone about Alexander. She had to understand that she couldn't go messing around with other people's lives like this. I waded into the cold water, felt the chill creep up my thighs, and became aware of the darkness and the sheer blackness of the sea.

My voice sounded faint in the dark, and as I called out to her, I kept thinking back to our conversation earlier that afternoon.

Shit, you know him, don't you? Alex. You know him?

Listen, Isa, please. Katie, James, Peter, they can't know about this. You must promise me. They can't ever know about this.

Wow, Mrs. L. I didn't realize you were so wild.

Isa, I'm serious. This has to stay between us. Please, Isa.

Yeah? Our little secret, eh? And why the hell should I keep quiet, huh?

Because I'm asking you to. I'm begging you. Don't do it.

I'll think about it.

No, Isa, you don't understand. There's nothing to think about. You can't talk to them. You can't tell anyone about this.

God, and what are you going to do about it then? How are you going to stop me?

Those words, so insolent, so disrespectful. *What are you going to do about it?* And the calm that came over me surprises me still. The clarity of the moment as I took in the situation. The two of us alone in the water, in the half light of the moon. No one to see us. No one knowing I was there. Peter at home asleep and thinking I was there beside him. And I thought of them then, Peter, Katie, James. They were all I ever wanted or needed. My family, the only thing that mattered. Isa floating under the moonlight, ignoring me, taunting me with her silence. In that moment she meant so little to me. Almost nothing.

If I wanted to, I thought, all I would need to do was wade over and get closer to her. All I would need to do was place my palms flat on her shoulders and push, then watch as her face was submerged. Watch as her eyes opened in panic as she realized what was happening. All I would need to do was push with the ball of my palms, and press my knee into her stomach, and hold her there. Then wait. Wait until I felt the limpness, wait until I could release her. Then watch her float away on the surface, eyes unblinking and opaque in the light of the moon. Gone.

And who would know? A foolish teenager, alone in the cold water, drugs and alcohol in her blood, her decision-making impaired by it all. And the rip current here, so treacherous, so dangerous, it caught out tourists every year. Isa would be a sad accident, nothing more.

And I thought of Katie then. The way she had looked over her shoulder and watched Isa floating there. Had she had the same thought? I wondered. I wasn't the only one frustrated by Isa's behavior. I wasn't the only one looking to teach her a lesson.

When she was within reach, I grabbed at her arm and pulled her towards me.

"Okay, Isa," I had said. "Enough with the fun and games."

And I pulled her closer, expecting her to stand up and push me away or protest. But she stayed there floating on the surface, looking up at the pale moon, her eyes bright and unblinking.

"Isa?" I said. "Isa?"

Nothing. Not a sound. Not a whimper. Nothing.

My voice becoming more panicked now, my heart rate faster. "Isa! Isa!"

But I knew, of course. She was gone. Floating there on the waves, her eyes to the heavens but seeing nothing.

But I had heard her laughing. In the sea with James. The two of them singing and laughing and splashing around in the water. It wasn't possible that in those few minutes from James and Katie leaving the beach to the moment I grabbed her arm, she had drowned. How?

And I remembered then, their singing, their laughter and something else. Katie calling out to James.

"Quit fooling around, James, and get out of the water."

The panic in her voice.

"Let go of me, James. Let go."

Yes, she had said that. I was sure she had said that. Three times, in fact. Three times she had told him to let her go. The playfighting, the fooling around, something else by then. Something dangerous. James pulling at her as he tried to steady himself in the water, and

Katie dragging him ashore. And Isa? Her head had gone under, James pushing down on her as he struggled to get out of the sea. And the terrible reality of what had happened hit me then.

"My God," I cried. "Oh James. My God."

And Isa floated there beside me, the silent witness to it all.

It's strange to think that momentous decisions can be made in such a spontaneous way. The course of your life can be altered in a few minutes. But that's how it was. I was faced with a choice, that was what I understood at that moment. Protect my family, protect myself, or call for help, raise the alarm, admit the truth. And the decision was easier to make than I imagined it would be. And I knew I would have to live with that. But the truth was, when I was forced to choose, I chose my family.

I waded back to the shore, and left Isa there in the water, floating in the dark and at the mercy of the ocean. I knew that come morning the current would carry her miles away, far from any traces of what had happened here at night on this dark stretch of beach.

So I let her go and waded ashore and walked home without looking back.

And as Isa was buffeted by the waves, I undressed and slipped into bed beside Peter and fell into a deep, and easy sleep.

CHAPTER THIRTY-FOUR

Katie

The bus ride to Fairview took around an hour. Despite the proximity of the city, there was always something peaceful about the cemetery. It felt as though it was right at the edge of the world, an in-between place, where concrete turns to green. There was a wildness to it. In winter, you could sometimes see deer roaming the grounds, and it almost seemed more like a woodland in places, where the crowns of the old growth trees touched one another, and the canopy entwined and darkened the paths even in the leaflessness of winter, as if nature was asserting itself, letting us know it would only be contained for so long.

I never brought flowers. I didn't want to leave any trace that I visited almost weekly. But it was a pilgrimage I knew I would maintain for the rest of my life. A penance. A request for forgiveness.

When I reached James' headstone, I hunkered down on the gravel and swept away the fallen leaves with my hands, into a pile to be scooped up later and stuffed into the bin.

"Hey, James," I said. "Here I am again."

In the beginning, I used to pretend he replied.

"Hey, Katie."

His voice as clear and strong as it was when he was alive. But lately, it had started to fade, and I worried that soon it would dissipate to nothing.

Today, if I listened closely, if I leaned against the headstone, I imagined I could hear him still. A faint hello coming through.

But beyond hello, I had nothing to tell him, no news or amusing anecdotes, so I sat in silence and looked around at his companions. The strange company he now kept. Almost all of them old. People who had led long, fruitful lives, I imagined. People who were loved still, if the fresh flowers were anything to go by.

My favorite was Leonard Dawes. I liked the simplicity of his plot. Just a small granite headstone with his name and the relevant dates. 1942–2011. Nothing else. No embellishments. No poetry or quotes from the Bible. I often imagined him. Stoical and to the point, and hoped that at night, when the cemetery was empty, or on those days when it rained, and the loneliness was unbearable, that Leonard called out to James, helping him along.

"Hey there, son," he would say. "You okay there?"

And James would tell him, "No," and repeat the sad story of his short life again, while Leonard listened and muttered a quiet, "That's just how it goes sometimes, son. That's just how it goes."

Sometimes I sat by Leonard's grave and thanked him for looking out for my brother.

"He's too young, really, to be lying here beside you," I told him.

But I never explained it. I could never admit that what I meant to say was that it was my fault my brother was there. *I could have helped him, but I didn't.*

It will become my own niggling doubt, and the guilt will nip at me for years, I know it will.

And sometimes I thought I could hear Leonard scolding me. "One day you'll pluck up the courage to tell someone the truth. Someone other than an old dead guy."

Good old Leonard. Never shy when it came to the truth.

Courage though, was that what I lacked? Or was it more an understanding that things were best left alone now? Because there was a symmetry to it all, I thought. A conclusion to events that made a strange, horrible sort of sense. Everyone with their own sad story. Each of us paying the price for our decisions and our actions. You could even find a sort of comfort in it. I knew Sarah had.

In the blur of James' funeral, I had found myself watching her, mesmerized by the strange serenity which seemed to have come over her.

I had put it down to exhaustion, at first. Another funeral, another trauma, another gathering at a graveside to lower a child into the ground. We were all numbed by events.

It was only when I saw Sarah smile, a tiny, barely discernible thing, just a small crease at the corner of her lips, that I understood.

Sarah was satisfied. There was something about it all that seemed like justice. And I felt sure that if I had asked Sarah, if I had walked up to her afterwards and said to her, "Now we know how it feels," Sarah would have nodded in agreement.

We were bound together by loss forever now.

A daughter, a brother, a son. Both gone. And I could not help but think that it was fair in a way, that the suffering should be shared equally in the end.

"And what do you think of that then, Leonard Dawes?" I had asked.

And I couldn't be sure, but I thought I heard him reply, "I'd say that's something you all need to learn to live with."

CHAPTER THIRTY-FIVE

Louise

The rooms smelled musty and mildewed, the months of stale air and winter dampness tinging everything with a forlorn aspect. Though it was always going to feel like this, I suppose. The events of that summer would forever linger in this place now. All that sadness and horror had seeped into the woodgrain, coated every surface, crept into every crack and crevice, and left a trace which could never be removed.

But I tried to. I threw open the windows and doors and let the air blow through the house while I sat on the porch and watched the sea.

A bright spring day, the sky blue as cornflowers, but chilly still, a stiff north-easterly wind shivering over the water, the sea shimmering with just a ripple of sun-kissed gold. It would be a month or two yet before the beaches came to life again with the sounds of summer.

Today, there were only a few walkers out on the sand with their dogs, leaning into the wind, and pulling the collars of their coats up tight around their throats.

But the emptiness, the chill, that last breath of spring cold still hanging in the air, was nicer than I imagined. And the solitude was as invigorating as it was calming.

I never came up here this time of year, though perhaps I should. The quiet and the solitude would do me good. I could recharge away from New York and its incessant buzz, simply gaze out at the sea and let the day pass by.

I didn't know what it was that had finally brought me back here. For more than a year we had stayed away. Taken a plane each break, just the three of us, to some far-flung destination. Anywhere but here seemed to be the consensus. As if we could flee. As if distance meant anything. Even on a white sandy beach in some Asian paradise it was impossible not to feel the loss. To look at the three of us and see only what was missing. The empty space where James was supposed to be.

Maybe that was it? The reason I had grabbed the car keys and driven here in the end? I knew now the memories lay inside. They were inescapable. A Thai beach, the dunes of Montauk, what difference did it make? He was always with me. That loss was the punishment I would always have to endure.

But I had not prepared myself for the shock I felt when I turned the key in the door and walked inside. The assault of memory. Isa and James lingering in every part of the house.

I could feel them when I went upstairs to air out Katie's room. Could hear Katie and Isa whispering and giggling. Caught the melody of a tune Isa sang in the shower.

In the kitchen, I thought I smelled pancakes, and saw James, then, sitting at the table, waiting for Peter to serve up breakfast.

On the porch, I looked at the hammock and imagined it still held the indentations of him. The dips and folds his body had made as he lay there and swung back and forth.

In the bathroom, a faint trace of coconut lingered, the smell of it provoking a memory of Isa's skin, so glistening and smooth and golden.

There were ghosts everywhere I looked. It was shocking to find them both here still. No amount of sea air, it seemed, could blow them away.

And it made me wonder if it had been a mistake after all, to come back. Perhaps we should just sell up and be done with it, I thought.

Though it saddened me to think of that: that this sanctuary could be lost to me, my retreat, sullied now, never to be retrieved.

Above the sound of gulls and the swish of waves, I heard my phone ring. Katie. No doubt she was wondering where I was, but I paused before answering, not sure if I wanted her to know. But she would only persist until I picked up, so better to get it over with.

"Hey, school's out early today then?" I said.

"Yeah, where are you?"

I could lie, I thought. Just say I was in town. But it would only be stalling. When I was still not home in a few hours she'd call me again. Ever since James died, she'd been so vigilant, calling me all the time, checking how I was. I guess she has good reason to. So, just tell her. Get it over with.

"I'm up in Montauk."

Her turn to pause. An intake of breath, then, "Oh."

"Listen, I might stay here a while."

"You want some company?"

"No, I'm okay. I need to be alone is all."

"Mom?"

"Yeah."

"You sure you're okay?"

"Yeah, honestly, I'm fine. Just remembering things I'd probably do better to forget."

"You sure you don't want me to come up?"

I ignored the question and just said I'd be home soon, then hung up and steadied myself. Waited for my breath to match the rhythm of the incoming tide, growing calm as I listened to the rise and fall of waves breaking on the sand, knowing that this was why I had come here, this was the thing I was seeking. The sound of the sea, the waves, the push and pull of them. I knew it was something I needed to fight. Knew also, that a day would come when the lure of it became too strong, the sound of the waves on the shore too loud and impossible to resist. Though for now, I would resist it. And that brought with it a peace, of sorts. To know the sea was there waiting for me and that I could choose to listen to it or turn away and reject its siren call, gave me energy for another day. Gave me hope that I might be strong enough to get through this, after all.

*

I lay in bed and listened to the sea and the gulls, watched the curtain billow in the breeze of the open window and breathed in the salty air. The dreaminess of the morning, the weight of sleep and the need to be alone, calming me. Perhaps I would stay another day or two. The thought of heading home to New York was too much. The thought of walking around there and trying to pretend that life would somehow carry on as normal, seemed absurd when I thought of it from this vantage point.

When I heard the front door creak open, heard a voice in the hallway call out to me, "Mom?," the wave of dread which filled me made me want to pull up the covers and disappear. And I thought of the sea again, the pull of the waves, and wanted more than ever to walk out there, into the water and then drop beneath the white crests forever and simply disappear.

A voice outside the bedroom door shattered my thoughts again. "Mom? You still sleeping?"

Katie opened the door just ajar and popped her head round.

"Hey there," I said.

She smiled and walked over to the bed and sat at the edge. "It's one thirty in the afternoon. I called you earlier and when you didn't pick up, I took the train straight here."

"You didn't need to do that, Katie," I said. "I'm fine. Just tired."

"Yeah, well, I worry about you. Too much has happened to stop me from worrying. You know that."

"I'm sorry. This is how I need to deal with it, is all. This place. The quiet. It feels like the right place to be."

She came and lay on the bed beside me and when I raised myself from the pillow, she was gazing at me in a way that left me longing for sleep or some other way to blot out the world.

"You don't think it's strange to be back here?" Katie said. "I mean, there are so many memories."

"Good ones, I hope."

"I don't know if that's possible, do you? Too much happened here, I don't think it can ever be good."

"I suppose not," I agreed. "When I walked around yesterday, it was as if they were both here still. Isa, James. It still seems impossible to think that they won't walk through the door."

She laid her head on my shoulder and sighed then took my hand and squeezed it.

"Why don't I make you some breakfast?" she said. "It's a beautiful day, we could drink a coffee and then go for a walk on the beach."

"That would be good," I told her. "But I'm not sure I'm ready for a walk."

"Okay, let's just have some coffee first and then see how we feel?"

"Sure."

She left me in bed, and I lay back on the pillows and listened to her working in the kitchen below, her energy something I needed to focus on. I needed it to fill me.

By the time I had washed and dressed, she was sitting on the porch, the coffee pot beside her on a small wicker table. When she saw me walk out, she poured two cups and smiled when I sat down, offering me a plate piled high with the small butter biscuits I always ate for breakfast.

She smiled when she saw my surprise. "I figured you'd have nothing here, so I brought these with me."

And she leaned over and kissed the top of my head as if I was the child needing comforting and she was the parent offering security and love.

"Are you okay?" I asked her.

"I suppose," she said. And she sipped her coffee and held my gaze. "It just seems like a whole lifetime ago that we last sat here drinking coffee."

I couldn't reply. Ever since I arrived, the events of that summer had played out in my head, but they had an unreal quality to them, as if my memories were false and what I was remembering was just some story I had read in the paper or seen on the news. Everything vivid and unreal at the same time. That whole lifetime belonged to someone else.

"Sometimes I think back to that night," she told me.

"Oh, you shouldn't, Katie. Don't torment yourself remembering that."

"But I can't help it. Being back here, it's so strange, don't you think? It's like we were different people then."

"Well, it has changed us. How can it not have?"

"I know, I just wish so much it had never happened."

"We can't change what happened that night. As much as we long to. We have to accept what happened and learn to live with it. I know I keep saying that. But it's true, isn't it? There's no other way I can think of, to carry on."

"Do you think we can? Carry on, I mean?"

I squeezed her hand tightly then and said, "Yes, I do. We have no choice." And I hoped my voice was steady enough, convincing enough. She could not doubt me, no matter how much I doubted myself. She had to believe I could help us all get through this.

"I should never have left her in the water though. If I'd gone back, I could have helped her. I could have saved her."

"No, Katie, please stop. We've been over this already. You can never know that for sure."

"Really? I don't know if that's true."

"You did the right thing that night, Katie. You did. And I need to know you believe that."

"Yeah? What did I do? I mean, I left Isa in the water. I left her to drown."

"No, you saved your brother. That's what you did. And don't ever forget that. You saved James."

"But he's not with us, is he? I mean, in the end, he wasn't saved."

"What happened to James was not your fault, Katie. And that night, when it mattered, when you saw him struggle in the sea, you helped him. You knew how drunk he was, you knew he'd taken drugs, and you knew you had to get him out of the water, because otherwise he would be in trouble. You saved him. When it mattered, you did the right thing."

"And I could have saved Isa too. I could have got James out of the water and gone back to help her. But I didn't."

"You had enough to do looking after James and getting him back to the safety of the party. Katie, you know this. You know it's true."

She took one of the biscuits and nibbled at it half-heartedly. I could tell she was unsure if she should carry on and I thought perhaps I should try, in the lull, to change the subject. But this was not the moment for small talk. She needed to talk to me about that night, and I had to give her the opportunity. I had to listen to her.

"I called out to her," she continued. "When she was in the sea. I told her to get out of the water, but she ignored me. She just stayed there, floating and staring at the sky. She didn't listen to me."

I took a sip of coffee and composed myself, my voice unwavering and calm when I spoke.

"That's not something you should blame yourself for. Isa was capable of making her own decisions. She could have gone back to the party with you, but she didn't. And we can always wonder why, but at the end of the day, that was Isa, wasn't it? It was who she was. Headstrong and a little wild and never one to listen to anyone. It was why we loved her. But it was also why she drove us all a little crazy."

"Then why does it not feel like I did the right thing?"

"Oh, Katie. It will always feel that way. How can it not? I don't think I'll ever stop thinking about James and what I could have done to protect him. It's all my heart wants—to have him here with me, to know I protected him. I'll always dream that I can change the past. I'll always imagine another future. It's what love does to you when someone close dies so unexpectedly. The need to imagine what life would be like if they were still here, it's natural. But you can't let it control you. You have to learn to accept what happened."

"That means accepting there is a future though, doesn't it? Without them, I mean."

"It does," I told her. "And it does exist, Katie. We can get there."

"You're going to have to help me," she said. "I don't think I can get there on my own."

"Oh, and I will. I promise you, I will."

And I saw her shudder then, as the slow flow of tears began, and all I could do was go and sit beside her and hold her close to me and tell her it would all be okay.

Overhead I heard a gull call out, its screech piercing the air and making me shiver. The clarity of its call, like an accusation. *Tell her the truth*, it seemed to suggest. *Tell her the truth.*

Perhaps one day I would. Perhaps one day I would be ready.

But for now, the truth was a burden I would need to bear alone. She was asking me to protect her and I had failed once. I had failed my son, but I would not fail her. I couldn't.

"We'll get through it," I told her again. "I promise you we will."

And she squeezed my hand, just a little too tightly, as if she knew she had to hold on to me, understood that I was the one who was in danger of falling. Then she lifted her head from my shoulder and stroked my hair and looked me in the eye, her gaze clear and assertive as if our conversation and the sea air and the coffee had helped her focus and come to some sort of decision.

"Maybe we should start now?" she said.

"What do you mean?"

And she stood up and reached out for me.

"Come on," she said. "Come with me. It's a beautiful day. Let's go and enjoy it."

She nodded to the beach and kept her hand held out towards me and I stood up and took hold of her.

"Ready?" she asked me.

"Yes, I'm ready."

Arm in arm we walked down the porch steps and headed to the beach. The sky so blue and so bright, the sun glinting off the water and blinding me momentarily, and I blinked and leaned against her, but kept on walking.

A LETTER FROM JENNIFER

Dear reader,

I want to say a huge thank you for choosing to read *Someone Else's Daughter*. When I first started writing this book, the idea that one day someone would read it seemed a very far off dream. Thank you for making my dream a reality.

For an author, there is nothing more inspiring than knowing there are readers out there in the world reading, and hopefully enjoying, your work. I hope this book is the beginning of a new and valued friendship and that *Someone Else's Daughter* is the first of my books you will read and enjoy. If you want to keep up to date with all my latest releases, just sign up at the following link. Your email address will never be shared and you can unsubscribe at any time.

www.bookouture.com/jennifer-harvey

If you did enjoy reading *Someone Else's Daughter*, I would be very grateful if you could write a review. I'd love to hear what you think, and it makes such a difference helping new readers to discover one of my books for the first time. Thank you!

I love hearing from my readers—you can get in touch through Twitter, Goodreads or my website.

Thanks,
Jennifer Harvey

@JenAnneHarvey1

www.jenharvey.net

ACKNOWLEDGMENTS

The idea for *Someone Else's Daughter* first came to me during a walk on the beach in early 2016. I had a vague inkling of what I wanted to write but I was daunted at the prospect of writing a full-length novel. Then fortune stepped in. Curtis Brown Creative announced a new six-week online course for writers looking to start their first novel and I signed up. I am so glad I did. During the course, I saw my vague idea take shape and, most importantly, become an achievable goal. Many thanks to Anna Davis at Curtis Brown Creative for developing such a useful course. This book would not exist without it.

On the long road to publication I have been extremely lucky to have the support of many people. Writing is a solitary occupation, but no book is written in isolation. I am very grateful to my sister, Elaine, who read a very rough draft of *Someone Else's Daughter* and offered me encouragement and insightful feedback. Thank you for everything.

Thank you too, Mum and Dad, for always believing this was possible and for never giving up on me. Knowing you are there cheering me on makes all the difference. This book is for you.

I also need to thank Caroline Ambrose and the whole team at The Bath Novel Award. Your continued support and enthusiasm for my writing has kept me going when I most needed it and my longlisting in 2017 was a much-needed morale boost at a time when my self-belief was dwindling. You are all wonderful.

An endless thank you to the amazing and tireless writing community of Twitter. The support of my fellow writers online has been vital. In particular, I want to thank the following friends who have always been there for me: Clare Archibald, you are a true inspiration and a trusted friend and critic, thank you for making me a better writer. Greg Collins, Andrew Moorhouse and Shirley

Golden, thank you for your unwavering support and kindness over the years, I truly appreciate it. Rachael Dunlop, Marie Gethins, Susi Holliday, Stephanie Hutton, Sophie van Llewyn, Louise Mangos, Jane Roberts, you all never cease to amaze me. Thank you for your enthusiasm and support, you inspire me in so many ways. Alva Holland, thank you for your warmth and kindness.

Thank you, Louise Newton-Clare, my dearest friend and lifelong cheerleader. I hope you enjoy reading this.

Thank you, Yvonne Kohler, for all the support. You have asked me so often about this book. I hope you enjoy it.

Many thanks to my colleagues Steve Campbell at Ellipsis Magazine, and Matthew Limpede and Anna Zumbahlen at Carve Magazine. It's a joy to work with you all.

To everyone at Bookouture, thank you for taking me on and helping to bring this book into the world. It is a dream come true for me and I couldn't wish for a better publisher. In particular I must thank Cara Chimirri. Your faith in my manuscript and your insightful edits have helped make this book so much better. I am so lucky to have such a kind and dedicated editor.

Thank you to Natasha Hodgson for the copyedits and to Alexandra Holmes for the editorial guidance.

Thanks also to Noelle Holten for the amazing marketing and promotion campaign, and to all the fantastic book bloggers for enthusiastically spreading the word. You are all wonderful.

Finally, Paolo and Helena, thank you for your love and patience. You have waited a long time for this book and now, here it is at last. I hope you enjoy it and I hope I can write many more for you.

Printed in Great Britain
by Amazon

43479029R00184